NOVEL LEARNING SERIES™

A Walk to Remember

For Teacher Resources,
visit NovelLearningSeries.com.

Also by Nicholas Sparks

The Notebook

Message in a Bottle

The Rescue

A Bend in the Road

Nights in Rodanthe

The Guardian

The Wedding

Three Weeks with My Brother
(with Micah Sparks)

True Believer

At First Sight

Dear John

The Choice

The Lucky One

The Last Song

Safe Haven

The Best of Me

NICHOLAS SPARKS

NOVEL LEARNING SERIES™

A Walk to Remember

GRAND CENTRAL
PUBLISHING

NEW YORK   BOSTON

Student Guide copyright © 2012 by Willow Holdings, Inc.
and Hachette Book Group, Inc.
A Walk to Remember is copyright © 1999 by Nicholas Sparks Enterprises, Inc.

A Walk to Remember was originally published by Hachette Book Group in 1999.

Grand Central Publishing
Hachette Book Group
237 Park Avenue
New York, NY 10017
www.HachetteBookGroup.com

Printed in the United States of America

RRD-C

First Student Guide Edition: April 2012
10 9 8 7 6 5 4 3 2 1

Grand Central Publishing is a division of Hachette Book Group, Inc.
The Grand Central Publishing name and logo is a trademark of
Hachette Book Group, Inc.

Novel Learning Series is a trademark of Willow Holdings, Inc.

The Hachette Speakers Bureau provides a wide range of authors for speaking events. To find out more, go to www.hachettespeakersbureau.com or call (866) 376-6591.

The publisher is not responsible for websites (or their content) that are not owned by the publisher.

The Library of Congress has cataloged the hardcover edition of
A Walk to Remember as follows:
Sparks, Nicholas.
A walk to remember / Nicholas Sparks.
p. cm.
ISBN 0-446-52553-7
I. Title.
PS3569. P363W35 1999
813'.54—dc21 99-12079
CIP

ISBN 978-1-4555-0856-3 (student guide)

For my parents, with love and memories.
Patrick Michael Sparks (1942–1996)
Jill Emma Marie Sparks (1942–1989)

And for my siblings, with all my heart and soul.
Micah Sparks
Danielle Lewis

Contents

Introduction to the Novel
Learning Series   1

Prologue   *3*

Questions and Explanations for the
Prologue   6

Chapter 1   *17*

Chapter 2   *35*

Questions and Explanations for
Chapters 1 and 2   48

Chapter 3   *61*

Chapter 4   *73*

Questions and Explanations for
Chapters 3 and 4   84

Chapter 5   *96*

Chapter 6   *105*

Questions and Explanations for
Chapters 5 and 6   116

Contents

Chapter 7   *128*

Chapter 8   *141*

Chapter 9   *147*

Questions and Explanations for
Chapters 7, 8, and 9   160

Chapter 10   *178*

Chapter 11   *190*

Questions and Explanations for
Chapters 10 and 11   203

Chapter 12   *214*

Chapter 13   *243*

Questions and Explanations for
Chapters 12 and 13   249

Post-Reading Questions and
Writing Assignments   260

About the Author   *289*

NOVEL LEARNING SERIES™

A Walk to Remember

Introduction to the
Novel Learning Series

The purpose of the Novel Learning Series is threefold:

1. to provide you with an opportunity to read and analyze a novel independently,
2. to provide study questions and writing prompts that are aligned with the Common Core State Standards for English Language Arts, and
3. to prepare you for rigorous high-stakes tests such as the SAT and ACT by providing multiple-choice questions that are similar in both form and content to the questions on those tests.

The first part of this book contains the novel *A Walk to Remember*, which is divided into seven sections for the purpose of this guide: the prologue, chapters 1 and 2; chapters 3 and 4; chapters 5 and 6; chapters 7, 8, and 9; chapters 10 and 11; and chapters 12 and 13. After each of these seven sections of the novel, there is a series of multiple-choice questions. You should read the chapters of the novel first, and then answer the questions. The information following each question explains *how* to answer the preceding question. If you are confident in your answer, use this information to confirm your thought process. If you are unsure of how to answer the question, the explanation can guide your decision-making process.

The final part of this guide contains critical reading questions related to a given passage, short answer assignments, and essay assignments. A rubric—a list of various essay elements and descriptions used to gauge quality in essay responses—is also provided. The rubric and the guide to understanding the rubric are designed to walk you through the writing process as you organize your thoughts and craft your response.

At this time, please turn the page, read the prologue, and answer the questions that follow.

Prologue

When I was seventeen, my life changed forever.

I know that there are people who wonder about me when I say this. They look at me strangely as if trying to fathom what could have happened back then, though I seldom bother to explain. Because I've lived here for most of my life, I don't feel that I have to unless it's on my terms, and that would take more time than most people are willing to give me. My story can't be summed up in two or three sentences; it can't be packaged into something neat and simple that people would immediately understand. Despite the passage of forty years, the people still living here who knew me that year accept my lack of explanation without question. My story in some ways is their story because it was something that all of us lived through.

It was I, however, who was closest to it.

I'm fifty-seven years old, but even now I can remember everything from that year, down to the smallest details. I relive that year often in my mind, bringing it back to life, and I realize that when I do, I always feel a strange combination of sadness and joy. There are moments when I wish I could roll back the clock and take all the sadness away, but I have the feeling that if I did, the joy would be gone as well. So I take the memories as they come, accepting them all, letting them guide me whenever I can. This happens more often than I let on.

It is April 12, in the last year before the millennium, and as I leave my house, I glance around. The sky is overcast and gray, but as I move down the street, I notice that the dogwoods and azaleas are blooming. I zip my jacket just a little. The temperature is cool, though I know it's only a matter of weeks before it will settle in to something comfortable and the gray skies give way to the kind of days that make North Carolina one of the most beautiful places in the world.

With a sigh, I feel it all coming back to me. I close my eyes and the years begin to move in reverse, slowly ticking backward, like the hands of a clock rotating in the wrong direction. As if through someone else's eyes, I watch myself grow younger; I see my hair changing from gray to brown, I feel the wrinkles around my eyes begin to smooth, my arms and legs grow sinewy. Lessons I've learned with age grow dimmer, and my innocence returns as that eventful year approaches.

Then, like me, the world begins to change: Roads narrow and some become gravel, suburban sprawl has been replaced with farmland, downtown streets teem with people, looking in windows as they pass Sweeney's bakery and Palka's meat shop. Men wear hats, women wear dresses. At the courthouse up the street, the bell tower rings...

I open my eyes and pause. I am standing outside the

Baptist church, and when I stare at the gable, I know exactly who I am.

My name is Landon Carter, and I'm seventeen years old.

This is my story; I promise to leave nothing out.

First you will smile, and then you will cry—don't say you haven't been warned.

Questions and Explanations for the Prologue

The questions in this book serve multiple purposes. Not only are they designed to check your comprehension and understanding of *A Walk to Remember*, they also encourage you to think critically about the literary text. It's important not only to know what happens in the novel, but to be able to analyze the text and make connections outside of it. In addition, the questions check your knowledge of essential literary terms and your knowledge of standard grammar and usage rules, as well as your vocabulary. The formats of the questions mirror those found in important standardized tests, such as the ACT and SAT.

You should do your best to answer each question. If you are having difficulty, a detailed explanation to guide your reasoning process is provided after each question. It is designed to teach you *how* to answer the question rather than just providing you the correct answer. Reading the explanation will be beneficial even if you are certain of your response; use it to verify that you have the correct response.

The ten questions on the prologue focus on grammar and usage, vocabulary, literary terms, characterization, and style. Some of the questions combine two or more of these areas, requiring you to synthesize your knowledge, make inferences, and interpret the text. The questions are designed to determine both your current level of understanding of the novel and your ability to answer higher-level questions.

The following sentence tests your ability to recognize grammar and usage errors. The sentence contains either a single error or no error at all. If the sentence contains an error, select the one underlined part that must be changed to make the sentence correct. If there is no error, select answer choice D.

1. Between 1959 <u>to</u> 1999, Landon <u>lived with</u> the memories

          A   B
   of the events <u>that</u> occurred when he was seventeen

                 C
   years old. <u>No error</u>

           D

In order to answer this question, you must discern what is being asked. Choice A requires knowing the difference between using *to* and *and* for inclusive dates; choice B is questioning the tense of the verb *live*, and choice C requires you to differentiate between *that* and *which*.

For choice A, recognize that two expressions exist to discuss a range of dates. The word *and* is used with the word *between*, and the word *to* is used with the word *from*. Which is being used here?

7

For choice B, recognize that the past tense is used to express action or make a statement about something that occurred in the past, and the present tense is used to express action that is occurring now, at the present time. Determine whether there is an appropriate usage of tense.

For choice C, determine whether the information in the clause *that occurred when he was seventeen years old* is essential to the sentence or not.

The following two questions test your vocabulary. Choose the word or set of words that, when inserted in the sentence, best fits the meaning of the sentence as a whole.

2. Landon's description of his town as it was forty years ago initially sounds _____, but he makes it clear that this narrative is going to be _____.

    A. strange...prudent

    B. idealized...realistic

    C. quaint...graphic

    D. hostile...pleasant

In addition to understanding the vocabulary words in the answers, you can determine the relationship between the words as determined by reading the context clues in the sentence. The words *initially* and *but* indicate that the correct answers will have contrasting, if not opposite, definitions.

Strange means curious, odd, or queer; *prudent* means wise in practical affairs, discreet. *Idealized* suggests that he's seeing the past through rose-colored glasses, a conception of perfection; *realistic* refers to the presentation of things as they really are. Something *quaint* has an old-fashioned attractiveness and charm, and something *graphic* is a vivid account. A *hostile* account would be antagonistic, and a *pleasant* account would be agreeable and enjoyable.

3. Landon's teenage muscles are tough, firm, and strong; thus, his description of his teenage self includes the word _____.

   A. sinewy

   B. lanky

   C. fibrous

   D. corporeal

The purpose of this question is to discern differences between words that might be considered synonyms– different words that have similar meanings. The context clues in the sentence will help differentiate among the choices. *Sinewy* means muscular and brawny. *Lanky* is bony and gaunt. *Fibrous* means resembling fibers. And *corporeal* means referring to the body. Although more than one of these terms may accurately describe Landon's teenage self, which is the best choice based on the other information in the sentence?

Question 4 tests your knowledge of <u>literary terms</u>.

4. Landon begins the story by telling us that his life changed when he was seventeen years old, thus preparing readers

for the profound events that he will never forget. The opening sentence refers to a time in the past, an event that occurred long before the current time period. This is an example of what literary device?

A. flashback

B. foreshadowing

C. hyperbole

D. onomatopoeia

This question is checking your knowledge of essential literary terms. A *flashback* is an event or a scene that takes place before the current time. For example, in *Harry Potter and the Prisoner of Azkaban*, when the Dementors frighten Harry, he experiences memories of his parents' deaths. That scene is a flashback. *Foreshadowing* is the providing of hints or clues to future events. For example, in *Romeo and Juliet*, when Benvolio suggests to Romeo that finding a new female beauty may help Romeo get over his love for Rosaline, that foreshadows Romeo's falling in love with Juliet when he sees her later in the play. *Hyperbole* is an overexaggeration used to illustrate a point. For example, if someone says, "I told you a million times what that is," you know that this person really didn't tell you a million times, just many, many times. And *onomatopoeia* is the use of a word that suggests the very sound it describes, like the noise made by the breakfast cereal Rice Krispies (*Snap, Crackle, Pop*) or the sound of a firework explosion—*kaboom*.

Question 5 asks you to determine the meaning of words and phrases as they are used in the text.

5. Landon's assertion that "I promise to leave nothing out" is an indication that:

   A. he feels compelled to finally tell the truth

   B. none of the details are sketchy

   C. he is suffering from an early onset of Alzheimer's

   D. he wants to be considered a reliable narrator

In order to answer a question like this, you must read all the answers to determine which one is the *best* possible answer. Sometimes, a part of an answer will be incorrect, thus eliminating that choice; other times an answer may be correct, but it will not be as complete or thorough as another option.

The key word in choice A is *compelled*. You must determine whether Landon's promise is the result of some pressure or sense of duty that he is currently feeling. For choice B, you must determine if it is possible for someone to "leave nothing out," yet still be sketchy on a couple of the details.

Choice C may or may not be true, but is the onset of Alzheimer's an indication that he won't leave anything out? A *reliable narrator* distances himself from the personal relationships and events in order to provide a more objective account. A *desire* to be a reliable narrator would not necessarily indicate that the objective is met.

Question 6 asks you to use textual evidence to draw a conclusion regarding character development.

6. What generalization can you make about Landon's character from reading the prologue?

A. He is truthful and straightforward.

B. He is insensitive to the memories of what occurred when he was seventeen years old.

C. He wishes it would be the beginning of spring.

D. He is flippant and supercilious.

We know from reading the prologue that Landon clearly states, "This is my story," and he promises to leave nothing out. As readers, we are invited to share Landon's narrative through the memories held within his mind's eye. Landon is direct as he foreshadows both the sadness and joy that took place throughout the story he is about to relate. For choice A, consider whether the prologue is both truthful and straightforward. For choice B, you need to determine whether an *insensitive* character would feel the roller coaster of emotions Landon experiences while reminiscing. For choice C, think about the following: Although there is an indication of springtime—dogwoods and azaleas were beginning to bloom and in a few weeks the weather would be more comfortable—does this information reveal anything about Landon's character? For choice D, consider that someone who is *flippant* is disrespectful and lacking in seriousness, and someone who is *supercilious* is haughtily disdainful.

Question 7 tests your knowledge of <u>literary terms</u>.

7. The prologue, and the entire novel, is told in the form of a:

A. biography

B. flashback

C. ballad

D. simile

This question also checks your knowledge of essential literary terms. Choice A is *biography*, which is a true account of the series of events making up a person's life and is considered nonfiction. Choice B is *flashback*, a narrative technique that incorporates an event or a series of events that occurred prior to the current time. Choice C is *ballad*, a form of poetry that tells a story. And choice D is *simile*, a figure of speech in which two unlike objects are compared using the words *like*, *as*, or *than*.

Question 8 asks you to analyze the <u>impact of specific details on meaning</u>.

8. What is the most important significance of including the following details in the prologue: "Men wear hats, women wear dresses"?

   A. They reveal Landon's distaste for the fashion of his youth, thus developing his character.

   B. These details help establish the setting.

   C. They provide an intimacy to Landon's narrative voice.

   D. They thematically support the idea of memory and its importance in our lives.

All the information provided by the author or a character, stated either directly or indirectly, comprises the details.

Different details are included or excluded, depending on an author's purpose. The type of details themselves will enable you to determine their purpose in a particular passage.

In order for choice A to be correct, there needs to be a sense of distaste for the information. Is there? Remember that choice B, establishing setting, refers to both time and place. Choice C requires you to differentiate between objectivity and intimacy. Objectivity—being able to relate the facts without an emotional involvement, thus being objective—is not the same as intimacy, which is a sense of familiarity, a personal connection. Both objectivity and intimacy can be used to describe a narrative voice. In order for details to support a theme, the theme must be stated, either directly or indirectly. In order for choice D to be correct, you must decide if there is enough information to determine a thematic statement about the topic of memory.

Question 9 asks you to analyze the point of view and <u>analyze the impact of specific details</u> on character development.

9. The prologue is best described as being told from the point of view of:

   A. a bitter old man who has avoided his neighbors for years but is finally ready to speak

   B. an omniscient and objective narrator

   C. a man who wishes to share the most profound experience of his life

   D. an obsequious middle-aged man who is accustomed to entertaining others

The key word in choice A is *bitter*, one who is intensely antagonistic and hostile. First you must determine if Landon is bitter, and then determine if the rest of the answer is true. For choice B, realize that an *omniscient narrator* is a third-person narrator who by definition is all-knowing. Choice C requires you to know that a *profound* experience penetrates the depths of one's being. And for choice D, you need to know that one who is *obsequious* is characterized by being dutiful and fawning. Which of these choices is the best description of Landon and his point of view?

Question 10 asks you to analyze how an author's choices contribute to overall structure and meaning.

10. Stylistically, the three single-sentence paragraphs that conclude the prologue do all of the following EXCEPT:

   A. build suspense

   B. establish the narrative voice

   C. create the mood for the novel

   D. reveal the primary conflict of the plot

Building *suspense* means adding excitement and interest to the narrative, providing the readers with a desire and interest to keep reading to find out what is going to happen. The narrative *voice* refers to the way the story is being told—through the diction, details, imagery, tone, and syntax that is used to create the sentences. The *mood* is the atmosphere, the emotional aura that surrounds the setting and is based on the details, images, and sounds. The *conflict* is the problem. Conflict is either internal, external, or a combination of the two. Clearly, the final three sentences of the prologue are doing three of these choices. You can determine the correct answer by either eliminating the choices you know are accurate descriptions or realizing which one is a false description.

Chapter 1

In 1958, Beaufort, North Carolina, which is located on the coast near Morehead City, was a place like many other small southern towns. It was the kind of place where the humidity rose so high in the summer that walking out to get the mail made a person feel as if he needed a shower, and kids walked around barefoot from April through October beneath oak trees draped in Spanish moss. People waved from their cars whenever they saw someone on the street whether they knew him or not, and the air smelled of pine, salt, and sea, a scent unique to the Carolinas. For many of the people there, fishing in the Pamlico Sound or crabbing in the Neuse River was a way of life, and boats were moored wherever you saw the Intracoastal Waterway. Only three channels came in on the television, though television was never important to those of us who grew up there. Instead our lives were centered around the churches, of which there were eighteen within the town limits alone. They went by names like the Fellowship Hall Christian Church, the Church of the Forgiven People, the Church of Sunday Atonement, and then, of course, there were the Baptist churches. When I was growing up, it was far and away the most popular denomination around, and there were Baptist churches on practically every corner of town, though each considered itself superior to the others. There were Baptist churches of every type—Freewill Baptists, Southern Baptists, Congregational Baptists, Missionary Baptists, Independent Baptists...well, you get the picture.

Back then, the big event of the year was sponsored by the Baptist church downtown—Southern, if you really want to know—in conjunction with the local high school. Every year they put on their Christmas pageant at the Beaufort Playhouse, which was actually a play that had been written by Hegbert Sullivan, a minister who'd been with the church since Moses parted the Red Sea. Okay, maybe he wasn't that old, but he was old enough that you could almost see through the guy's skin. It was sort of clammy all the time, and translucent—kids would swear they actually saw the blood flowing through his veins—and his hair was as white as those bunnies you see in pet stores around Easter.

Anyway, he wrote this play called *The Christmas Angel,* because he didn't want to keep on performing that old Charles Dickens classic *A Christmas Carol.* In his mind Scrooge was a heathen, who came to his redemption only because he saw ghosts, not angels—and who was to say whether they'd been sent by God, anyway? And who was to say he wouldn't revert to his sinful ways if they hadn't been sent directly from heaven? The play didn't exactly tell you in the end—it sort of plays into faith and all—but Hegbert didn't trust ghosts if they weren't actually sent by God, which wasn't explained in plain language, and this was his big problem with it. A few years back he'd changed the end of the play—sort of followed it up with his own version, complete with old man Scrooge becoming a preacher and all, heading off to Jerusalem to find the place where Jesus once taught the scribes. It didn't fly too well—not even to the congregation, who sat in the audience staring wide-eyed at the spectacle—and the newspaper said things like "Though it was certainly interesting, it wasn't exactly the play we've all come to know and love…"

So Hegbert decided to try his hand at writing his own play. He'd written his own sermons his whole life, and some of them, we had to admit, were actually interesting, especially when he talked about the "wrath of God coming down on the fornicators" and all that good stuff. That really got his blood boiling, I'll tell you, when he talked about the fornicators. That was his real hot spot. When we were younger, my friends and I would hide behind the trees and shout, "Hegbert is a fornicator!" when we saw him walking down the street, and we'd giggle like idiots, like we were the wittiest creatures ever to inhabit the planet.

Old Hegbert, he'd stop dead in his tracks and his ears would perk up—I swear to God, they actually moved and he'd turn this bright shade of red, like he'd just drunk gasoline, and the big green veins in his neck would start sticking out all over, like those maps of the Amazon River that you see in *National Geographic*. He'd peer from side to side, his eyes narrowing into slits as he searched for us, and then, just as suddenly, he'd start to go pale again, back to that fishy skin, right before our eyes. Boy, it was something to watch, that's for sure.

So we'd be hiding behind a tree and Hegbert (what kind of parents name their kid Hegbert, anyway?) would stand there waiting for us to give ourselves up, as if he thought we'd be that stupid. We'd put our hands over our mouths to keep from laughing out loud, but somehow he'd always zero in on us. He'd be turning from side to side, and then he'd stop, those beady eyes coming right at us, right through the tree. "I know who you are, Landon Carter," he'd say, "and the Lord knows, too." He'd let that sink in for a minute or so, and then he'd finally head off again, and during the sermon that weekend he'd stare right at us and say something like "God is merciful to children, but the children must be worthy as well." And we'd sort of lower ourselves in the seats, not from embarrassment, but to hide a new round of giggles. Hegbert didn't understand us at all, which was really sort of strange, being that he had a kid and all. But then again, she was a girl. More on that, though, later.

Anyway, like I said, Hegbert wrote *The Christmas Angel* one year and decided to put on *that* play instead. The play itself wasn't bad, actually, which surprised everyone the first year it was performed. It's basically the story of a man who had lost his wife a few years back. This guy, Tom Thornton, used to be real religious, but he had a crisis of faith after his wife died during childbirth. He's raising this little girl all on his own, but he hasn't been the greatest father, and what the little girl really wants for Christmas is a special music box with an angel engraved on top, a picture of which she'd cut out from an old catalog. The guy searches long and hard to find the gift, but he can't find it anywhere. So it's Christmas Eve and he's still searching, and while he's out looking through the stores, he comes across a strange woman he's never seen before, and she promises to help him find the gift for his daughter. First, though, they help this homeless person (back then they were called bums, by the way), then they stop at an orphanage to see some kids, then visit a lonely old woman who just wanted some company on Christmas Eve. At this point the mysterious woman asks Tom Thornton what he wants for Christmas, and he says that he wants his wife back. She brings him to the city fountain and tells him to look in the water and he'll find what he's looking for. When he looks in the water, he sees the face of his little girl, and he breaks down and cries right there. While he's sobbing, the mysterious lady runs off, and Tom Thornton searches but can't find her anywhere. Eventually he heads home, the lessons from the evening playing in his mind. He walks into his little girl's room, and her sleeping figure makes him realize that she's all he has left of his wife, and he starts to cry again because he knows he hasn't been a good enough father to her. The next morning, magically, the music box is underneath the tree, and the angel that's engraved on it looks exactly like the woman he'd seen the night before.

So it wasn't that bad, really. If truth be told, people cried buckets whenever they saw it. The play sold out every year it was performed, and due to its popularity, Hegbert eventually had to move it from the church to the Beaufort Playhouse, which had a lot more seating. By the time I was a senior in high school, the performances ran twice to packed houses, which, considering who actually performed it, was a story in and of itself.

You see, Hegbert wanted young people to perform the play—seniors in high school, not the theater group. I reckon he thought it would be a good learning experience before the seniors headed off to college and came face-to-face with all the fornicators. He was that kind of guy, you know, always wanting to save us from temptation. He wanted us to know that God is out there watching you, even when you're away from home, and that if you put your trust in God, you'll be all right in the end. It was a lesson that I would eventually learn in time, though it wasn't Hegbert who taught me.

As I said before, Beaufort was fairly typical as far as southern towns went, though it did have an interesting history. Blackbeard the pirate once owned a house there, and his ship, *Queen Anne's Revenge,* is supposedly buried somewhere in the sand just offshore. Recently some archaeologists or oceanographers or whoever looks for stuff like that said they found it, but no one's certain just yet, being that it sank over 250 years ago and you can't exactly reach into the glove compartment and check the registration. Beaufort's come a long way since the 1950s, but it's still not exactly a major metropolis or anything. Beaufort was, and always will be, on the smallish side, but when I was growing up, it barely warranted a place on the map. To put it into perspective, the congressional district that included Beaufort covered the entire eastern part of the state—some twenty thousand square miles—and there wasn't a single town with more than twenty-five thousand people. Even compared with those towns, Beaufort was regarded as being on the small side. Everything east of Raleigh and north of Wilmington, all the way to the Virginia border, was the district my father represented.

I suppose you've heard of him. He's sort of a legend, even now. His name is Worth Carter, and he was a congressman for almost thirty years. His slogan every other year during the election season was "Worth Carter represents———," and the person was supposed to fill in the city name where he or she lived. I can remember, driving on trips when me and Mom had to make our appearances to show the people he was a true family man, that we'd see those bumper stickers, stenciled in with names like Otway and Chocawinity and Seven Springs. Nowadays stuff like that wouldn't fly, but back then that was fairly sophisticated publicity. I imagine if he tried to do that now, people opposing him would insert all sorts of foul language in the blank space, but we never saw it once. Okay, maybe once. A farmer from Duplin County once wrote the word *shit* in the blank space, and when my mom saw it, she covered my eyes and said a prayer asking for forgiveness for the poor ignorant bastard. She didn't say exactly those words, but I got the gist of it.

So my father, Mr. Congressman, was a bigwig, and everyone but everyone knew it, including old man Hegbert. Now, the two of them didn't get along, not at all, despite the fact that my father went to Hegbert's church whenever he was in town, which to be frank wasn't all that often. Hegbert, in addition to his belief that fornicators were destined to clean the urinals in hell, also believed that communism was "a sickness that doomed mankind to heathenhood." Even though heathenhood wasn't a word—I can't find it in any dictionary—the congregation knew what he meant. They also knew that he was directing his words specifically to my father, who would sit with his eyes closed and pretend not to listen. My father was on one of the House committees that oversaw the "Red influence" supposedly infiltrating every aspect of the country, including national defense, higher education, and even tobacco farming. You have to remember that this was during the cold war; tensions were running high, and we North Carolinians needed something to bring it down to a more personal level. My father had consistently looked for facts, which were irrelevant to people like Hegbert.

Afterward, when my father would come home after the service, he'd say something like "Reverend Sullivan was in rare form today. I hope you heard that part about the Scripture where Jesus was talking about the poor..."

Yeah, sure, Dad...

My father tried to defuse situations whenever possible. I think that's why he stayed in Congress for so long. The guy could kiss the ugliest babies known to mankind and still come up with something nice to say. "He's such a gentle child," he'd say when a baby had a giant head, or, "I'll bet she's the sweetest girl in the world," if she had a birthmark over her entire face. One time a lady showed up with a kid in a wheelchair. My father took one look at him and said, "I'll bet you ten to one that you're the smartest kid in your class." And he was! Yeah, my father was great at stuff like that. He could fling it with the best of 'em, that's for sure. And he wasn't such a bad guy, not really, especially if you consider the fact that he didn't beat me or anything.

But he wasn't there for me growing up. I hate to say that because nowadays people claim that sort of stuff even if their parent *was* around and use it to excuse their behavior. *My dad...he didn't love me...that's why I became a stripper and performed on* The Jerry Springer Show...I'm not using it to excuse the person I've become, I'm simply saying it as a fact. My father was gone nine months of the year, living out of town in a Washington, D.C., apartment three hundred miles away. My mother didn't go with him because both of them wanted me to grow up "the same way they had."

Of course, my father's father took him hunting and fishing, taught him to play ball, showed up for birthday parties, all that small stuff that adds up to quite a bit before adulthood. My father, on the other hand, was a stranger, someone I barely knew at all. For the first five years of my life I thought all fathers lived somewhere else. It wasn't until my best friend, Eric Hunter, asked me in kindergarten who that guy was who showed up at my house the night before that I realized something wasn't quite right about the situation.

"He's my father," I said proudly.

"Oh," Eric said as he rifled through my lunch-box, looking for my Milky Way, "I didn't know you had a father."

Talk about something whacking you straight in the face.

So, I grew up under the care of my mother. Now she was a nice lady, sweet and gentle, the kind of mother most people dream about. But she wasn't, nor could she ever be, a manly influence in my life, and that fact, coupled with my growing disillusionment with my father, made me become something of a rebel, even at a young age. Not a bad one, mind you. Me and my friends might sneak out late and soap up car windows now and then or eat boiled peanuts in the graveyard behind the church, but in the fifties that was the kind of thing that made other parents shake their heads and whisper to their children, "You don't want to be like that Carter boy. He's on the fast track to prison."

Me. A bad boy. For eating boiled peanuts in the graveyard. Go figure.

Anyway, my father and Hegbert didn't get along, but it wasn't only because of politics. No, it seems that my father and Hegbert knew each other from way back when. Hegbert was about twenty years older than my father, and back before he was a minister, he used to work for my father's father. My grandfather—even though he spent lots of time with my father—was a true bastard if there ever was one. He was the one, by the way, who made the family fortune, but I don't want you to imagine him as the sort of man who slaved over his business, working diligently and watching it grow, prospering slowly over time. My grandfather was much shrewder than that. The way he made his money was simple—he started as a bootlegger, accumulating wealth throughout Prohibition by running rum up from Cuba. Then he began buying land and hiring sharecroppers to work it. He took ninety percent of the money the sharecroppers made on their tobacco crop, then loaned them money whenever they needed it at ridiculous interest rates. Of course, he never intended to collect the money—instead he would foreclose on any land or equipment they happened to own. Then, in what he called "his moment of inspiration," he started a bank called Carter Banking and Loan. The only other bank in a two-county radius had mysteriously burned down, and with the onset of the Depression, it never reopened. Though everyone knew what had really happened, not a word was ever spoken for fear of retribution, and their fear was well placed. The bank wasn't the only building that had mysteriously burned down.

His interest rates were outrageous, and little by little he began amassing more land and property as people defaulted on their loans. When the Depression hit hardest, he foreclosed on dozens of businesses throughout the county while retaining the original owners to continue to work on salary, paying them just enough to keep them where they were, because they had nowhere else to go. He told them that when the economy improved, he'd sell their business back to them, and people always believed him.

Never once, however, did he keep his promise. In the end

he controlled a vast portion of the county's economy, and he abused his clout in every way imaginable.

I'd like to tell you he eventually went to a terrible death, but he didn't. He died at a ripe-old age while sleeping with his mistress on his yacht off the Cayman Islands. He'd outlived both his wives and his only son. Some end for a guy like that, huh? Life, I've learned, is never fair. If people teach anything in school, that should be it.

But back to the story...Hegbert, once he realized what a bastard my grandfather really was, quit working for him and went into the ministry, then came back to Beaufort and started ministering in the same church we attended. He spent his first few years perfecting his fire-and-brimstone act with monthly sermons on the evils of the greedy, and this left him scant time for anything else. He was forty-three before he ever got married; he was fifty-five when his daughter, Jamie Sullivan, was born. His wife, a wispy little thing twenty years younger than he, went through six miscarriages before Jamie was born, and in the end she died in childbirth, making Hegbert a widower who had to raise a daughter on his own.

Hence, of course, the story behind the play.

People knew the story even before the play was first performed. It was one of those stories that made its rounds whenever Hegbert had to baptize a baby or attend a funeral. Everyone knew about it, and that's why, I think, so many people got emotional whenever they saw the Christmas play. They knew it was based on something that happened in real life, which gave it special meaning.

Jamie Sullivan was a senior in high school, just like me, and she'd already been chosen to play the angel, not that anyone else even had a chance. This, of course, made the play extra special that year. It was going to be a big deal, maybe the biggest ever—at least in Miss Garber's mind. She was the drama teacher, and she was already glowing about the possibilities the first time I met her in class.

Now, I hadn't really planned on taking drama that year. I really hadn't, but it was either that or chemistry II. The thing was, I thought it would be a blow-off class, especially when compared with my other option. No papers, no tests, no tables where I'd have to memorize protons and neutrons and combine elements in their proper formulas...what could possibly be better for a high school senior? It seemed like a sure thing, and when I signed up for it, I thought I'd just be able to sleep through most every class, which, considering my late night peanut eating, was fairly important at the time.

On the first day of class I was one of the last to arrive, coming in just a few seconds before the bell rang, and I took a seat in the back of the room. Miss Garber had her back turned to the class, and she was busy writing her name in big cursive letters, as if we didn't know who she was. Everyone knew her—it was impossible not to. She was big, at least six feet two, with flaming red hair and pale skin that showed her freckles well into her forties. She was also overweight—I'd say honestly she pushed two fifty—and she had a fondness for wearing flower-patterned muumuus. She had thick, dark, horn-rimmed glasses, and she greeted every one with, "Helloooooo," sort of singing the last syllable. Miss Garber was one of a kind, that's for sure, and she was single, which made it even worse. A guy, no matter how old, couldn't help but feel sorry for a gal like her.

Beneath her name she wrote the goals she wanted to accomplish that year. "Self-confidence" was number one, followed by

"Self-awareness" and, third, "Self-fulfillment." Miss Garber was big into the "self" stuff, which put her really ahead of the curve as far as psychotherapy is concerned, though she probably didn't realize it at the time. Miss Garber was a pioneer in that field. Maybe it had something to do with the way she looked; maybe she was just trying to feel better about herself.

But I digress.

It wasn't until the class started that I noticed something unusual. Though Beaufort High School wasn't large, I knew for a fact that it was pretty much split fifty-fifty between males and females, which was why I was surprised when I saw that this class was at least ninety percent female. There was only one other male in the class, which to my thinking was a good thing, and for a moment I felt flush with a "look out world, here I come" kind of feeling. Girls, girls, girls... I couldn't help but think. Girls and girls and no tests in sight.

Okay, so I wasn't the most forward-thinking guy on the block.

So Miss Garber brings up the Christmas play and tells everyone that Jamie Sullivan is going to be the angel that year. Miss Garber started clapping right away—she was a member of the church, too—and there were a lot of people who thought she was gunning for Hegbert in a romantic sort of way. The first time I heard it, I remember thinking that it was a good thing they were too old to have children, if they ever did get together. Imagine—translucent with freckles? The very thought gave everyone shudders, but of course, no one ever said anything about it, at least within hearing distance of Miss Garber and Hegbert. Gossip is one thing, hurtful gossip is completely another, and even in high school we weren't *that* mean.

Miss Garber kept on clapping, all alone for a while, until all of us finally joined in, because it was obvious that was what she wanted. "Stand up, Jamie," she said. So Jamie stood up and turned around, and Miss Garber started clapping even faster, as if she were standing in the presence of a bona fide movie star.

Now Jamie Sullivan was a nice girl. She really was. Beaufort was small enough that it had only one elementary school, so we'd been in the same classes our entire lives, and I'd be lying if I said I never talked to her. Once, in second grade, she'd sat in the seat right next to me for the whole year, and we'd even had a few conversations, but it didn't mean that I spent a lot of time hanging out with her in my spare time, even back then. Who I saw in school was one thing; who I saw *after* school was something completely different, and Jamie had never been on my social calendar.

It's not that Jamie was unattractive—don't get me wrong. She wasn't hideous or anything like that. Fortunately she'd taken after her mother, who, based on the pictures I'd seen, wasn't half-bad, especially considering who she ended up marrying. But Jamie wasn't exactly what I considered attractive, either. Despite the fact that she was thin, with honey blond hair and soft blue eyes, most of the time she looked sort of . . . *plain,* and that was when you noticed her at all. Jamie didn't care much about outward appearances, because she was always looking for things like "inner beauty," and I suppose that's part of the reason she looked the way she did. For as long as I'd known her— and this was going way back, remember—she'd always worn her hair in a tight bun, almost like a spinster, without a stitch of makeup on her face. Coupled with her usual brown cardigan and plaid skirt, she always looked as though she were on her way to interview for a job at the library. We used to think it was just a phase and that she'd eventually grow out of it, but she never had. Even through our first three years of high school, she hadn't changed at all. The only thing that had changed was the size of her clothes.

But it wasn't just the way Jamie looked that made her different; it was also the way she acted. Jamie didn't spend any time hanging out at Cecil's Diner or going to slumber parties with other girls, and I knew for a fact that she'd never had a boyfriend her entire life. Old Hegbert would probably have had a heart attack if she had. But even if by some odd turn of events Hegbert had allowed it, it still wouldn't have mattered. Jamie carried her Bible wherever she went, and if her looks and Hegbert didn't keep the boys away, the Bible sure as heck did. Now, I liked the Bible as much as the next teenage boy, but Jamie seemed to enjoy it in a way that was completely foreign to me. Not only did she go to vacation Bible school every August, but she would read the Bible during lunch break at school. In my mind that just wasn't normal, even if she was the minister's daughter. No matter how you sliced it, reading Paul's letters to the Ephesians wasn't nearly as much fun as flirting, if you know what I mean.

But Jamie didn't stop there. Because of all her Bible reading, or maybe because of Hegbert's influence, Jamie believed it was important to help others, and helping others is exactly what she did. I knew she volunteered at the orphanage in Morehead City, but for her that simply wasn't enough. She was always in charge of one fund-raiser or another, helping everyone from the Boy Scouts to the Indian Princesses, and I know that when she was fourteen, she spent part of her summer painting the outside of an elderly neighbor's house. Jamie was the kind of girl who would pull weeds in someone's garden without being asked or stop traffic to help little kids cross the road. She'd save her allowance to buy a new basketball for the orphans, or she'd turn around and drop the money into the church basket on Sunday. She was, in other words, the kind of girl who made the rest of us look bad, and whenever she glanced my way, I couldn't help but feel guilty, even though I hadn't done anything wrong.

Nor did Jamie limit her good deeds to people. If she ever came across a wounded animal, for instance, she'd try to help it, too. Opossums, squirrels, dogs, cats, frogs...it didn't matter to her. Dr. Rawlings, the vet, knew her by sight, and he'd shake his head whenever he saw her walking up to the door carrying a cardboard box with yet another critter inside. He'd take off his eyeglasses and wipe them with his handkerchief while Jamie explained how she'd found the poor creature and what had happened to it. "He was hit by a car, Dr. Rawlings. I think it was in the Lord's plan to have me find him and try to save him. You'll help me, won't you?"

With Jamie, everything was in the Lord's plan. That was another thing. She always mentioned the Lord's plan whenever you talked to her, no matter what the subject. The baseball game's rained out? Must be the Lord's plan to prevent something worse from happening. A surprise trigonometry quiz that everyone in class fails? Must be in the Lord's plan to give us challenges. Anyway, you get the picture.

Then, of course, there was the whole Hegbert situation, and this didn't help her at all. Being the minister's daughter couldn't have been easy, but she made it seem as if it were the most natural thing in the world and that she was lucky to have been blessed in that way. That's how she used to say it, too. "I've been so blessed to have a father like mine." Whenever she said it, all we could do was shake our heads and wonder what planet she actually came from.

Despite all these other strikes, though, the one thing that *really* drove me crazy about her was the fact that she was always so damn cheerful, no matter what was happening around her. I swear, that girl never said a bad thing about anything or anyone, even to those of us who weren't that nice to her. She would hum to herself as she walked down the street, she would wave to strangers driving by in their cars. Sometimes ladies would come running out of their house if they saw her walking by, offering her pumpkin bread if they'd been baking all day or lemonade if the sun was high in the sky. It seemed as if every adult in town adored her. "She's such a nice young lady," they'd say whenever Jamie's name came up. "The world would be a better place if there were more people like her."

But my friends and I didn't quite see it that way. In our minds, one Jamie Sullivan was plenty.

I was thinking about all this while Jamie stood in front of us on the first day of drama class, and I admit that I wasn't much interested in seeing her. But strangely, when Jamie turned to face us, I kind of got a shock, like I was sitting on a loose wire or something. She wore a plaid skirt with a white blouse under the same brown cardigan sweater I'd seen a million times, but there were two new bumps on her chest that the sweater couldn't hide that I swore hadn't been there just three months earlier. She'd never worn makeup and she still didn't, but she had a tan, probably from Bible school, and for the first time she looked—well, almost pretty. Of course, I dismissed that thought right away, but as she looked around the room, she stopped and smiled right at me, obviously glad to see that I was in the class. It wasn't until later that I would learn the reason why.

Chapter 2

After high school I planned to go to the University of North Carolina at Chapel Hill. My father wanted me to go to Harvard or Princeton like some of the sons of other congressmen did, but with my grades it wasn't possible. Not that I was a bad student. I just didn't focus on my studies, and my grades weren't exactly up to snuff for the Ivy Leagues. By my senior year it was pretty much touch and go whether I'd even get accepted at UNC, and this was my father's alma mater, a place where he could pull some strings. During one of his few weekends home, my father came up with the plan to put me over the top. I'd just finished my first week of school and we were sitting down for dinner. He was home for three days on account of Labor Day weekend.

"I think you should run for student body president," he said. "You'll be graduating in June, and I think it would look good on your record. Your mother thinks so, too, by the way."

My mother nodded as she chewed a mouthful of peas. She didn't speak much when my father had the floor, though she winked at me. Sometimes I think my mother liked to see me squirm, even though she was sweet.

"I don't think I'd have a chance at winning," I said. Though I was probably the richest kid in school, I was by no means the most popular. That honor belonged to Eric Hunter, my best friend. He could throw a baseball at almost ninety miles an hour, and he'd led the football team to back-to-back state titles as the star quarterback. He was a stud. Even his name sounded cool.

"Of course you can win," my father said quickly. "We Carters always win."

That's another one of the reasons I didn't like spending time with my father. During those few times he was home, I think he wanted to mold me into a miniature version of himself. Since I'd grown up pretty much without him, I'd come to resent having him around. This was the first conversation we'd had in weeks. He rarely talked to me on the phone.

"But what if I don't want to?"

My father put down his fork, a bite of his pork chop still on the tines. He looked at me crossly, giving me the once-over. He was wearing a suit even though it was over eighty degrees in the house, and it made him even more intimidating. My father always wore a suit, by the way.

"I think," he said slowly, "that it would be a good idea."

I knew that when he talked that way the issue was settled. That's the way it was in my family. My father's word was law. But the fact was, even after I agreed, I didn't want to do it. I didn't want to waste my afternoons meeting with teachers after school—after school!—every week for the rest of the year, dreaming up themes for school dances or trying to decide what colors the streamers should be. That's really all the class presidents did, at least back when I was in high school. It wasn't like students had the power to actually decide anything meaningful.

But then again, I knew my father had a point. If I wanted to go to UNC, I had to do something. I didn't play football or basketball, I didn't play an instrument, I wasn't in the chess club or the bowling club or anything else. I didn't excel in the classroom—hell, I didn't excel at much of anything. Growing despondent, I started listing the things I actually could do, but to be honest, there really wasn't that much. I could tie eight different types of sailing knots, I could walk barefoot across hot asphalt farther than anyone I knew, I could balance a pencil vertically on my finger for thirty seconds . . . but I didn't think that any of those things would really stand out on a college application. So there I was, lying in bed all night long, slowly coming to the sinking realization that I was a loser. Thanks, Dad.

The next morning I went to the principal's office and added my name to the list of candidates. There were two other people running—John Foreman and Maggie Brown. Now, John didn't stand a chance, I knew that right off. He was the kind of guy who'd pick lint off your clothes while he talked to you. But he was a good student. He sat in the front row and raised his hand every time the teacher asked a question. If he was called to give the answer, he would almost always give the right one, and he'd turn his head from side to side with a smug look on his face, as if proving how superior his intellect was when compared with those of the other peons in the room. Eric and I used to shoot spitballs at him when the teacher's back was turned.

Maggie Brown was another matter. She was a good student as well. She'd served on the student council for the first three years and had been the junior class president the year before. The only real strike against her was the fact that she wasn't very attractive, and she'd put on twenty pounds that summer. I knew that not a single guy would vote for her.

After seeing the competition, I figured that I might have a chance after all. My entire future was on the line here, so I formulated my strategy. Eric was the first to agree.

"Sure, I'll get all the guys on the team to vote for you, no problem. If that's what you really want."

"How about their girlfriends, too?" I asked.

That was pretty much my entire campaign. Of course, I went to the debates like I was supposed to, and I passed out those dorky "What I'll do if I'm elected president" fliers, but in the end it was Eric Hunter who probably got me where I needed to be. Beaufort High School had only about four hundred students, so getting the athletic vote was critical, and most of the jocks didn't give a hoot who they voted for anyway. In the end it worked out just the way I planned.

I was voted student body president with a fairly large majority of the vote. I had no idea what trouble it would eventually lead me to.

When I was a junior I went steady with a girl named Angela Clark. She was my first real girlfriend, though it lasted for only a few months. Just before school let out for the summer, she dumped me for a guy named Lew who was twenty years old and worked as a mechanic in his father's garage. His primary attribute, as far as I could tell, was that he had a really nice car. He always wore a white T-shirt with a pack of Camels folded into the sleeve, and he'd lean against the hood of his Thunderbird, looking back and forth, saying things like "Hey, baby" whenever a girl walked by. He was a real winner, if you know what I mean.

Well, anyway, the homecoming dance was coming up, and because of the whole Angela situation, I still didn't have a date. Everyone on the student council had to attend—it was mandatory. I had to help decorate the gym and clean up the next day—and besides, it was usually a pretty good time. I called a couple of girls I knew, but they already had dates, so I called a few more. They had dates, too. By the final week the pickings were getting pretty slim. The pool was down to the kinds of girls who had thick glasses and talked with lisps. Beaufort was never exactly a hotbed for beauties anyway, but then again I had to find somebody. I didn't want to go to the dance without a date— what would that look like? I'd be the only student body president ever to attend the homecoming dance alone. I'd end up being the guy scooping punch all night long or mopping up the barf in the bathroom. That's what people without dates usually did.

Growing sort of panicky, I pulled out the yearbook from the year before and started flipping through the pages one by one, looking for anyone who might not have a date. First I looked through the pages with the seniors. Though a lot of them were off at college, a few of them were still around town. Even though I didn't think I had much of a chance with them, I called anyway, and sure enough, I was proven right. I couldn't find anyone, at least not anyone who would go with me. I was getting pretty good at handling rejection, I'll tell you, though that's not the sort of thing you brag about to your grandkids. My mom knew what I was going through, and she finally came into my room and sat on the bed beside me.

"If you can't get a date, I'll be happy to go with you," she said.

"Thanks, Mom," I said dejectedly.

When she left the room, I felt even worse than I had before. Even my mom didn't think I could find somebody. And if I showed up with her? If I lived a hundred years, I'd never live that down.

There was another guy in my boat, by the way. Carey Dennison had been elected treasurer, and he still didn't have a date, either. Carey was the kind of guy no one wanted to spend time with at all, and the only reason he'd been elected was because he'd run unopposed. Even then I think the vote was fairly close. He played the tuba in the marching band, and his body looked all out of proportion, as if he'd stopped growing halfway through puberty. He had a great big stomach and gangly arms and legs, like the Hoos in Hooville, if you know what I mean. He also had a high-pitched way of talking—it's what made him such a good tuba player, I reckon—and he never stopped asking questions. "Where did you go last weekend? Was it fun? Did you see any girls?" He wouldn't even wait for an answer, and he'd move around constantly as he asked so you had to keep turning your head to keep him in sight. I swear he was probably the most annoying person I'd ever met. If I didn't get a date, he'd stand off on one side with me all night long, firing questions like some deranged prosecutor.

So there I was, flipping through the pages in the junior class section, when I saw Jamie Sullivan's picture. I paused for just a second, then turned the page, cursing myself for even thinking about it. I spent the next hour searching for anyone halfway decent looking, but I slowly came to the realization that there wasn't anyone left. In time I finally turned back to her picture and looked again. She wasn't bad looking, I told myself, and she's really sweet. She'd probably say yes, I thought...

I closed the yearbook. Jamie Sullivan? Hegbert's daughter? No way. Absolutely not. My friends would roast me alive.

But compared with dating your mother or cleaning up puke or even, God forbid...Carey Dennison?

I spent the rest of the evening debating the pros and cons of my dilemma. Believe me, I went back and forth for a while, but in the end the choice was obvious, even to me. I had to ask Jamie to the dance, and I paced around the room thinking of the best way to ask her.

It was then that I realized something terrible, something absolutely frightening. Carey Dennison, I suddenly realized, was probably doing the exact same thing I was doing right now. He was probably looking through the yearbook, too! He was weird, but he wasn't the kind of guy who liked cleaning up puke, either, and if you'd seen his mother, you'd know that his choice was even worse than mine. What if he asked Jamie first? Jamie wouldn't say no to him, and realistically she was the only option he had. No one besides her would be caught dead with him. Jamie helped everyone—she was one of those equal opportunity saints. She'd probably listen to Carey's squeaky voice, see the goodness radiating from his heart, and accept right off the bat.

So there I was, sitting in my room, frantic with the possibility that Jamie might not go to the dance with me. I barely slept that night, I tell you, which was just about the strangest thing I'd ever experienced. I don't think anyone ever fretted about asking Jamie out before. I planned to ask her first thing in the morning, while I still had my courage, but Jamie wasn't in school. I assumed she was working with the orphans over in Morehead City, the way she did every month. A few of us had tried to get out of school using that excuse, too, but Jamie was

41

the only one who ever got away with it. The principal knew she was reading to them or doing crafts or just sitting around playing games with them. She wasn't sneaking out to the beach or hanging out at Cecil's Diner or anything. That concept was absolutely ludicrous.

"Got a date yet?" Eric asked me in between classes. He knew very well that I didn't, but even though he was my best friend, he liked to stick it to me once in a while.

"Not yet," I said, "but I'm working on it."

Down the hall, Carey Dennison was reaching into his locker. I swear he shot me a beady glare when he thought I wasn't looking.

That's the kind of day it was.

The minutes ticked by slowly during my final class. The way I figured it—if Carey and I got out at the same time, I'd be able to get to her house first, what with those gawky legs and all. I started to psych myself up, and when the bell rang, I took off from school running at a full clip. I was flying for about a hundred yards or so, and then I started to get kind of tired, and then a cramp set in. Pretty soon all I could do was walk, but that cramp really started to get to me, and I had to bend over and hold my side while I kept moving. As I made my way down the streets of Beaufort, I looked like a wheezing version of the Hunchback of Notre Dame.

Behind me I thought I heard Carey's high-pitched laughter. I turned around, digging my fingers into my gut to stifle the pain, but I couldn't see him. Maybe he was cutting through someone's backyard! He was a sneaky bastard, that guy. You couldn't trust him even for a minute.

I started to stumble along even faster, and pretty soon I reached Jamie's street. By then I was sweating all over—my shirt was soaked right through—and I was still wheezing something fierce. Well, I reached her front door, took a second to catch my breath, and finally knocked. Despite my fevered rush to her house, my pessimistic side assumed that Carey would be the one who opened the door for me. I imagined him smiling at me with a victorious look in his eye, one that essentially meant "Sorry, partner, you're too late."

But it wasn't Carey who answered, it was Jamie, and for the first time in my life I saw what she'd look like if she were an ordinary person. She was wearing jeans and a red blouse, and though her hair was still pulled up into a bun, she looked more casual than she usually did. I realized she could actually be cute if she gave herself the opportunity.

"Landon," she said as she held open the door, "this is a surprise!" Jamie was always glad to see everyone, including me, though I think my appearance startled her. "You look like you've been exercising," she said.

"Not really," I lied, wiping my brow. Luckily the cramp was fading fast.

"You've sweat clean through your shirt."

"Oh, that?" I looked at my shirt. "That's nothing. I just sweat a lot sometimes."

"Maybe you should have it checked by a doctor."

"I'll be okay, I'm sure."

"I'll say a prayer for you anyway," she offered as she smiled. Jamie was always praying for someone. I might as well join the club.

"Thanks," I said.

She looked down and sort of shuffled her feet for a moment. "Well, I'd invite you in, but my father isn't home, and he doesn't allow boys in the house while he's not around."

"Oh," I said dejectedly, "that's okay. We can talk out here, I guess." If I'd had my way, I would have done this inside.

"Would you like some lemonade while we sit?" she asked. "I just made some."

"I'd love some," I said.

"I'll be right back." She walked back into the house, but she left the door open and I took a quick glance around. The house, I noticed, was small but tidy, with a piano against one wall and a sofa against the other. A small fan sat oscillating in the corner. On the coffee table there were books with names like *Listening to Jesus* and *Faith Is the Answer*. Her Bible was there, too, and it was opened to the chapter of Luke.

A moment later Jamie returned with the lemonade, and we took a seat in two chairs near the corner of the porch. I knew she and her father sat there in the evenings because I passed by their house now and then. As soon as we were seated, I saw Mrs. Hastings, her neighbor across the street, wave to us. Jamie waved back while I sort of scooted my chair so that Mrs. Hastings couldn't see my face. Even though I was going to ask Jamie to the dance, I didn't want anyone—even Mrs. Hastings—to see me there on the off chance that she'd already accepted Carey's offer. It was one thing to actually go with Jamie, it was another thing to be rejected by her in favor of a guy like Carey.

"What are you doing?" Jamie asked me. "You're moving your chair into the sun."

"I like the sun," I said. She was right, though. Almost immediately I could feel the rays burning through my shirt and making me sweat again.

"If that's what you want," she said, smiling. "So, what did you want to talk to me about?"

Jamie reached up and started to adjust her hair. By my

reckoning, it hadn't moved at all. I took a deep breath, trying to gather myself, but I couldn't force myself to come out with it just yet.

"So," I said instead, "you were at the orphanage today?"

Jamie looked at me curiously. "No. My father and I were at the doctor's office."

"Is he okay?"

She smiled. "Healthy as can be."

I nodded and glanced across the street. Mrs. Hastings had gone back inside, and I couldn't see anyone else in the vicinity. The coast was finally clear, but I still wasn't ready.

"Sure is a beautiful day," I said, stalling.

"Yes, it is."

"Warm, too."

"That's because you're in the sun."

I looked around, feeling the pressure building. "Why, I'll bet there's not a single cloud in the whole sky."

This time Jamie didn't respond, and we sat in silence for a few moments.

"Landon," she finally said, "you didn't come here to talk about the weather, did you?"

"Not really."

"Then why are you here?"

The moment of truth had arrived, and I cleared my throat.

"Well...I wanted to know if you were going to the home-coming dance."

"Oh," she said. Her tone made it seem as if she were unaware that such a thing existed. I fidgeted in my seat and waited for her answer.

"I really hadn't planned on going," she finally said.

"But if someone asked you to go, you might?"

45

It took a moment for her to answer.

"I'm not sure," she said, thinking carefully. "I suppose I might go, if I got the chance. I've never been to a homecoming dance before."

"They're fun," I said quickly. "Not *too* much fun, but fun." Especially when compared to my other options, I didn't add.

She smiled at my turn of phrase. "I'd have to talk to my father, of course, but if he said it was okay, then I guess I could."

In the tree beside the porch, a bird started to chirp noisily, as if he knew I wasn't supposed to be here. I concentrated on the sound, trying to calm my nerves. Just two days ago I couldn't have imagined myself even thinking about it, but suddenly there I was, listening to myself as I spoke the magic words.

"Well, would you like to go to the dance with me?"

I could tell she was surprised. I think she believed that the little lead-up to the question probably had to do with someone else asking her. Sometimes teenagers sent their friends out to "scout the terrain," so to speak, so as not to face possible rejection. Even though Jamie wasn't much like other teenagers, I'm sure she was familiar with the concept, at least in theory.

Instead of answering right away, though, Jamie glanced away for a long moment. I got a sinking feeling in my stomach because I assumed she was going to say no. Visions of my mother, puke, and Carey flooded through my mind, and all of a sudden I regretted the way I'd behaved toward her all these years. I kept remembering all the times I'd teased her or called her father a fornicator or simply made fun of her behind her back. Just when I was feeling awful about the whole thing and imagining how I would ever be able to avoid Carey for five hours, she turned and faced me again. She had a slight smile on her face.

"I'd love to," she finally said, "on one condition."

I steadied myself, hoping it wasn't something *too* awful.

"Yes?"

"You have to promise that you won't fall in love with me."

I knew she was kidding by the way she laughed, and I couldn't help but breathe a sigh of relief. Sometimes, I had to admit, Jamie had a pretty good sense of humor.

I smiled and gave her my word.

Questions and Explanations for Chapters 1 and 2

The fourteen questions on chapters 1 and 2 focus on grammar and usage, vocabulary, literary terms, characterization, and the effect of both setting and allusions. Some of the questions combine two or more of these areas, requiring you to synthesize your knowledge, make inferences, and interpret the text. The questions are designed to determine both your current level of understanding of the novel and your ability to answer higher-level questions.

The following sentence tests your ability to recognize grammar and usage errors. Part of the following sentence is underlined; beneath the sentence are four ways of phrasing the underlined material. Select the option that produces the best sentence. If you think the original phrasing produces a better sentence than any of the alternatives, select choice A.

1. Jamie Sullivan volunteered for sundry good causes, <u>many of them were</u> helping the poor, downtrodden, and homeless.

   A. many of them were

   B. many of which were

   C. many were

   D. and many of them were

For choice A to be correct, there must not be an error in the original sentence or the original wording must be better than the other choices. Substitute the suggested changes in place of the underlined words and compare them to the original.

Choice B eliminates the comma splice of the original by creating a subordinate clause. A comma splice is when a comma is used to connect two main clauses without using a coordinating conjunction. A comma splice is also one kind of a run-on sentence—for example, "John likes *The Lord of the Rings*, Jane prefers *Twilight*." Each clause in this example is a complete thought, and connecting them with only a comma is incorrect. The error can be corrected a few different ways: "John likes *The Lord of the Rings*, but Jane prefers *Twilight*" (using a comma and a coordinating conjunction to create a compound sentence, a sentence with two or more main clauses); "John likes *The Lord of the Rings*; Jane prefers *Twilight*" (using a semicolon to create a compound sentence); "John likes *The Lord of the Rings*, although Jane prefers *Twilight*" (using a comma and a subordinating conjunction to create a complex sentence, a sentence with one main clause and at least one dependent clause). Stylistically, a complex sentence is usually preferable to a compound sentence.

Although choice C tightens the second half of the sentence, it still retains the comma splice of the original. Choice D creates a grammatically correct compound sentence. Stylistically, which is the strongest sentence?

Questions 2 and 3 test your vocabulary. Choose the word or set of words that, when inserted in the sentence, best fits the meaning of the sentence as a whole.

2. Reverend Hegbert Sullivan was _____ by the _____ manner in which Landon's grandfather treated people.

   A. repelled...peaceful

   B. weakened...amusing

   C. amazed...generous

   D. annoyed...unethical

The context clues in the sentence reveal that the two words must have a similar connotation; they must be similar in nature, as well as being part of an accurate statement based on the information found in the chapter.

Repelled means having a distaste or aversion toward, and *peaceful* means free from strife or commotion. *Weakened* means reduced in strength or impaired, and *amusing* means pleasantly entertaining. *Amazed* means greatly surprised and astounded; *generous* means liberal in giving, unselfish. *Annoyed* means disturbed or bothered, and *unethical* means not moral, upright, or honest.

3. The fact that public school drama class students could be mandated to participate in a religious Christmas play demonstrates how _____ school, community, and religion were in the 1950s.

   A. secular

   B. complimentary

   C. short-sighted

   D. interrelated

This question is designed to discern the *best* possible answer, even when a number of choices may be potentially correct. It's important to recognize what the statement intends to convey, rather than interpreting it based on your personal beliefs. *Secular* means concerned with nonreligious subjects. *Complimentary* is politely flattering (and not to be confused with *complementary*, which means fitting well together). *Short-sighted* means lacking in foresight. And *interrelated* means mutually related.

Based on the context clues in the sentence and what you've read in the novel, the relationship between school, community, and religion was clearly quite connected in the 1950s.

Question 4 asks you to analyze the impact of specific word choices on meaning and to use textual evidence to support inferences drawn from the text.

4. Which group of words from chapter 1 best illustrates the culture in Beaufort, North Carolina, in the late 1950s?

A. "the humidity rose so high in the summer that walking out to get the mail made a person feel as if he needed a shower"

B. "kids walked around barefoot from April through October beneath oak trees draped in Spanish moss"

C. "fishing in the Pamlico Sound or crabbing in the Neuse River was a way of life"

D. "our lives were centered around the churches, of which there were eighteen within the town limits alone"

This question is asking you to determine what is most important to the beliefs of the people in Beaufort. The answer is the one that best illustrates the culture, or the ideas, beliefs, and values, of the town.

Choice A is a factual description. But what does the humidity reveal about a culture? Choice B depicts something about the way of life—how kids dressed and played. Choice C mentions "a way of life," but those words actually describe only those who were fishing or crabbing—that is, only a subset of the culture of Beaufort and not the whole of the town. And choice D states that the behaviors and beliefs of the townspeople are focused on their beliefs in the church's tradition. Decide which of these correct pieces of information best answers the question.

Question 5 tests your knowledge of literary terms.

5. It is said that Hegbert Sullivan, the minister, has "been with the church since Moses parted the Red Sea." This quotation makes use of which literary device?

 A. personification

 B. alliteration

 C. metaphor

 D. symbolism

This is another question that checks both your knowledge and application of literary terms. *Personification*, choice A, is giving nonhuman things human characteristics—for example, "The leaves danced in the wind." *Alliteration*, choice B, is the repetition of the initial sound in a series of words—for example, "Becky bought Bill a bad bugle." A *metaphor*, choice C, is a comparison between unlike things without using a connective word—for example, "LeBron James is an animal on the basketball court." And *symbolism*, choice D, is the sustained use of objects to stand for something else. Thus, a symbol is any object that not only has meaning in and of itself but also is representative of something else. For example, the American flag is a piece of fabric with stars and stripes on it (literally, it is a flag), but it symbolizes, among other things, democracy, freedom, and the fifty states.

Question 6 asks you to use textual evidence to support analysis of what the text explicitly says.

6. In chapter 1, we learn about the family dynamics within the Carter household and the roles that each member plays. It is apparent that Mrs. Carter has to play the roles of both parents during the nine months every year that Landon's father, the congressman, is away in Washington. How do you think the lack of a male influence impacted Landon's life?

A. He loved his mother very much and was happy that she chose to remain at home with him and not to go to Washington with his father.

B. His father didn't beat him, so he felt it was fine that his father had little interaction with him.

C. He became disillusioned about his father's relationship with him and became a rebel because of it.

D. Because his father was rarely at home, Landon was able to establish himself as the man of the house.

In order to select the correct answer, you have to make sure your choice directly answers the question. Landon clearly loves his mother, and you need to determine if that love is the result of a lack of a male influence. Landon's father clearly doesn't beat him, and you need to determine if Landon is fine with this lack of interaction. Landon admits to becoming somewhat of a rebel, but is it because he is disillusioned with his relationship (or lack thereof)? You need to determine if Landon has established himself as the man of the house.

Question 7 asks you to analyze the development of a central idea of the text.

7. In the novel, the minister Hegbert Sullivan wrote *The Christmas Angel*, a Christmas play that was loved by the entire town. The play was seemingly autobiographical, detailing the personal story of his life after his wife's death and his search for love and the meaning of life with his daughter. What do you think is the overarching theme that resonates from the protagonist, Tom Thornton?

> A. He lost his faith when his wife died during childbirth, and he wants her back.
>
> B. He wants a special music box for his daughter.
>
> C. He knows that he hasn't been a good enough father for his daughter.
>
> D. If you put your faith in God, things will work out in the end.

All of the information in the choices is correct, but the question is asking what the overarching theme is. Thus, the best answer won't be just about the plot or about a character. Instead, it will be a statement about a thematic topic.

Question 8 tests your comprehension and vocabulary, as well as your ability to draw an inference based on textual evidence.

8. In most ways, Jamie is quite different from the other teenage girls in her school. Which of the following words would NOT represent Jamie's image of herself?

> A. adventurous
>
> B. helpful
>
> C. selfless
>
> D. dependable

The word *not* indicates that three out of the four responses do represent Jamie's image of herself. Don't get confused by the word *not*, for the wrong answers to this question are actually accurate descriptions of Jamie. An *adventurous* person is inclined to participate in exciting undertakings. One who is *helpful* provides aid and assistance. Someone who is *self-less* has little concern for himself or herself. And one who is *dependable* is worthy of trust and is reliable.

Question 9 tests your comprehension and vocabulary, as well as your ability to draw an inference based on textual evidence.

9. In chapters 1 and 2, Landon is characterized as all of the following EXCEPT:

   A. immature

   B. sarcastic

   C. regretful

   D. pious

This question is just like the previous one, with the word *except* functioning the same way as the word *not* does in question 8. An *immature* person is juvenile and childish. A *sarcastic* person often makes sneering or cutting remarks. A *regretful* person has a sense of regret or guilt for some wrongdoing, and a *pious* person shows reverence for God.

Question 10 asks you to analyze how an author's choices contribute to the novel's overall structure and meaning.

10. The setting of *A Walk to Remember*, as established in chapters 1 and 2, does all of the following EXCEPT:

   A. provide background for the time period of the novel

   B. help create the mood of the novel

    C. state explicitly the theme of the novel

    D. aid in the understanding of Landon as a character

The format of this question is the same as that of the previous two, but now you need to recognize the various functions of the setting and analyze what effect the setting has in the first two chapters. Either eliminate the choices you know are examples of how the setting functions in the first two chapters or select the choice that represents a function of setting that *is not* fulfilled in these chapters.

Remember that setting refers to both time and place. Think about what life in a small southern town in 1958 would be like. Does knowing the time and place give you a sense of the era and help establish a feeling of what life was like? Does it directly state a theme of the novel? Do we get a better understanding of Landon knowing where and when he went to high school?

Question 11 asks you to analyze how an author's choices contribute to the novel's overall structure and meaning.

11. What effect does Reverend Hegbert Sullivan's seeming obsession with "fornicators" have?

    A. It supports the interpretation that he is a dirty old man.

    B. It provides humor and simultaneously establishes the reverend's character.

    C. It demonstrates Landon's mature narrative voice.

    D. It undermines his credibility as a father and a minister.

In order to answer this question, you need to have read and understood the characterization of Reverend Sullivan as viewed from Landon's perspective. Does Landon view him as a dirty old man, as suggested in choice A? Is the anecdote humorous, and does it reveal something about how Reverend Sullivan thinks, speaks, and acts, as stated in choice B? Is Landon speaking maturely as he relates this story, as choice C claims? Finally, would a father and minister be concerned about premarital sex? And if so, would that concern undermine his credibility, as choice D suggests?

Rewording the choices into questions provides a fresh way to think about and analyze them, enabling you to select the correct one.

Question 12 asks you to analyze how an author's choices contribute to the novel's overall structure and meaning.

12. Stylistically, the summary of the play *The Christmas Angel* in the novel achieves all of the following EXCEPT which one?

   A. It demonstrates Landon's reliability as a narrator.

   B. The life of the young female character in the play parallels Jamie's life, so Landon is essentially describing Jamie.

   C. It suggests the importance of Landon's involvement in the production.

   D. It foreshadows the relationship between Hegbert and Jamie.

A *reliable narrator* demonstrates knowledge of the situations and characters involved in the story, presenting them in an objective manner. The personal involvement of a reliable narrator does not typically impede a truthful account of the story. Does the female character in the play parallel the character of Jamie? If so, then it does provide a description of her. Likewise, if the characters in the play are autobiographical, then it also foreshadows the father-daughter relationship. The amount of time spent on summarizing the plot of the play suggests that it must be important, and therefore would indicate that the narrator was intimately involved with the production. Three of the choices describe effects of the play's summary and can be eliminated as possible correct answers for this question.

Question 13 tests your comprehension as well as your knowledge of literary terms.

13. Landon's father, Worth Carter, serves as a *foil* for which character?

    A. Landon

    B. Jamie

    C. Reverend Hegbert

    D. Eric Hunter

You need to know what a literary *foil* is in order to answer this question. A literary *foil* is a character who provides contrast for another character. For example, in the Twilight series, Jacob and Edward are foils for each other. The best way to answer this question is to determine which character is most unlike, or the opposite of, Landon's father.

Question 14 tests your knowledge of literary terms as well as your ability to draw inferences based on textual evidence.

14. Landon's allusion to the "Hoos in Hooville" (a misspelling of Dr. Seuss's "Whos") does all of the following EXCEPT:

    A. enable readers to understand better the physical description of Carey Dennison

    B. demonstrate Landon's sarcastic nature

    C. reveal Landon's own immaturity

    D. foreshadow Landon's own transformation

Though knowledge of the allusion to Dr. Seuss's Whos of Whoville from the book *How the Grinch Stole Christmas* is not essential for answering this question, it might make it a bit easier. The reference to the "Hoos" is used in a metaphor comparing Carey to the "Hoos," providing a visual image of his body type. Although comparing Carey to a Who isn't necessarily a nice thing to say, you need to determine if Landon's tone is serious or sarcastic, sneering, and taunting. What does the metaphor suggest about the type of person who would make such a comparison? And the title character in the book—the Grinch—is initially a bad guy but eventually has a conversion, learning the true meaning of Christmas.

Chapter 3

As a general rule, Southern Baptists don't dance. In Beaufort, however, it wasn't a rule that was ever strictly enforced. The minister before Hegbert—don't ask me what his name was—took sort of a lax view about school dances as long as they were chaperoned, and because of that, they'd become a tradition of sorts. By the time Hegbert came along, it was too late to change things. Jamie was pretty much the only one who'd never been to a school dance and frankly, I didn't know whether she even knew how to dance at all.

I admit that I also had some concerns about what she would wear, though it wasn't something I would tell her. When Jamie went to the church socials—which were encouraged by Hegbert—she usually wore an old sweater and one of the plaid skirts we saw in school every day, but the homecoming dance was supposed to be special. Most of the girls bought new dresses and the boys wore suits, and this year we were bringing in a photographer to take our pictures. I knew Jamie wasn't going to buy a new dress because she wasn't exactly well-off. Ministering wasn't a profession where people made a lot of money, but of course ministers weren't in it for monetary gain, they were in it for the long haul, if you know what I mean. But I didn't want her to wear the same thing she wore to school every day, either. Not so much for me—I'm not that cold-hearted—but because of what others might say. I didn't want people to make fun of her or anything.

The good news, if there was any, was that Eric didn't rib me too bad about the whole Jamie situation because he was too busy thinking about his own date. He was taking Margaret Hays, who was the head cheerleader at our school. She wasn't the brightest bulb on the Christmas tree, but she was nice in her own way. By nice, of course, I'm talking about her legs. Eric offered to double-date with me, but I turned him down because I didn't want to take any chances with Eric teasing Jamie or anything like that. He was a good guy, but he could be kind of heartless sometimes, especially when he had a few shots of bourbon in him.

The day of the dance was actually quite busy for me. I spent most of the afternoon helping to decorate the gym, and I had to get to Jamie's about a half hour early because her father wanted to talk to me, though I didn't know why. Jamie had sprung that one on me just the day before, and I can't say I was exactly thrilled by the prospect of it. I figured he was going to talk about temptation and the evil path it can lead us to. If he brought up fornication, though, I knew I would die right there on the spot. I said small prayers all day long in the hope of avoiding this conversation, but I wasn't sure if God would put my prayers on the front burner, if you know what I mean, because of the way I'd behaved in the past. I was pretty nervous just thinking about it.

After I showered I put on my best suit, swung by the florist to pick up Jamie's corsage, then drove to her house. My mom had let me borrow the car, and I parked it on the street directly in front of Jamie's house. We hadn't turned the clocks back yet, so it was still light out when I got there, and I strolled up the cracked walkway to her door. I knocked and waited for a moment, then knocked again. From behind the door I heard Hegbert say, "I'll be right there," but he wasn't exactly racing to the door. I must have stood there for two minutes or so, looking at the door, the moldings, the little cracks in the windowsills. Off to the side were the chairs that Jamie and I had sat in just a few days back. The one I sat in was still turned in the opposite direction. I guess they hadn't sat there in the last couple of days.

Finally the door creaked open. The light coming from the lamp inside shadowed Hegbert's face slightly and sort of reflected through his hair. He was old, like I said, seventy-two years by my reckoning. It was the first time I'd ever seen him up close, and I could see all the wrinkles on his face. His skin really was translucent, even more so than I'd imagined.

"Hello, Reverend," I said, swallowing my trepidation. "I'm here to take Jamie to the homecoming dance."

"Of course you are," he said. "But first, I wanted to talk with you."

"Yes, sir, that's why I came early."

"C'mon in."

In church Hegbert was a fairly snappy dresser, but right now he looked like a farmer, dressed in overalls and a T-shirt. He motioned for me to sit on the wooden chair he'd brought in from the kitchen. "I'm sorry it took a little while to open the door. I was working on tomorrow's sermon," he said.

I sat down.

"That's okay, sir." I don't know why, but you just had to call him "sir." He sort of projected that image.

"All right, then, so tell me about yourself."

I thought it was a fairly ridiculous question, with him having such a long history with my family and all. He was also the one who had baptized me, by the way, and he'd seen me in church every Sunday since I'd been a baby.

"Well, sir," I began, not really knowing what to say, "I'm the student body president. I don't know whether Jamie mentioned that to you."

He nodded. "She did. Go on."

"And...well, I hope to go to the University of North Carolina next fall. I've already received the application."

He nodded again. "Anything else?"

I had to admit, I was running out of things after that. Part of me wanted to pick up the pencil off the end table and start balancing it, giving him the whole thirty seconds' worth, but he wasn't the kind of guy who would appreciate it.

"I guess not, sir."

"Do you mind if I ask you a question?"

"No, sir."

He sort of stared at me for a long time, as if thinking about it.

"Why did you ask my daughter to the dance?" he finally said.

I was surprised, and I know that my expression showed it.

"I don't know what you mean, sir."

"You're not planning to do anything to...embarrass her, are you?"

"No, sir," I said quickly, shocked by the accusation. "Not at all. I needed someone to go with, and I asked her. It's as simple as that."

"You don't have any pranks planned?"

"No, sir. I wouldn't do that to her . . ."

This went on for a few more minutes—his grilling me about my true intentions, I mean—but luckily Jamie stepped out of the back room, and her father and I both turned our heads at the same moment. Hegbert finally stopped talking, and I breathed a sigh of relief. She'd put on a nice blue skirt and a white blouse I'd never seen before. Fortunately she'd left her sweater in the closet. It wasn't too bad, I had to admit, though I knew she'd still be underdressed compared with others at the dance. As always, her hair was pulled up in a bun. Personally I think it would have looked better if she'd kept it down, but that was the last thing I wanted to say. Jamie looked like . . . well, Jamie looked exactly like she usually did, but at least she wasn't planning on bringing her Bible. That would have just been too much to live down.

"You're not giving Landon a hard time, are you?" she said cheerfully to her father.

"We were just visiting," I said quickly before he had a chance to respond. For some reason I didn't think he'd told Jamie about the kind of person he thought I was, and I didn't think that now would be a good time.

"Well, we should probably go," she said after a moment. I think she sensed the tension in the room. She walked over to her father and kissed him on the cheek. "Don't stay up too late working on the sermon, okay?"

"I won't," he said softly. Even with me in the room, I could tell he really loved her and wasn't afraid to show it. It was how he felt about me that was the problem.

We said good-bye, and on our way to the car I handed Jamie her corsage and told her I'd show her how to put it on once we got in the car. I opened her door for her and walked around the other side, then got in as well. In that short period of time, Jamie had already pinned on the flower.

"I'm not exactly a dimwit, you know. I do know how to pin on a corsage."

I started the car and headed toward the high school, with the conversation I'd just had with Hegbert running through my mind.

"My father doesn't like you very much," she said, as if knowing what I was thinking.

I nodded without saying anything.

"He thinks you're irresponsible."

I nodded again.

"He doesn't like your father much, either."

I nodded once more.

"Or your family."

I get the picture.

"But do you know what I think?" she asked suddenly.

"Not really." By then I was pretty depressed.

"I think that all this was in the Lord's plan somehow. What do you think the message is?"

Here we go, I thought to myself.

I doubt if the evening could have been much worse, if you want to know the truth. Most of my friends kept their distance, and Jamie didn't have many friends to begin with, so we spent most of our time alone. Even worse, it turned out that my presence wasn't even required anymore. They'd changed the rule owing to the fact that Carey couldn't get a date, and that left me feeling pretty miserable about the whole thing as soon as I found out about it. But because of what her father had said to me, I couldn't exactly take her home early, now, could I? And more than that, she was really having a good time; even I could see that. She loved the decorations I'd helped put up, she loved the music, she loved everything about the dance. She kept telling me how wonderful everything was, and she asked me whether I might help her decorate the church someday, for one of their socials. I sort of mumbled that she should call me, and even though I said it without a trace of energy, Jamie thanked me for being so considerate. To be honest, I was depressed for at least the first hour, though she didn't seem to notice.

Jamie had to be home by eleven o'clock, an hour before the dance ended, which made it somewhat easier for me to handle. Once the music started we hit the floor, and it turned out that she was a pretty good dancer, considering it was her first time and all. She followed my lead pretty well through about a dozen songs, and after that we headed to the tables and had what resembled an ordinary conversation. Sure, she threw in words like "faith" and "joy" and even "salvation," and she talked about helping the orphans and scooping critters off the highway, but she was just so damn happy, it was hard to stay down for long.

So things weren't too terrible at first and really no worse than I had expected. It wasn't until Lew and Angela showed up that everything really went sour.

They showed up a few minutes after we arrived. He was wearing that stupid T-shirt, Camels in his sleeve, and a glop of hair gel on his head. Angela hung all over him right from the beginning of the dance, and it didn't take a genius to realize she'd had a few drinks before she got there. Her dress was really flashy—her mother worked in a salon and was up on all the latest fashions—and I noticed she'd picked up that ladylike habit called chewing gum. She really worked that gum, chewing it almost like a cow working her cud.

Well, good old Lew spiked the punch bowl, and a few more people started getting tipsy. By the time the teachers found out, most of the punch was already gone and people were getting that glassy look in their eyes. When I saw Angela gobble up her second glass of punch, I knew I should keep my eye on her. Even though she'd dumped me, I didn't want anything bad to happen to her. She was the first girl I'd ever French-kissed, and even though our teeth clanked together so hard the first time we tried it that I saw stars and had to take aspirin when I got home, I still had feelings for her.

So there I was, sitting with Jamie, barely listening as she described the wonders of Bible school, watching Angela out of the corner of my eye, when Lew spotted me looking at her. In one frenzied motion he grabbed Angela around the waist and dragged her over to the table, giving me one of those looks, the one that "means business." You know the one I'm talking about.

"Are you staring at my girl?" he asked, already tensing up.

"No."

"Yeah, he was," Angela said, kind of slurring out the words. "He was staring right at me. This is my old boyfriend, the one I told you about."

His eyes turned into little slits, just like Hegbert's were prone to do. I guess I have this effect on lots of people.

"So you're the one," he said, sneering.

Now, I'm not much of a fighter. The only real fight I was ever in was in third grade, and I pretty much lost that one when I started to cry even before the guy punched me. Usually I didn't have much trouble staying away from things like this because of my passive nature, and besides, no one ever messed with me when Eric was around. But Eric was off with Margaret somewhere, probably behind the bleachers.

"I wasn't staring," I said finally, "and I don't know what she told you, but I doubt if it was true."

His eyes narrowed. "Are you calling Angela a liar?" he sneered.

Oops.

I think he would have hit me right there, but Jamie suddenly worked her way into the situation.

"Don't I know you?" she said cheerfully, looking right at him. Sometimes Jamie seemed oblivious of situations that were happening right in front of her. "Wait—yes, I do. You work in the garage downtown. Your father's name is Joe, and your grandma lives out on Foster Road, by the railroad crossing."

A look of confusion crossed Lew's face, as though he were trying to put together a puzzle with too many pieces.

"How do you know all that? What he'd do, tell you about me, too?"

"No," Jamie said, "don't be silly." She laughed to herself. Only Jamie could find humor at a time like this. "I saw your picture in your grandma's house. I was walking by, and she needed some help bringing in the groceries. Your picture was on the mantel."

Lew was looking at Jamie as though she had cornstalks growing out of her ears.

Meanwhile Jamie was fanning herself with her hand. "Well, we were just sitting down to take a breather from all that dancing. It sure gets hot out there. Would you like to join us? We've got a couple of chairs. I'd love to hear how your grandma is doing."

She sounded so happy about it that Lew didn't know what to do. Unlike those of us who were used to this sort of thing, he'd never come across someone like Jamie before. He stood there for a moment or two, trying to decide if he should hit the guy with the girl who'd helped his grandma. If it sounds confusing to you, imagine what it was doing to Lew's petroleum-damaged brain.

He finally skulked off without responding, taking Angela with him. Angela had probably forgotten how the whole thing started anyway, owing to the amount she'd had to drink. Jamie and I watched him go, and when he was a safe distance away, I exhaled. I hadn't even realized I'd been holding my breath.

"Thanks," I mumbled sheepishly, realizing that Jamie—Jamie!—was the one who'd saved me from grave bodily harm.

Jamie looked at me strangely. "For what?" she asked, and when I didn't exactly spell it out for her, she went right back into her story about Bible school, as if nothing had happened at all. But this time I found myself actually listening to her, at least with one of my ears. It was the least I could do.

It turns out that it wasn't the last we saw of either Lew or Angela that evening. The two glasses of punch had really done Angela in, and she threw up all over the ladies' restroom. Lew, being the classy guy he was, left when he heard her retching, sort of slinking out the way he came in, and that was the last I saw of him. Jamie, as fate would have it, was the one who found Angela in the bathroom, and it was obvious that Angela wasn't doing too well. The only option was to clean her up and take her home before the teachers found out about it. Getting drunk was a big deal back then, and she'd be looking at suspension, maybe even expulsion, if she got caught.

Jamie, bless her heart, didn't want that to happen any more than I did, though I would have thought otherwise if you'd asked me beforehand, owing to the fact that Angela was a minor and in violation of the law. She'd also broken another one of Hegbert's rules for proper behavior. Hegbert frowned on lawbreaking *and* drinking, and though it didn't get him going like fornication, we all knew he was deadly serious, and we assumed Jamie felt the same way. And maybe she did, but her helper instinct must have taken over. She probably took one look at Angela and thought "wounded critter" or something like that and took immediate charge of the situation. I went off and located Eric behind the bleachers, and he agreed to stand guard at the bathroom door while Jamie and I went in to tidy it up. Angela had done a marvelous job, I tell you. The puke was everywhere except the toilet. The walls, the floor, the sinks—even on the ceiling, though don't ask me how she did that. So there I was, perched on all fours, cleaning up puke at the homecoming dance in my best blue suit, which was exactly what I had wanted to avoid in the first place. And Jamie, my date, was on all fours, too, doing exactly the same thing.

I could practically hear Carey laughing a squeaky, maniacal laugh somewhere in the distance.

We ended up sneaking out the back door of the gym, keeping Angela stable by walking on either side of her. She kept asking where Lew was, but Jamie told her not to worry. She had a real soothing way of talking to Angela, though Angela was so far gone, I doubt if she even knew who was speaking. We loaded Angela into the backseat of my car, where she passed out almost immediately, although not before she'd vomited once more on the floor of the car. The smell was so awful that we had to roll down the windows to keep from gagging, and the drive to Angela's house seemed extra long. Her mother answered the door, took one look at her daughter, and brought her inside without so much as a word of thanks. I think she was embarrassed, and we really didn't have much to say to her anyway. The situation pretty much spoke for itself.

By the time we dropped her off it was ten forty-five, and we drove straight back to Jamie's. I was really worried when we got there because of the way she looked and smelled, and I said a silent prayer hoping that Hegbert wasn't awake. I didn't want to have to explain this to him. Oh, he'd probably listen to Jamie if she was the one who told him about it, but I had the sinking feeling that he'd find a way to blame me anyway.

So I walked her to the door, and we stood outside under the porch light. Jamie crossed her arms and smiled a little, looking just as if she'd come in from an evening stroll where she'd contemplated the beauty of the world.

"Please don't tell your father about this," I said.

"I won't," she said. She kept on smiling when she finally turned my way. "I had a good time tonight. Thank you for taking me to the dance."

Here she was, covered in puke, actually thanking me for the evening. Jamie Sullivan could really drive a guy crazy sometimes.

Chapter 4

In the two weeks following the homecoming dance, my life pretty much returned to normal. My father was back in Washington, D.C., which made things a lot more fun around my house, primarily because I could sneak out the window again and head to the graveyard for my late night forays. I don't know what it was about the graveyard that attracted us so. Maybe it had something to do with the tombstones themselves, because as far as tombstones went, they were actually fairly comfortable to sit on.

We usually sat in a small plot where the Preston family had been buried about a hundred years ago. There were eight tombstones there, all arranged in a circle, making it easy to pass the boiled peanuts back and forth between us. One time my friends and I decided to learn what we could about the Preston family, and we went to the library to find out if anything had been written about them. I mean, if you're going to sit on someone's tombstone, you might as well know something about them, right?

It turns out that there wasn't much about the family in the historical records, though we did find out one interesting tidbit of information. Henry Preston, the father, was a one-armed lumberjack, believe it or not. Supposedly he could cut down a tree as fast as any two-armed man. Now the vision of a one-armed lumberjack is pretty vivid right off the bat, so we talked about him a lot. We used to wonder what else he could do with only one arm, and we'd spend long hours discussing how fast he could pitch a baseball or whether or not he'd be able to swim across the Intracoastal Waterway. Our conversations weren't exactly highbrow, I admit, but I enjoyed them nonetheless.

Well, Eric and me were out there one Saturday night with a couple of other friends, eating boiled peanuts and talking about Henry Preston, when Eric asked me how my "date" went with Jamie Sullivan. He and I hadn't seen much of each other since the homecoming dance because the football season was already in the play-offs and Eric had been out of town the past few weekends with the team.

"It was okay," I said, shrugging, doing my best to play it cool.

Eric playfully elbowed me in the ribs, and I grunted. He outweighed me by at least thirty pounds.

"Did you kiss her good night?"

"No."

He took a long drink from his can of Budweiser as I answered. I don't know how he did it, but Eric never had trouble buying beer, which was strange, being that everyone in town knew how old he was.

He wiped his lips with the back of his hand, tossing me a sidelong glance.

"I would have thought that after she helped you clean the bathroom, you would have at least kissed her good night."

"Well, I didn't."

"Did you even try?"

"No."

"Why not?"

"She's not that kind of girl," I said, and even though we all knew it was true, it still sounded like I was defending her.

Eric latched on to that like a leech.

"I think you like her," he said.

"You're full of crap," I answered, and he slapped my back, hard enough to force the breath right out of me. Hanging out with Eric usually meant that I'd have a few bruises the following day.

"Yeah, I might be full of crap," he said, winking at me, "but you're the one who's smitten with Jamie Sullivan."

I knew we were treading on dangerous ground.

"I was just using her to impress Margaret," I said. "And with all the love notes she's been sending me lately, I reckon it must have worked."

Eric laughed aloud, slapping me on the back again.

"You and Margaret—now *that's* funny . . ."

I knew I'd just dodged a major bullet, and I breathed a sigh of relief as the conversation spun off in a new direction. I joined in now and then, but I wasn't really listening to what they were saying. Instead I kept hearing this little voice inside me that made me wonder about what Eric had said.

The thing was, Jamie was probably the best date I could have had that night, especially considering how the evening turned out. Not many dates—heck, not many people, period—would have done what she did. At the same time, her being a good date didn't mean I liked her. I hadn't talked to her at all since the dance, except when I saw her in drama class, and even then it was only a few words here and there. If I liked her at all, I told myself, I would have wanted to talk to her. If I liked her, I would have offered to walk her home. If I liked her, I would have wanted to bring her to Cecil's Diner for a basket of hushpuppies and some RC cola. But I didn't want to do any of those things. I really didn't. In my mind, I'd already served my penance.

The next day, Sunday, I was in my room, working on my application to UNC. In addition to the transcripts from my high school and other personal information, they required five essays of the usual type. If you could meet one person in history, who would that person be and why? Name the most significant influence in your life and why you feel that way. What do you look for in a role model and why? The essay questions were fairly predictable—our English teacher had told us what to expect—and I'd already worked on a couple of variations in class as homework.

English was probably my best subject. I'd never received anything lower than an A since I first started school, and I was glad the emphasis for the application process was on writing. If it had been on math, I might have been in trouble, especially if it included those algebra questions that talked about the two trains leaving an hour apart, traveling in opposite directions at forty miles an hour, etc. It wasn't that I was bad in math—I usually pulled at least a C—but it didn't come naturally to me, if you know what I mean.

Anyway, I was writing one of my essays when the phone rang. The only phone we had was located in the kitchen, and I had to run downstairs to grab the receiver. I was breathing so loudly that I couldn't make out the voice too well, though it sounded like Angela. I immediately smiled to myself. Even though she'd been sick all over the place and I'd had to clean it up, she was actually pretty fun to be around most of the time. And her dress really had been something, at least for the first hour. I figured she was probably calling to thank me or even to get together for a barbecue sandwich and hushpuppies or something.

"Landon?"

"Oh, hey," I said, playing it cool, "what's going on?"

There was a short pause on the other end.

"How are you?"

It was then that I suddenly realized I wasn't speaking to Angela. Instead it was Jamie, and I almost dropped the phone. I can't say that I was happy about hearing from her, and for a second I wondered who had given her my phone number before I realized it was probably in the church records.

"Landon?"

"I'm fine," I finally blurted out, still in shock.

"Are you busy?" she asked.

"Sort of."

"Oh...I see...," she said, trailing off. She paused again.

"Why are you calling me?" I asked.

It took her a few seconds to get the words out.

"Well...I just wanted to know if you wouldn't mind coming by a little later this afternoon."

"Coming by?"

"Yes. To my house."

"Your house?" I didn't even try to disguise the growing surprise in my voice. Jamie ignored it and went on.

"There's something I want to talk to you about. I wouldn't ask if it wasn't important."

"Can't you just tell me over the phone?"

"I'd rather not."

"Well, I'm working on my college application essays all after-noon," I said, trying to get out of it.

"Oh...well...like I said, it's important, but I suppose I can talk to you Monday at school..."

With that, I suddenly realized that she wasn't going to let me off the hook and that we'd end up talking one way or the other. My brain suddenly clicked through the scenarios as I tried to figure out which one I should do—talk to her where my friends would see us or talk at her house. Though neither option was particularly good, there was something in the back of my mind, reminding me that she'd helped me out when I'd really needed it, and the least I could do was to listen to what she had to say. I may be irrespon-sible, but I'm a *nice* irresponsible, if I do say so myself.

Of course, that didn't mean everyone else had to know about it.

"No," I said, "today is fine..."

We arranged to meet at five o'clock, and the rest of the after-noon ticked by slowly, like the drips from Chinese water tor-ture. I left my house twenty minutes early so I'd have plenty of time to get there. My house was located near the waterfront in the historic part of town, just a few doors down from where Blackbeard used to live, overlooking the Intracoastal Water-way. Jamie lived on the other side of town, across the railroad tracks, so it would take me about that long to get there.

It was November, and the temperature was finally cooling down. One thing I really liked about Beaufort was the fact that the springs and falls lasted practically forever. It might get hot in the summer or snow once every six years, and there might be a cold spell that lasted a week or so in January, but for the most part all you needed was a light jacket to make it through the winter. Today was one of those perfect days—mid-seventies without a cloud in the sky.

I made it to Jamie's house right on time and knocked on her door. Jamie answered it, and a quick peek inside revealed that Hegbert wasn't around. It wasn't quite warm enough for sweet tea or lemonade, and we sat in the chairs on the porch again, without anything to drink. The sun was beginning to lower itself in the sky, and there wasn't anyone on the street. This time I didn't have to move my chair. It hadn't been moved since the last time I'd been there.

"Thank you for coming, Landon," she said. "I know you're busy, but I appreciate your taking the time to do this."

"So, what's so important?" I said, wanting to get this over with as quickly as possible.

Jamie, for the first time since I'd known her, actually looked nervous as she sat with me. She kept bringing her hands together and pulling them apart.

"I wanted to ask you a favor," she said seriously.

"A favor?"

She nodded.

At first I thought she was going to ask me to help her decorate the church, like she'd mentioned at homecoming, or maybe she needed me to use my mother's car to bring some stuff to the orphans. Jamie didn't have her license, and Hegbert needed their car anyway, being that there was always a funeral or something he had to go to. But it still took a few seconds for her to get the words out.

She sighed, her hands coming together again.

"I'd like to ask you if you wouldn't mind playing Tom Thornton in the school play," she said.

Tom Thornton, like I said before, was the man in search of the music box for his daughter, the one who meets the angel. Except for the angel, it was far and away the most important role.

"Well…I don't know," I said, confused. "I thought Eddie Jones was going to be Tom. That's what Miss Garber told us."

Eddie Jones was a lot like Carey Dennison, by the way. He was really skinny, with pimples all over his face, and he usually talked to you with his eyes all squinched up. He had a nervous tic, and he couldn't help but squinch his eyes whenever he got nervous, which was practically all the time. He'd probably end up spouting his lines like a psychotic blind man if you put him, in front of a crowd. To make things worse, he had a stutter, too, and it took him a long time to say anything at all. Miss Garber had given him the role because he'd been the only one who offered to do it, but even then it was obvious she didn't want him, either. Teachers were human, too, but she didn't have much of an option, since no one else had come forward.

"Miss Garber didn't say that exactly. What she said was that Eddie could have the role if no one else tried out for it."

"Can't someone else do it instead?"

But there really wasn't anyone else, and I knew it. Because of Hegbert's requirement that only seniors perform, the play was in a bind that year. There were about fifty senior boys at the high school, twenty-two of whom were on the football team, and with the team still in the running for the state title, none of them would have the time to go to the rehearsals. Of the thirty or so who were left, more than half were in the band and they had after-school practice as well. A quick calculation showed that there were maybe a dozen other people who could possibly do it.

Now, I didn't want to do the play at all, and not only because I'd come to realize that drama was just about the most boring class ever invented. The thing was, I'd already taken Jamie to homecoming, and with her as the angel, I just couldn't bear the thought that I'd have to spend every afternoon with her for the next month or so. Being seen with her once was bad enough . . . but being seen with her every day? What would my friends say?

But I could tell this was really important to her. The simple fact that she'd asked made that clear. Jamie never asked anyone for a favor. I think deep down she suspected that no one would ever do her a favor because of who she was. The very realization made me sad.

"What about Jeff Bangert? He might do it," I offered.

Jamie shook her head. "He can't. His father's sick, and he has to work in the store after school until his father gets back on his feet."

"What about Darren Woods?"

"He broke his arm last week when he slipped on the boat. His arm is in a sling."

"Really? I didn't know that," I said, stalling, but Jamie knew what I was doing.

"I've been praying about it, Landon," she said simply, and sighed for the second time. "I'd really like this play to be special this year, not for me, but because of my father. I want it to be the best production ever. I know how much it will mean to him to see me be the angel, because this play reminds him of my mother . . ." She paused, collecting her thoughts. "It would be terrible if the play was a failure this year, especially since I'm involved."

She stopped again before going on, her voice becoming more emotional as she went on.

"I know Eddie would do the best he could, I really do. And I'm not embarrassed to do the play with him, I'm really not. Actually, he's a very nice person, but he told me that he's having second thoughts about doing it. Sometimes people at school can be so...so...cruel, and I don't want Eddie to be hurt. But..." She took a deep breath. "But the real reason I'm asking is because of my father. He's such a *good* man, Landon. If people make fun of his memory of my mother while I'm playing the part...well, that would break my heart. And with Eddie and me...you know what people would say."

I nodded, my lips pressed together, knowing that I would have been one of those people she was talking about. In fact, I already was. Jamie and Eddie, the dynamic duo, we called them after Miss Garber had announced that they'd be the ones doing the roles. The very fact that it was I who had started it up made me feel terrible, almost sick to my stomach.

She straightened up a little in her seat and looked at me sadly, as if she already knew I was going to say no. I guess she didn't know how I was feeling. She went on.

"I know that challenges are always part of the Lord's plan, but I don't want to believe that the Lord is cruel, especially to someone like my father. He devotes his life to God, he gives to the community. And he's already lost his wife and has had to raise me on my own. And I love him so much for it..."

Jamie turned away, but I could see the tears in her eyes. It was the first time I'd ever seen her cry. I think part of me wanted to cry, too.

"I'm not asking you to do it for me," she said softly, "I'm

really not, and if you say no, I'll still pray for you. I promise. But if you'd like to do something kind for a wonderful man who means so much to me . . . Will you just think about it?"

Her eyes looked like those of a cocker spaniel that had just messed on the rug. I looked down at my feet.

"I don't have to think about it," I finally said. "I'll do it."

I really didn't have a choice, did I?

Questions and Explanations for Chapters 3 and 4

The eleven questions on chapters 3 and 4 focus on grammar and usage, vocabulary, literary terms, characterization, and effects of style. Some of the questions combine two or more of these areas, requiring you to synthesize your knowledge, make inferences, and interpret the text. The questions are designed to determine both your current level of understanding of the novel and your ability to answer higher-level questions.

The following sentence tests your ability to recognize grammar and usage errors. The sentence contains either a single error or no error at all. If the sentence contains an error, select the one underlined part that must be changed to make the sentence correct. If there is no error, select answer choice D.

1. During adolescence, the desire for an acceptable reputation is a significant <u>problem,</u> it <u>affects</u> a number of
                            A   **B**
   high school students during <u>their</u> teenage years. <u>No</u>
                                     C
   <u>error</u>
   D

In order to answer this question correctly, you need to know what you are expected to be evaluating. Choice A requires you to consider two things—the word and the punctuation mark, a comma, following it. You must determine if the noun form of *problem* is correct, and if the comma is being used correctly.

Choice B also requires you to look at two things: the subject-verb agreement between *it* and *affects*; and the homophones—two words that sound the same but have different meanings, such as *to, too,* and *two—affect* and *effect. Affect* is typically used as a verb, meaning to act on. *Effect* is typically a noun, meaning something that is produced. If someone or something is doing something, usually the correct word choice is *affect*—for example, "Research has shown that rereading a passage will affect a student's level of comprehension." Choice C requires you to make sure the pronoun *their* agrees in number, gender, and case with its antecedent. *Number* refers to singular or plural. For example, *my, his,* and *her* are singular; and *our* and *their* are plural. *Gender* refers to male or female. You wouldn't say, "Mark ate her spinach," because Mark isn't a girl. You would write, "Mark ate his spinach." *Case* refers to the type of pronoun it is. A subjective pronoun is the doer of an action—for example, "*I* read the novel." The possessive case shows ownership—for example, "I read *my* novel." And the objective case is when the pronoun is used as either a direct or an indirect object or the object of a preposition—for example, "The teacher gave *me* the assignment."

Questions 2 and 3 test your vocabulary. Choose the word or set of words that, when inserted in the sentence, best fits the meaning of the sentence as a whole.

2. Although there were some homecoming dance decorating tasks that Landon could _____, others he had to _____ himself.

    A. endorse...perform

    B. practice...institute

    C. disregard...ignore

    D. delegate...attend to

In order to answer this question, you need to understand the context clue provided by the word *although* at the beginning of the sentence. The word indicates a contrast between the two choices. In addition, realize that both words need to make logical sense. Place both words into the sentence and make sure the sentence is complete as a whole.

Endorse means to approve or support; *perform* means to carry out. *Practice* means to learn by repetition, and *institute* means to establish. When you *disregard* something, you dismiss it or bar it from consideration, and when you *ignore* something you refuse to acknowledge it. To transfer power to someone is to *delegate*. To pay attention to something means to *attend to* it.

3. Because of their tenuous relationship, Landon felt a little _____ before talking to Reverend Sullivan the night of the dance, for he was unsure of what Jamie's father might say.

A. acclivity

B. murmur

C. trepidation

D. vehemence

Answering this question requires knowledge of the word *tenuous*, as well as knowledge of your four choices. You also need to recognize from the context clues that Landon was unsure of Reverend Sullivan's remarks. Knowing that *tenuous* means weak and recognizing Landon's uncertainty, you should realize that the correct answer will reinforce these ideas.

An *acclivity* is an upward slope. A *murmur* is a low, continuous sound. *Trepidation* is a state of fear or anxiety. And *vehemence* is a forcefulness of expression.

Question 4 asks you to draw an inference from the textual evidence.

4. Throughout these two chapters, Landon often says, "If you know what I mean." What is the primary purpose of this repetition?

    A. to capture Landon's teenage narrative voice

    B. to clarify Landon's memory of the past

    C. to emphasize the contrast between Landon and Jamie

    D. to reinforce the significance of the events

Authors use repetition as a means of drawing attention to something. In order to determine the effect of the repetition, you need to analyze *what* is being repeated and *when* it is being repeated. Once you do those two things, you should be able to determine *why* it is repeated, and thus understand its purpose.

Because all of these choices could be the purpose of some type of repetition, you need to look at the particular words being repeated to determine what singular effect they have in the chapter. Then, look at the verbs at the beginning of each choice and determine what each choice is stating.

Choice A means that these words would represent the words of a teenage narrator. Choice B implies that Landon's memory is unclear and the repetition frees the memories from ambiguity. Choice C focuses on the word *I*, emphasizing that Jamie and Landon have different understandings of what he says. Choice D states that the repetition strengthens the importance of the events Landon recounts.

Question 5 tests your comprehension as well as your ability to use strong and thorough textual evidence to draw an inference from the text.

5. Chapter 3 shows the beginning of Landon's maturation process. All of the following are examples of this EXCEPT which one?

   A. He is considerate of Jamie's feelings, demonstrating true concern about what others might say about her at the dance.

   B. He separates himself from his friends in order to avoid the humiliation of dating someone outside of his social circle.

   C. He attempts to protect Jamie from the potential jeering she may experience at the hands of his friends.

D. He is aghast when Reverend Sullivan asks him if he plans on embarrassing Jamie in any way.

Three out of the four choices are examples of Landon's maturation. To answer this question correctly, you may either eliminate choices that illustrate maturation, or you can find the one choice that is not an example of his maturation process. Is concern about someone else's feelings a part of maturity? If so, you can eliminate choice A. Does a mature person separate himself from friends in order to avoid perceived humiliation? If yes, then eliminate choice B. If protecting others is an example of maturity, then eliminate choice C. And if a mature person is amazed that someone would question whether their actions and intentions would potentially embarrass another, then eliminate choice D.

Question 6 checks your ability to differentiate among different types of irony.

6. While Jamie and Landon are at the dance, Landon sees his former girlfriend Angela and her boyfriend Lew arrive. He describes the couple and mentions Angela's gum chewing. Landon initially says, "I noticed she'd picked up that ladylike habit called chewing gum." This statement is an example of what?

A. cosmic irony

B. dramatic irony

C. situational irony

D. verbal irony

Understanding *irony*, a situation where there's a contrast between appearance and reality, is essential to interpreting most literary texts. *Cosmic irony*, also known as irony of fate, is the situation where no matter what a character attempts to do, he cannot escape his fate. The most famous example of this is in the Greek myth of Oedipus, who was fated to grow up and kill his father and marry his mother, no matter what he or anyone else tried to do to prevent it. *Dramatic irony* is when the reader knows something that the character in the text does not know. An example of dramatic irony is when the audience knows that Juliet isn't dead but Romeo does not; when he arrives at the Capulet tomb, he is devastated at her death, and the audience is devastated that he doesn't know the truth. *Situational irony* is the incongruity between the expected outcome and what actually occurs. An example would be if Erik studies quite hard for a test yet fails it, but Mitch doesn't prepare at all for it and aces it. *Verbal irony* is meaning the opposite of what is stated; sarcasm is a form of verbal irony. In *Julius Caesar*, Mark Antony's standing over Caesar's dead body and repeatedly stating, "And Brutus is an honorable man" when he means that Brutus is anything but honorable is an example of verbal irony.

Question 7 tests your knowledge of literary terms.

7. Landon goes on to describe Angela, stating, "She really worked that gum, chewing it almost like a cow working her cud." This direct quotation contains which figure of speech?

    A. allusion

    B. metaphor

C. simile

D. allegory

Knowledge of figures of speech will enable you to answer this question. An *allusion*, choice A, is an indirect reference. Some of the most common types of allusions are historical, such as making a reference to Napoleon by saying that someone met his Waterloo; biblical, such as John Coffey in *The Green Mile* being a Christ figure; mythological, a reference to a Greek or Roman myth, such as someone having the Midas touch; and literary, a reference to a character in a work of literature, such as an ill-fated couple being like Romeo and Juliet.

A *metaphor*, choice B, is a comparison between two unlike things not using a connective word—for example, Olympian Michael Phelps was a flying fish in the pool. And a *simile*, choice C, is a comparison of unlike things using a connective word, such as *like*, *as*, or *than*—for example, "She looked as fresh as the morning snow."

An *allegory*, choice D, is a narrative that exists on two levels—the literal and the symbolic. *The Lord of the Flies* is often considered an allegory. On the surface, it's a novel about British boys stranded on an island, but on a deeper level, the boys as a whole represent humanity. The island stands for the world, and the fighting is essentially a war. The novel explores the notion of savagery and civilization, on the island specifically and in the world beyond the island generally.

Read the following passage, which comes after Jamie asks Landon to play the part of Tom Thornton in the school play, and then answer questions 8 and 9. Question 8 requires you to analyze the passage in order

to identify the impact certain words have on Jamie's tone; and question 9 asks you to draw an inference from the passage regarding Landon's self-perception.

"I know Eddie would do the best he could, I really do. And I'm not embarrassed to do the play with him, I'm really not. . . . Sometimes people at school can be so . . . so . . . cruel, and I don't want Eddie to be hurt. But . . ." She took a deep breath. "But the real reason I'm asking is because of my father. He's such a good man, Landon. If people make fun of his memory of my mother while I'm playing the part . . . well, that would break my heart. And with Eddie and me . . . you know what people would say."

[Landon] nodded, knowing that [he] would have been one of those people [Jamie] was talking about.

8. Jamie's tone in this passage is chiefly:

   A. jovial

   B. contentious

   C. determined

   D. apathetic

First you need to know that *tone* means attitude; tone can refer to the author's attitude about characters and subject matter, as well as the specific attitude that a character has. *Jovial* refers to hearty, joyous humor. *Contentious* is quarrelsome. One who is *determined* is staunch, resolute, and resolved; and one who is *apathetic* shows little or no emotion or interest.

9. How do you think Landon feels about himself at this point?

    A. He is feeling trapped because he really doesn't want to participate in the play.

    B. He knows that he doesn't have a choice.

    C. He feels dreadful that he is one of the people in school who had been an instigator for such hurtful behavior.

    D. He doesn't want his friends to know that he is spending time with Jamie.

In order to answer this question, you need to understand the development of Landon's character in the chapter as well as have closely read the passage to understand Landon's reaction to Jamie's comments. Choice A indicates that his primary concern right now is focused on himself and his lack of interest in participating in the play. Choice B is a matter-of-fact response to the situation. Choice C indicates that Landon feels empathetic toward Jamie and understands the concern she is expressing for both Eddie and her father. Choice D suggests that Landon is more focused on what his friends would think about his spending time with Jamie.

Question 10 requires you to use textual evidence to draw an inference regarding Landon's attitude toward Jamie.

10. By the end of chapter 4, Landon's attitude toward Jamie Sullivan is most likely one of:

    A. unadulterated shame

    B. reluctant admiration

C. undying respect

D. unknowing intimidation

To answer this question, you need to know the descriptive words and then be able to apply them to Landon and his attitude toward Jamie at this point in the novel. *Unadulterated shame* is absolute disgrace. *Reluctant admiration* is a disinclined feeling of pleasure and approval. *Undying respect* suggests that his esteem for her is unending, and *unknowing intimidation* means that Landon is ignorant of the fact that Jamie makes him feel timid or afraid.

Question 11 tests your comprehension and asks you to use details and examples from the text to draw an inference regarding Jamie's character.

11. The description of Jamie Sullivan throughout chapters 3 and 4 indicates all of the following about her EXCEPT that:

   A. she is kind and compassionate

   B. she is nonjudgmental

   C. she is persistent

   D. she is impetuous

Three out of the four answer choices are accurate descriptions and thus can be eliminated as possible correct answers to this question. In order for choice A to be eliminated, you must be able to find an example of Jamie being kind and compassionate. In order for choice B to be correct, Jamie must be judgmental; if she is not, then it must be eliminated. If Jamie perseveres, then you can eliminate choice C. An impetuous person is characterized by rash and sudden actions; if this is the case with Jamie, then eliminate choice D.

Chapter 5

The next day I talked to Miss Garber, went through the audition, and got the part. Eddie, by the way, wasn't upset at all. In fact, I could tell he was actually relieved about the whole thing. When Miss Garber asked him if he'd be willing to let me play the role of Tom Thornton, his face sort of relaxed right there and one of his eyes popped back open. "Y-y-yes, a-a-absolutely," he said, stuttering. "I—I—I un-un-understand." It took him practically ten seconds to get the words out.

For his generosity, however, Miss Garber gave him the role of the bum, and we knew he'd do fairly well in that role. The bum, you see, was completely mute, but the angel always knew what he was thinking. At one point in the play she has to tell the mute bum that God will always watch out for him because God especially cares for the poor and downtrodden. That was one of the tip-offs to the audience that she'd been sent from heaven.

Like I said earlier, Hegbert wanted it to be real clear who offered redemption and salvation, and it certainly wasn't going to be a few rickety ghosts who just popped up out of nowhere.

Rehearsals started the next week, and we rehearsed in the classroom, because the Playhouse wouldn't open their doors for us until we'd got all the "little bugs" out of our performance. By little bugs, I mean our tendency to accidentally knock over the props. The props had been made about fifteen years ago, when the play was in its first year, by Toby Bush, a sort of roving handyman who had done a few projects for the Playhouse in the past. He was a roving handyman because he drank beer all day long while he worked, and by about two o'clock or so he'd really be flying. I guess he couldn't see straight, because he'd accidentally whack his fingers with the hammer at least once a day. Whenever that happened, he'd throw down the hammer and jump up and down, holding his fingers, cursing everyone from his mother to the devil. When he finally calmed down, he'd have another beer to soothe the pain before going back to work. His knuckles were the size of walnuts, permanently swollen from years of whacking, and no one was willing to hire him on a permanent basis. The only reason Hegbert had hired him at all was because he was far and away the lowest bidder in town.

But Hegbert wouldn't allow drinking or cursing, and Toby really didn't know how to work within such a strict environment. As a result, the work was kind of sloppy, though it wasn't obvious right off the bat. After a few years the props began to fall apart, and Hegbert took it upon himself to keep the things together. But while Hegbert was good at thumping the Bible, he wasn't too good at thumping nails, and the props had bent, rusty nails sticking out all over, poking through the plywood in so many places that we had to be careful to walk exactly where we were supposed to. If we bumped them the wrong way, we'd either cut ourselves or the props would topple over, making little nail holes all over the stage floor. After a couple of years the Playhouse stage had to be resurfaced, and though they couldn't exactly close their doors to Hegbert, they made a deal with him to be more careful in the future. That meant we had to practice in the classroom until we'd worked out the "little bugs."

Fortunately Hegbert wasn't involved with the actual production of the play, because of all his ministering duties. That role fell to Miss Garber, and the first thing she told us to do was to memorize our lines as quickly as possible. We didn't have as much time as was usually allotted for rehearsals because Thanksgiving came on the last possible day in November, and Hegbert didn't want the play to be performed too close to Christmas, so as not to interfere with "its true meaning." That left us only three weeks to get the play just right, which was about a week shorter than usual.

The rehearsals began at three o'clock, and Jamie knew all her lines the first day there, which wasn't really surprising. What was surprising was that she knew all my lines, too, as well as everyone else's. We'd be going over a scene, she'd be doing it without the script, and I'd be looking down at a stack of pages, trying to figure out what my next line should be, and whenever I looked up she had this real shiny look about her, as if waiting for a burning bush or something. The only lines I knew were the mute bum's, at least on that first day, and all of a sudden I was actually envious of Eddie, at least in that regard. This was going to be a lot of work, not exactly what I'd expected when I'd signed up for the class.

My noble feelings about doing the play had worn off by the second day of rehearsals. Even though I knew I was doing the "right thing," my friends didn't understand it at all, and they'd been riding me since they'd found out. "You're doing what?" Eric asked when he learned about it. "You're doing the play with Jamie Sullivan? Are you insane or just plain stupid?" I sort of mumbled that I had a good reason, but he wouldn't let it drop, and he told everyone around us that I had a crush on her. I denied it, of course, which just made them assume it was true, and they'd laugh all the louder and tell the next person they saw. The stories kept getting wilder, too—by lunchtime I'd heard from Sally that I was thinking of getting engaged. I actually think Sally was jealous about it. She'd had a crush on me for years, and the feeling might have been mutual except for the fact that she had a glass eye, and that was something I just couldn't ignore. Her bad eye reminded me of something you'd see stuffed into the head of a mounted owl in a tacky antique shop, and to be honest, it sort of gave me the willies.

I guess that was when I started to resent Jamie again. I know it wasn't her fault, but I was the one who was taking the arrows for Hegbert, who hadn't exactly gone out of his way the night of homecoming to make me feel welcome. I began to stumble through my lines in class for the next few days, not really even attempting to learn them, and occasionally I'd crack a joke or two, which everyone laughed at, except for Jamie and Miss Garber. After rehearsal was over I'd head home to put the play out of my mind, and I wouldn't even bother to pick up the script. Instead I'd joke with my friends about the weird things Jamie did and tell fibs about how it was Miss Garber who had forced me into the whole thing.

Jamie, though, wasn't going to let me off that easy. No, she got me right where it hurts, right smack in the old ego.

I was out with Eric on Saturday night following Beaufort's third consecutive state championship in football, about a week after rehearsals had started. We were hanging out at the waterfront outside of Cecil's Diner, eating hushpuppies and watching people cruising in their cars, when I saw Jamie walking down the street. She was still a hundred yards away, turning her head from side to side, wearing that old brown sweater again and carrying her Bible in one hand. It must have been nine o'clock or so, which was late for her to be out, and it was even stranger to see her in this part of town. I turned my back to her and pulled the collar up on my jacket, but even Margaret—who had banana pudding where her brain should have been—was smart enough to figure out who she was looking for.

"Landon, your girlfriend is here."

"She's not my girlfriend," I said. "I don't have a girlfriend."

"Your fiancée, then."

I guess she'd talked to Sally, too.

"I'm not engaged," I said. "Now knock it off."

I glanced over my shoulder to see if she'd spotted me, and I guess she had. She was walking toward us. I pretended not to notice.

"Here she comes," Margaret said, and giggled.

"I know," I said.

Twenty seconds later she said it again.

"She's still coming." I told you she was quick.

"I know," I said through gritted teeth. If it wasn't for her legs, she could almost drive you as crazy as Jamie.

I glanced around again, and this time Jamie knew I'd seen her and she smiled and waved at me. I turned away, and a moment later she was standing right beside me.

"Hello, Landon," she said to me, oblivious of my scorn. "Hello, Eric, Margaret . . ." She went around the group. Everyone sort of mumbled "hello" and tried not to stare at the Bible.

Eric was holding a beer, and he moved it behind his back so she wouldn't see it. Jamie could even make Eric feel guilty if she was close enough to him. They'd been neighbors at one time, and Eric had been on the receiving end of her talks before. Behind her back he called her "the Salvation Lady," in obvious reference to the Salvation Army. "She would have been a brigadier general," he liked to say. But when she was standing right in front of him, it was another story. In his mind she had an in with God, and he didn't want to be in her bad graces.

"How are you doing, Eric? I haven't seen you around much recently." She said this as if she still talked to him all the time.

He shifted from one foot to the other and looked at his shoes, playing that guilty look for all it was worth.

"Well, I haven't been to church lately," he said.

Jamie smiled that glittery smile. "Well, that's okay, I suppose, as long as it doesn't become a habit or anything."

"It won't."

Now I've heard of confession—that thing when Catholics sit behind a screen and tell the priest about all their sins—and that's the way Eric was when he was next to Jamie. For a second I thought he was going to call her "ma'am."

"You want a beer?" Margaret asked. I think she was trying to be funny, but no one laughed.

Jamie put her hand to her hair, tugging gently at her bun. "Oh . . . no, not really . . . thank you, though."

She looked directly at me with a really sweet glow, and right away I knew I was in trouble. I thought she was going to ask me off to the side or something, which to be honest I thought would turn out better, but I guess that wasn't in her plans.

"Well, you did really well this week at rehearsals," she said to me. "I know you've got a lot of lines to learn, but I'm sure you're going to get them all real soon. And I just wanted to thank you for volunteering like you did. You're a real gentleman."

"Thanks," I said, a little knot forming in my stomach. I tried to be cool, but all my friends were looking right at me, suddenly wondering if I'd been telling them the truth about Miss Garber forcing it on me and everything. I hoped they missed it.

"Your friends should be proud of you," Jamie added, putting that thought to rest.

"Oh, we are," Eric said, pouncing. "Very proud. He's a good guy, that Landon, what with his volunteering and all."

Oh no.

Jamie smiled at him, then turned back to me again, her old cheerful self. "I also wanted to tell you that if you need any help, you can come by anytime. We can sit on the porch like we did before and go over your lines if you need to."

I saw Eric mouth the words "like we did before" to Margaret. This really wasn't going well at all. By now the pit in my stomach was as big as Paul Bunyan's bowling ball.

"That's okay," I mumbled, wondering how I could squirm my way out of this. "I can learn them at home."

"Well, sometimes it helps if someone's there to read with you, Landon," Eric offered.

I told you he'd stick it to me, even though he was my friend.

"No, really," I said to him, "I'll learn the lines on my own."

"Maybe," Eric said, smiling, "you two should practice in

front of the orphans, once you've got it down a little better. Sort of a dress rehearsal, you know? I'm sure they'd love to see it."

You could practically see Jamie's mind start clicking at the mention of the word *orphans*. Everyone knew what her hot button was. "Do you think so?" she asked.

Eric nodded seriously. "I'm sure of it. Landon was the one who thought of it first, but I know that if I was an orphan, I'd love something like that, even if it wasn't exactly the real thing."

"Me too," Margaret chimed in.

As they spoke, the only thing I could think about was that scene from *Julius Caesar* where Brutus stabs him in the back. *Et tu, Eric?*

"It was Landon's idea?" she asked, furrowing her brow. She looked at me, and I could tell she was still mulling it over.

But Eric wasn't about to let me off the hook that easy. Now that he had me flopping on the deck, the only thing left to do was gut me. "You'd like to do that, wouldn't you, Landon?" he said. "Helping the orphans, I mean."

It wasn't exactly something you could answer no to, was it?

"I reckon so," I said under my breath, staring at my best friend. Eric, despite the remedial classes he was in, would have been one hell of a chess player.

"Good, then, it's all settled. That's if it's okay with you, Jamie." His smile was so sweet, it could have flavored half the RC cola in the county.

"Well...yes, I suppose I'll have to talk to Miss Garber and the director of the orphanage, but if they say it's okay, I think it would be a fine idea."

And the thing was, you could tell she was really happy about it.

Checkmate.

*   *   *

The next day I spent fourteen hours memorizing my lines, cursing my friends, and wondering how my life had spun so out of control. My senior year certainly wasn't turning out the way I thought it would when it began, but if I had to perform for a bunch of orphans, I certainly didn't want to look like an idiot.

Chapter 6

The first thing we did was talk to Miss Garber about our plans for the orphans, and she thought it was a marvelous idea. That was her favorite word, by the way—*marvelous*—after she'd greeted you with "Helloooo." On Monday, when she realized that I knew all my lines, she said, "Marvelous!" and for the next two hours whenever I'd finish up a scene, she'd say it again. By the end of the rehearsal, I'd heard it about four zillion times.

But Miss Garber actually went our idea one better. She told the class what we were doing, and she asked if other members of the cast would be willing to do their parts as well, so that the orphans could really enjoy the whole thing. The way she asked meant that they really didn't have a choice, and she looked around the class, waiting for someone to nod so she could make it official. No one moved a muscle, except for Eddie. Somehow he'd inhaled a bug up his nose at that exact moment, and he sneezed violently. The bug flew out his nose, shot across his desk, and landed on the floor right by Norma Jean's leg. She jumped out of her chair and screamed out loud, and the people on either side of her shouted, "Eww...gross!" The rest of the class started looking around and craning their necks, trying to see what happened, and for the next ten seconds there was total pandemonium in the classroom. For Miss Garber, that was as good of an answer as she needed.

"Marvelous," she said, closing the discussion.

Jamie, meanwhile, was getting really excited about performing for the orphans. During a break in rehearsals she pulled me aside and thanked me for thinking of them. "There's no way you would know," she said almost conspiratorially, "but I've been wondering what to do for the orphanage this year. I've been praying about it for months now because I want this Christmas to be the most special one of all."

"Why is this Christmas so important?" I asked her, and she smiled patiently, as if I'd asked a question that didn't really matter.

"It just is," she said simply.

The next step was to talk it over with Mr. Jenkins, the director of the orphanage. Now I'd never met Mr. Jenkins before, being that the orphanage was in Morehead City, which was across the bridge from Beaufort, and I'd never had any reason to go there. When Jamie surprised me with the news the following day that we'd be meeting him later that evening, I was sort of worried that I wasn't dressed nice enough. I know it was an orphanage, but a guy wants to make a good impression. Even though I wasn't as excited about it as Jamie was (no one was as excited as Jamie), I didn't want to be regarded as the Grinch who ruined Christmas for the orphans, either.

Before we went to the orphanage for our meeting, we had

to walk to my house to pick up my mom's car, and while there, I planned on changing into something a little nicer. The walk took about ten minutes or so, and Jamie didn't say much along the way, at least until we got to my neighborhood. The homes around mine were all large and well kept, and she asked who lived where and how old the houses were. I answered her questions without much thought, but when I opened the front door to my house, I suddenly realized how different this world was compared with her own. She had a shocked expression on her face as she looked around the living room, taking in her surroundings.

No doubt it was the fanciest home she'd ever been in. A moment later I saw her eyes travel to the paintings that lined the walls. My ancestors, so to speak. As with many southern families, my entire lineage could be traced in the dozen faces that lined the walls. She stared at them, looking for a resemblance, I think, then turned her attention to the furnishings, which still looked practically new, even after twenty years. The furniture had been handmade, assembled or carved from mahogany and cherry, and designed specifically for each room. It *was* nice, I had to admit, but it wasn't something I really thought about. To me, it was just a house. My favorite part of it was the window in my room that led to the porch on the upper level. That was my escape hatch.

I showed her around, though, giving her a quick tour of the sitting room, the library, the den, and the family room, Jamie's eyes growing wider with each new room. My mom was out on the sun porch, sipping a mint julep and reading, and heard us poking around. She came back inside to say hello.

I think I told you that every adult in town adored Jamie, and that included my mom. Even though Hegbert was always giving the kinds of sermons that had our family's name written all over them, my mom never held it against Jamie, because of how sweet she was. So they talked while I was upstairs rifling through my closet for a clean shirt and a tie. Back then boys wore ties a lot, especially when they were meeting someone in a position of authority. When I came back down the stairs fully dressed, Jamie had already told my mom about the plan.

"It's a wonderful idea," Jamie said, beaming at me. "Landon's really got a special heart."

My mom—after making sure she'd heard Jamie correctly—faced me with her eyebrows raised. She stared at me like I was an alien.

"So this was your idea?" my mom asked. Like everyone else in town, she knew Jamie didn't lie.

I cleared my throat, thinking of Eric and what I still wanted to do to him. It involved molasses and fire ants, by the way.

"Kind of," I said.

"Amazing." It was the only word she could get out. She didn't know the details, but she knew I must have been boxed into a corner to do something like this. Mothers always know stuff like that, and I could see her peering closely at me and trying to figure it out. To escape her inquisitive gaze, I checked my watch, feigned surprise, and casually mentioned to Jamie that we'd better be going. My mom got the car keys from her pocketbook and handed them to me, still giving me the once-over as we headed out the door. I breathed a sigh of relief, imagining that I'd somehow gotten away with something, but as I walked Jamie to the car, I heard my mother's voice again.

"Come on over anytime, Jamie!" my mom shouted. "You're always welcome here."

Even mothers could stick it to you sometimes.

I was still shaking my head as I got in the car.

"Your mother's a wonderful lady," Jamie said.

I started the engine. "Yeah," I said, "I guess so."

"And your house is beautiful."

"Uh-huh."

"You should count your blessings."

"Oh," I said, "I do. I'm practically the luckiest guy alive."

Somehow she didn't catch the sarcastic tone of my voice.

We got to the orphanage just about the time it was getting dark. We were a couple of minutes early, and the director was on the phone. It was an important call and he couldn't meet with us right away, so we made ourselves comfortable. We were waiting on a bench in the hallway outside his door, when Jamie turned to me. Her Bible was in her lap. I guess she wanted it for support, but then again, maybe it was just her habit.

"You did really well today," she said. "With your lines, I mean."

"Thanks," I said, feeling proud and dejected at exactly the same time. "I still haven't learned my beats, though," I offered. There was no way we could practice *those* on the porch, and I hoped she wasn't going to suggest it.

"You will. They're easy once you know all the words."

"I hope so."

Jamie smiled, and after a moment she changed the subject, sort of throwing me off track. "Do you ever think about the future, Landon?" she asked.

I was startled by her question because it sounded...so *ordinary*.

"Yeah, sure. I guess so," I answered cautiously.

"Well, what do you want to do with your life?"

I shrugged, a little wary of where she was going with this. "I don't know yet. I haven't figured that part out. I'm going to UNC next fall, at least I hope so. I have to get accepted first."

"You will," she said.

"How do you know?"

"Because I've prayed for that, too."

When she said it, I thought we were heading into a discussion about the power of prayer and faith, but Jamie tossed yet another curveball at me.

"How about after college? What do you want to do then?"

"I don't know," I said, shrugging. "Maybe I'll be a one-armed lumberjack."

She didn't think it was funny.

"I think you should become a minister," she said seriously. "I think you're good with people, and they'd respect what you have to say."

Though the concept was absolutely ridiculous, with her I just knew it came from the heart and she intended it as a compliment.

"Thanks," I said. "I don't know if I'll do that, but I'm sure I'll find something." It took a moment for me to realize that the conversation had stalled and that it was my turn to ask a question.

"How about you? What do you want to do in the future?"

Jamie turned away and got a far-off gaze in her eyes, making me wonder what she was thinking, but it vanished almost as quickly as it came.

"I want to get married," she said quietly. "And when I do, I want my father to walk me down the aisle and I want everyone I know to be there. I want the church bursting with people."

"That's all?" Though I wasn't averse to the idea of marriage, it seemed kind of silly to hope for that as your life's goal.

"Yes," she said. "That's all I want."

The way she answered made me suspect that she thought she'd end up like Miss Garber. I tried to make her feel better, even though it still seemed silly to me.

"Well, you'll get married someday. You'll meet some guy and the two of you will hit it off, and he'll ask you to marry him. And I'm sure that your father will be happy to walk you down the aisle."

I didn't mention the part about having a big crowd in the church. I guess it was the one thing that even I couldn't imagine.

Jamie thought carefully about my answer, really pondering the way I said it, though I didn't know why.

"I hope so," she said finally.

I could tell she didn't want to talk about it anymore, don't ask me how, so I moved on to something new.

"So how long have you been coming to the orphanage?" I asked conversationally.

"Seven years now. I was ten years old the first time I came. I was younger than a lot of the kids here."

"Do you enjoy it, or does it make you sad?"

"Both. Some of the children here came from really horrible situations. It's enough to break your heart when you hear about it. But when they see you come in with some books from the library or a new game to play, their smiles just take all the sadness away. It's the greatest feeling in the world."

She practically glowed when she spoke. Though she wasn't saying it to make me feel guilty, that was exactly the way I felt. It was one of the reasons it was so hard to put up with her, but by then I was getting fairly used to it. She could twist you every way but normal, I'd come to learn.

At that moment, Mr. Jenkins opened the door and invited us in. The office looked almost like a hospital room, with black-and-white tiled floors, white walls and ceilings, a metal cabinet against the wall. Where the bed would normally have been, there was a metal desk that looked like it had been stamped off the assembly line. It was almost neurotically clean of anything personal. There wasn't a single picture or anything.

Jamie introduced me, and I shook Mr. Jenkins's hand. After we sat down, Jamie did most of the talking. They were old friends, you could see that right off, and Mr. Jenkins had given her a big hug as soon as she'd entered. After smoothing out her skirt, Jamie explained our plan. Now, Mr. Jenkins had seen the play a few years back, and he knew exactly what she was talking about almost as soon as she started. But even though Mr. Jenkins liked Jamie a lot and knew she meant well, he didn't think it was a good idea.

"I don't think it's a good idea," he said.

That's how I knew what he was thinking.

"Why not?" Jamie asked, her brow furrowed. She seemed genuinely perplexed by his lack of enthusiasm.

Mr. Jenkins picked up a pencil and started tapping it on his desk, obviously thinking about how to explain himself. In time, he put down the pencil and sighed.

"Even though it's a wonderful offer and I know you'd like to do something special, the play is about a father who eventually comes to realize how much he loves his daughter." He let that sink in for a moment and picked up the pencil again. "Christmas is hard enough around here without reminding the kids of what they're missing. I think that if the children see something like that..."

He didn't even have to finish. Jamie put her hands to her

mouth. "Oh my," she said right away, "you're right. I hadn't thought about that."

Neither had I, to tell you the truth. But it was obvious right off the bat that Mr. Jenkins made sense.

He thanked us anyway and chatted for a while about what he planned to do instead. "We'll have a small tree and a few gifts— something that all of them can share. You're welcome to visit Christmas Eve..."

After we said our good-byes, Jamie and I walked in silence without saying anything. I could tell she was sad. The more I hung around Jamie, the more I realized she had lots of different emotions—she wasn't always cheerful and happy. Believe it or not, that was the first time I recognized that in some ways she was just like the rest of us.

"I'm sorry it didn't work out," I said softly.

"I am, too."

She had that faraway look in her eyes again, and it was a moment before she went on.

"I just wanted to do something different for them this year. Something special that they would remember forever. I thought for sure this was it..." She sighed. "The Lord seems to have a plan that I just don't know about yet."

She was quiet for a long time, and I looked at her. Seeing Jamie feeling bad was almost worse than feeling bad because of her. Unlike Jamie, I deserved to feel bad about myself—I knew what kind of person I was. But with her...

"While we're here, do you want to stop in to see the kids?" I asked into the silence. It was the only thing I could think to do that might make her feel better. "I could wait out here while you talk to them, or go to the car if you want."

"Would you visit them with me?" she asked suddenly.

To be honest, I wasn't sure I could handle it, but I knew she really wanted me there. And she was feeling so down that the words came out automatically.

"Sure, I'll go."

"They'll be in the rec room now. That's where they usually are at this time," she said.

We walked down the corridors to the end of the hall, where two doors opened into a good-size room. Perched in the far corner was a small television with about thirty metal folding chairs placed all around it. The kids were sitting in the chairs, crowded around it, and you could tell that only the ones in the front row had a good view of the thing.

I glanced around. In the corner was an old Ping-Pong table. The surface was cracked and dusty, the net nowhere to be seen. A couple of empty Styrofoam cups sat on top of it, and I knew it hadn't been used in months, maybe years. Along the wall next to the Ping-Pong table were a set of shelves, with a few toys here and there—blocks and puzzles, a couple of games. There weren't too many, and the few that were there looked as if they'd been in this room for a long time. Along the near walls were small individual desks piled with newspapers, scribbled on with crayons.

We stood in the doorway for just a second. We hadn't been noticed yet, and I asked what the newspapers were for.

"They don't have coloring books," she whispered, "so they use newspapers." She didn't look at me as she spoke—instead her attention was directed at the kids. She'd begun to smile again.

"Are these all the toys they have?" I asked.

She nodded. "Yes, except for the stuffed animals. They're allowed to keep those in their rooms. This is where the rest of the things are kept."

I guess she was used to it. To me, though, the sparseness of the room made the whole thing depressing. I couldn't imagine growing up in a place like this.

Jamie and I finally walked into the room, and one of the kids turned around at the sound of our steps. He was about eight or so, with red hair and freckles, his two front teeth missing.

"Jamie!" he shouted happily when he saw her, and all of a sudden all the other heads turned. The kids ranged in age from about five to twelve, more boys than girls. After twelve they had to be sent to live with foster parents, I later learned.

"Hey, Roger," Jamie said in response, "how are you?"

With that, Roger and some of the others began to crowd around us. A few of the other kids ignored us and moved closer to the television now that there were free seats in the front row. Jamie introduced me to one of the older kids who'd come up and asked if I was her boyfriend. By his tone, I think that he had the same opinion of Jamie that most of the kids in our high school had.

"He's just a friend," she said. "But he's very nice."

Over the next hour, we visited with the children. I got a lot of questions about where I lived and whether my house was big or what kind of car I owned, and when we finally had to leave, Jamie promised that she'd be back soon. I noticed that she didn't promise I would be with her.

While we were walking back to the car, I said, "They're a nice bunch of kids." I shrugged awkwardly. "I'm glad that you want to help them."

Jamie turned to me and smiled. She knew there wasn't much to add after that, but I could tell she was still wondering what she was going to do for them that Christmas.

Questions and Explanations for
Chapters 5 and 6

The twelve questions on chapters 5 and 6 focus on grammar and usage, vocabulary, literary terms, characterization, and stylistic choices. Some of the questions combine two or more of these areas, requiring you to synthesize your knowledge, make inferences, and interpret the text. The questions are designed to determine both your current level of understanding of the novel and your ability to answer higher-level questions.

The following statements (1 and 2) test your ability to recognize grammar and usage errors. Each sentence contains either a single error or no error at all. If the sentence contains an error, select the one underlined part that must be changed to make the sentence correct. If there is no error, select answer choice D.

1. You could practically see <u>Jamie's</u> <u>mind start clicking</u> at
   _A _B
   the mention of the <u>orphan's</u>. <u>No error</u>
   _C _D

In order to answer this question correctly, you need to know what you are asked to evaluate. Choice A is questioning whether the apostrophe is used correctly. Choice B is pointing out the use of an idiomatic expression (a common phrase or saying whose meaning cannot be understood by its individual words or elements). Choice C is also drawing attention to the use of an apostrophe. An apostrophe is used to create a contraction and to show possession.

2. "<u>Well…yes,</u> I suppose I'll have to talk to Miss Garber
   _A
   and the <u>director of the orphanage,</u> but if they say <u>it's</u>
   _B _C
   okay, I think it would be a fine idea." <u>No error</u>
   _D

Choice A is calling attention to the use of an ellipsis and the use of a comma. Choice B requires you to understand and apply comma rules, and choice C is questioning your understanding of how to use an apostrophe.

Question 3 asks you to determine the meaning of a word as it is used in the text.

3. "My noble feelings about doing the play had worn off by the second day of rehearsals. Even though I knew I was doing the 'right thing,' my friends didn't understand it at all, and they'd been <u>riding me</u> since they'd found out."

What word would be best to replace "riding" in Landon's quotation in the previous sentence?

A. degrading

B. congratulating

C. upsetting

D. teasing

To answer this question, first recognize the context clues and realize that what Landon's friends have been doing is somewhat contrary to doing the "right thing." Context clues are the words in a sentence that surround an unfamiliar or difficult word or phrase, making it easier to understand. For example, in the sentence "The noxious fumes caused both vomiting and headaches," you know that the fumes created two undesirable results; thus the word *noxious* must mean harmful or injurious.

Next you can substitute the word in each choice for the underlined phrase above and determine if the sentence makes sense as a whole. Choice A, *degrading* means to lower in dignity. Choice B, *congratulating*, means showing praise, and choice C, *upsetting*, means disturbing mentally and emotionally. Choice D, *teasing*, means irritating with petty distractions.

Question 4 asks you to analyze how an author's choice concerning structure contributes to the overall meaning of the text.

4. Landon thinks of himself as irresponsible, yet Jamie sees the genuine version of him. "Unlike Jamie," Landon

says, "I deserved to feel bad about myself—I knew what kind of person I was. But with her..." Which statements illustrate the author's implication of "But with her..."?

A. Landon feels like he is failing.

B. Landon feels as though he is a better person with her influence.

C. Landon is resentful of Jamie's hold on him.

D. Landon begins to think of himself in a new light.

Notice that the question, with the word *statements*, indicates there will be more than one correct answer. The word *but* indicates a contrast and the ellipsis requires readers to fill in the gaps. If the quotation indicates Landon's shortcomings, select choice A. If Landon feels that Jamie has the capacity to change him, based on her words and actions, then select choice B. If Landon is bothered by the effect Jamie has on him, then select choice C. If Landon's opinion of himself is improving, select choice D.

Question 5 tests your knowledge of literary terms.

5. "Whenever I looked up she had this real shiny look about her, as if waiting for a burning bush or something." The phrase "burning bush" is an example of what rhetorical device?

A. allusion

B. anaphora

C. metaphor

D. simile

Knowledge of literary terms and the ability to apply them to specific passages will enable you to answer this question. An *allusion*, choice A, is an indirect reference to something outside of the story itself. Some of the most common types of allusions are historical, biblical, mythological, and literary. In the sentence, "I felt like Katniss," those who have read *The Hunger Games* will understand the reference to the protagonist of that series.

Anaphora, choice B, is the repetition of a word or group of words at the beginning of successive clauses or sentences—for example, "I want you to know the word *anaphora*. I want you to recognize the effect of anaphora in a passage. I want you to attempt to use anaphora in your own writing."

A *metaphor*, choice C, is a comparison between two unlike things not using a connective word, such as Shakespeare's assertion that "all the world's a stage." And a *simile*, choice D, is a comparison of unlike things using a connective word, such as *like*, *as*, or *than*; an example would be "My love is like a red, red rose."

Question 6 checks your comprehension and asks you to analyze how an author's choice concerning structure contributes to the overall meaning of the text; it also requires you to make an inference based on textual evidence.

6. After Eric credits Landon with the idea of performing the play for the orphans and it's clear Jamie is really

happy about the idea, there is a single-word sentence and paragraph: "Checkmate." Stylistically, this sentence does all of the following EXCEPT:

A. conclude the analogy used to characterize Eric

B. mark the end of the discussion and the section of the chapter

C. illustrate Landon's feeling of being trapped and defeated

D. delineate the nature of the game that the boys are playing at Jamie's expense

Three out of the four choices indicate an accurate stylistic effect. First, you need to understand what the word *checkmate* means: It describes the situation at the end of a game of chess when one competitor positions his pieces to capture his opponent's king piece and thus wins the game. To answer this question correctly, you may either eliminate the choices that illustrate accurate stylistic effects of capture and defeat, or you can find the correct answer, the one that is not an example of an effect of the single-word sentence.

Choice A states that this single-word paragraph is the end of the comparison between what Eric is doing and someone playing a game of chess. Choice B states that the word brings the end of the discussion as well as the end of a section of the chapter. Choice C indicates that Landon has feelings that mirror those of someone on the losing end of a chess game. Choice D states that both Eric and Landon are playing a game that is similar to chess.

Question 7 tests your ability to understand an allusion as well as determine the meaning of words as they are used in the text and draw inferences from the textual evidence.

7. In chapter 5, the allusion to *Julius Caesar* does each of the following EXCEPT:

   A. compare explicitly Landon's deeds to those of the Roman emperor

   B. foreshadow the tragedy at the end of the novel

   C. develop Landon's feeling of betrayal

   D. mirror the character development of co-protagonists Caesar and Brutus against that of Jamie and Landon

In order to determine the effect of an allusion—an indirect reference—you must understand it. Julius Caesar was a Roman emperor who was betrayed by his friends. Centuries later, Shakespeare wrote a play about his assassination called *The Tragedy of Julius Caesar*. Many critics consider Julius Caesar—the title character—to be the main character, yet others consider Brutus the protagonist of the tragedy because the play revolves around Brutus's thoughts and actions. Three out of the four answer choices relate to the idea of betrayal by a friend or the death of a character—they are examples of how the allusion is effective. One of the choices will not do this, and that one is the correct answer.

Choice A indicates that Landon acts like Julius Caesar, particularly the manner in which he treats people. Choice B hints that there may be a tragic ending at the end of the novel. Choice C focuses solely on Landon's feelings of betrayal by his friend.

Choice D suggests that either Landon or Jamie could be considered the protagonist of *A Walk to Remember*.

Question 8 tests your application of literary terms.

8. "By the end of the rehearsal, I'd heard it about four zillion times." The phrase "four zillion times" is an example of which figure of speech?

   A. allusion

   B. hyperbole

   C. onomatopoeia

   D. personification

Again, knowledge of literary terms will help you to identify their use in a particular passage. An *allusion*, choice A, is an indirect reference. "He had the patience of Job" is a biblical allusion. *Hyperbole*, choice B, is an obvious and intentional exaggeration, as in "This learning guide has discussed hyperbole about four million times." *Onomatopoeia*, choice C, is a word that suggests the very sound it describes, such as *buzz*, *sizzle*, and *boom*. *Personification*, choice D, is giving nonhuman things a human characteristic, such as in "Opportunity knocked on his door."

Question 9 tests your ability to draw inferences based on the textual evidence.

9. Landon's maturation is positively affected by all of the following EXCEPT:

   A. Jamie's visit to his house

   B. his visit to the orphanage

   C. Jamie's suggestion regarding his future

   D. his friendship with Eric

Three out of the four choices somehow impacted Landon for the better when he was growing up. Those events that had a beneficial effect on his maturation process can be eliminated, and the single correct answer is the one that *does not* impact Landon's growing up or has a negative effect.

Choice A suggests that either something occurs or Landon notices or realizes something when Jamie is visiting his house. Consider the similarities and differences between their two lives and their two homes. For choice B to be eliminated Landon's visit to the orphanage must have affected Landon in a positive—and probably unexpected—way. In order to consider choice C, you need to know what suggestion Jamie makes regarding Landon's future. Specifically, you should consider what career she suggested for Landon. For choice D to be eliminated Eric must have been a positive influence on Landon, probably because of the maturity that Eric himself demonstrates.

Question 10 asks you to draw an inference by first determining the meaning of words as they are used in the text.

10. When Jamie suggests that Landon become a minister, his response is, "Though the concept was absolutely ridiculous, with her I just knew it came from the heart and she intended it as a compliment." What can you infer about Landon's reaction to Jamie's idea?

A. He is being sarcastic as usual.

B. He will never take anything seriously.

C. He demonstrates empathy for the first time in the novel.

D. He is being ironic, for we already know that he indeed becomes a minister.

If Landon's words are sarcastic, then you should select choice A. If Landon is not responding seriously to her suggestion, then select choice B. If Landon is identifying with Jamie's feelings, thoughts, and attitudes, select choice C. And if Landon is planning on becoming a minister, select choice D.

Question 11 asks you to make an inference based on strong and thorough textual evidence.

11. Considered as a whole, what is the primary purpose of chapter 5?

A. to advance the plot

B. to develop the theme of sacrifice

C. to provide a realistic portrayal of Landon's character

D. to contrast Eric and Landon

In order to answer this question correctly, you need to not only read the chapter but also realize what is going on throughout the chapter. Then you must determine how the chapter fits into the novel as a whole. Although all of these choices may exist in chapter 5, you must determine what the most important or principal purpose of the chapter is, and you do that by comparing and contrasting the choices, and using the cumulative weight of the evidence—the details and examples from the text—to select the strongest choice.

If the most important function of the chapter is to advance the story line, then select choice A. If the thematic topic of surrendering, or giving up something, is central to the chapter, then select choice B. If the chapter is mostly about Landon and presenting him as a true teenage boy, select choice C. If the majority of the chapter is spent comparing and contrasting Landon with his friend Eric, then select choice D.

Question 12 tests your comprehension as well as your ability to analyze details and examples from the text to draw a conclusion regarding character development.

12. Jamie's assertion that "Landon's really got a special heart" and the effect of her words on others does each of the following EXCEPT:

   A. illustrate Jamie's sincere feelings

   B. enable readers to get a better understanding of Landon's mother

   C. serve as an example of verbal irony

   D. serve as another comment that helps Landon change his own view of himself

It is important to understand not only a character's words and the reasons for those words, but also how these words impact and affect other characters. If you think Jamie *is not* being sincere, select choice A. If you *do not* learn anything new about Landon's mother, based on her response to Jamie's words, select choice B. If Jamie's words *are not* ironic, select choice C. And if Jamie's words *do not* enable Landon to continue to change and develop his own vision of himself, select choice D.

Chapter 7

By early December, just over two weeks into rehearsals, the sky was winter dark before Miss Garber would let us leave, and Jamie asked me if I wouldn't mind walking her home. I don't know why she wanted me to. Beaufort wasn't exactly a hotbed of criminal activity back then. The only murder I'd ever heard about had occurred six years earlier when a guy was stabbed outside of Maurice's Tavern, which was a hangout for people like Lew, by the way. For an hour or so it caused quite a stir, and phone lines buzzed all over town while nervous women wondered about the possibility of a crazed lunatic wandering the streets, preying on innocent victims. Doors were locked, guns were loaded, men sat by the front windows, looking for anyone out of the ordinary who might be creeping down the street. But the whole thing was over before the night was through when the guy walked into the police station to give himself up, explaining that it was a bar fight that got out of hand. Evidently the victim had welshed on a bet. The guy was charged with second-degree murder and got six years in the state penitentiary. The policemen in our town had the most boring jobs in the world, but they still liked to strut around with a swagger or sit in coffee shops while they talked about the "big crime," as if they'd cracked the case of the Lindbergh baby.

But Jamie's house was on the way to mine, and I couldn't say no without hurting her feelings. It wasn't that I liked her or anything, don't get the wrong idea, but when you've had to spend a few hours a day with someone, and you're going to continue doing that for at least another week, you don't want to do anything that might make the next day miserable for either of you.

The play was going to be performed that Friday and Saturday, and lots of people were already talking about it. Miss Garber had been so impressed by Jamie and me that she kept telling everyone it was going to be the best play the school had ever done. She had a real flair for promotion, too, we found out. We had one radio station in town, and they interviewed her over the air, not once, but twice. "It's going to be marvelous," she pronounced, "absolutely marvelous." She'd also called the newspaper, and they'd agreed to write an article about it, primarily because of the Jamie–Hegbert connection, even though everyone in town already knew about it. But Miss Garber was relentless, and just that day she'd told us the Playhouse was going to bring in extra seats to accommodate the extra-large crowd expected. The class sort of oohed and aahed, like it was a big deal or something, but then I guess it was to some of them. Remember, we had guys like Eddie in class. He probably thought that this would be the only time in his life when someone might be interested in him. The sad thing was, he was probably right.

You might think I'd be getting excited about it, too, but I really wasn't. My friends were still teasing me at school, and I hadn't had an afternoon off in what seemed like forever. The only thing that kept me going was the fact that I was doing the "right thing." I know it's not much, but frankly, it was all I had. Occasionally I even felt sort of good about it, too, though I never admitted it to anyone. I could practically imagine the angels in heaven, standing around and staring wistfully down at me with little tears filling the corners of their eyes, talking about how wonderful I was for all my sacrifices.

So I was walking her home that first night, thinking about this stuff, when Jamie asked me a question.

"Is it true you and your friends sometimes go to the grave-yard at night?"

Part of me was surprised that she was even interested. Though it wasn't exactly a secret, it didn't seem like the sort of thing she'd care about at all.

"Yeah," I said, shrugging. "Sometimes."

"What do you do there, besides eat peanuts?"

I guess she knew about that, too.

"I don't know," I said. "Talk...joke around. It's just a place we like to go."

"Does it ever scare you?"

"No," I answered. "Why? Would it scare you?"

"I don't know," she said. "It might."

"Why?"

"Because I'd worry that I might do something wrong."

"We don't do anything bad there. I mean, we don't knock over the tombstones or leave our trash around," I said. I didn't want to tell her about our conversations about Henry Preston because I knew that wasn't the sort of thing Jamie would want to hear about. Last week Eric had wondered aloud how fast a guy like that could lie in bed and . . . well . . . you know.

"Do you ever just sit around and listen to the sounds?" she asked. "Like the crickets chirping, or the rustling of leaves when the wind blows? Or do you ever just lie on your backs and stare at the stars?"

Even though she was a teenager and had been for four years, Jamie didn't know the first thing about teenagers, and trying to understand teenage *boys* for her was like trying to decipher the theory of relativity.

"Not really," I said.

She nodded a little. "I think that's what I'd do if I were there, if I ever go, I mean. I'd just look around to really see the place, or sit quietly and listen."

This whole conversation struck me as strange, but I didn't press it, and we walked in silence for a few moments. And since she'd asked a little about me, I sort of felt obliged to ask her about herself. I mean, she hadn't brought up the Lord's plan or anything, so it was the least I could do.

"So, what do you do?" I asked. "Besides working with the orphans or helping critters or reading the Bible, I mean?" It sounded ridiculous, even to me, I admit, but *that's what she did*.

She smiled at me. I think she was surprised by my question, and even more surprised at my interest in her.

"I do a lot of things. I study for my classes, I spend time with my dad. We play gin rummy now and then. Things like that."

"Do you ever just go off with friends and goof around?"

"No," she said, and I could tell by the way she answered that even to her, it was obvious that no one wanted her around much.

"I'll bet you're excited about going off to college next year," I said, changing the subject.

It took her a moment to answer.

"I don't think I'm going to go," she said matter-of-factly. Her answer caught me off guard. Jamie had some of the highest grades in our senior class, and depending on how the last semester went, she might even end up valedictorian. We had a running pool going as to how many times she would mention the Lord's plan in her speech, by the way. My bet was fourteen, being that she only had five minutes.

"What about Mount Sermon? I thought that's where you were planning to go. You'd love a place like that," I offered.

She looked at me with a twinkle in her eye. "You mean I'd fit right in there, don't you?"

Those curveballs she sometimes threw could smack you right between the eyeballs.

"I didn't mean it that way," I said quickly. "I just meant that I'd heard about how excited you were to be going there next year."

She shrugged without really answering me, and to be honest, I didn't know what to make of it. By then we'd reached the front of her house, and we stopped on the sidewalk out front. From where I was standing, I could make out Hegbert's shadow in the living room through the curtains. The lamp was on, and he was sitting on the sofa by the window. His head was bowed, like he was reading something. I assumed it was the Bible.

"Thank you for walking me home, Landon," she said, and she glanced up at me for a moment before finally starting up the walk.

As I watched her go, I couldn't help but think that of all the times I'd ever talked to her, this was the strangest conversation we'd ever had. Despite the oddness of some of her answers, she seemed practically normal.

The next night, as I was walking her home, she asked me about my father.

"He's all right, I reckon," I said. "But he's not around much."

"Do you miss that? Not growing up with him around?"

"Sometimes."

"I miss my mom, too," she said, "even though I never even knew her."

It was the first time I'd ever considered that Jamie and I might have something in common. I let that sink in for a while.

"It must be hard for you," I said sincerely. "Even though my father's a stranger to me, at least he's still around."

She looked up at me as we walked, then faced forward again. She tugged gently at her hair again. I was beginning to notice that she did this whenever she was nervous or wasn't sure what to say.

"It is, sometimes. Don't get me wrong—I love my father with all my heart—but there are times when I wonder what it would have been like to have a mother around. I think she and I would have been able to talk about things in a way that my father and I can't."

I assumed she was talking about boys. It wasn't until later that I learned how wrong I was.

"What's it like, living with your father? Is he like how he is in church?"

"No. He's actually got a pretty good sense of humor."

"Hegbert?" I blurted out. I couldn't even imagine it.

I think she was shocked to hear me call him by his first name, but she let me off the hook and didn't respond to my comment. Instead she said, "Don't look so surprised. You'll like him, once you get to know him."

"I doubt if I'll ever get to know him."

"You never know, Landon," she said, smiling, "what the Lord's plan is."

I hated when she said things like that. With her, you just knew she talked to the Lord every day, and you never knew what the "Big Guy upstairs" had told her. She might even have a direct ticket into heaven, if you know what I mean, being as how good a person she was.

"How would I get to know him?" I asked.

She didn't answer, but she smiled to herself, as if she knew some secret that she was keeping from me. Like I said, I hated it when she did that.

The next night we talked about her Bible.

"Why do you always carry it with you?" I asked. Now, I assumed she carried the Bible around simply because she was the minister's daughter. It wasn't that big of an assumption, given how Hegbert felt about Scripture and all. But the Bible she carried was old and the cover was kind of ratty looking, and I figured that she'd be the kind of person who would buy a new one every year or so just to help out the Bible publishing industry or to show her renewed dedication to the Lord or something.

She walked a few steps before answering.

"It was my mother's," she said simply.

"Oh..." I said it like I'd stepped on someone's pet turtle, squashing it under my shoe.

She looked at me. "It's okay, Landon. How could you have known?"

"I'm sorry I asked..."

"Don't be. You didn't mean anything by it." She paused. "My mother and father were given this Bible for their wedding, but my mom was the one who claimed it first. She read it all the time, especially whenever she was going through a hard time in her life."

I thought about the miscarriages. Jamie went on.

"She loved to read it at night, before she went to sleep, and she had it with her in the hospital when I was born. When my father found out that she had died, he carried the Bible and me out of the hospital at the same time."

"I'm sorry," I said again. Whenever someone tells you something sad, it's the only thing you can think to say, even if you've already said it before.

"It just gives me a way to...to be a part of her. Can you understand that?" She wasn't saying it sadly, just more to let me know the answer to my question. Somehow that made it worse.

After she told me the story, I thought of her growing up with Hegbert again, and I didn't really know what to say. As I was thinking about my answer, though, I heard a car blare its horn from behind us, and both Jamie and I stopped and turned around at the same time as we heard it pulling over to the side.

Eric and Margaret were in the car, Eric on the driver's side, Margaret on the side closest to us.

"Well, lookee who we have here," Eric said as he leaned over the steering wheel so that I could see his face. I hadn't told him I'd been walking Jamie home, and in the curious way that teenage minds work, this new development took priority over anything that I was feeling about Jamie's story.

"Hello, Eric. Hello, Margaret," Jamie said cheerfully.

"Walking her home, Landon?" I could see the little devil behind Eric's smile.

"Hey, Eric," I said, wishing he'd never seen me.

"It's a beautiful night for strolling, isn't it?" Eric said. I think that because Margaret was between him and Jamie, he felt a little bolder than he usually was in Jamie's presence. And there was no way he could let this opportunity pass without sticking it to me.

Jamie looked around and smiled. "Yes, it is."

Eric looked around, too, with this wistful look in his eyes before taking a deep breath. I could tell he was faking it. "Boy, it really is nice out there." He sighed and glanced toward us as he shrugged. "I'd offer you a ride, but it wouldn't be half as nice as actually walking under the stars, and I wouldn't want you two to miss it." He said this like he was doing us both a favor.

"Oh, we're almost to my house anyway," Jamie said. "I was going to offer Landon a cup of cider. Would you like to meet us there? We have plenty."

A cup of cider? At her house? She hadn't mentioned that . . .

I put my hands in my pockets, wondering if this could get any worse.

"Oh, no . . . that's all right. We were just heading off to Cecil's Diner."

"On a school night?" she asked innocently.

"Oh, we won't be out too late," he promised, "but we should probably be going. Enjoy your cider, you two."

"Thanks for stopping to say hello," Jamie said, waving.

Eric got the car rolling again, but slowly. Jamie probably thought he was a safe driver. He really wasn't, though he was good at getting out of trouble when he'd crashed into something. I remember one time when he'd told his mother that a cow had jumped out in front of the car and that's why the grille and fender were damaged. "It happened so fast, Mom, the cow came out of nowhere. It just darted out in front of me, and I couldn't stop in time." Now, everyone knows cows don't exactly *dart* anywhere, but his mother believed him. She used to be a head cheerleader, too, by the way.

Once they'd pulled out of sight, Jamie turned to me and smiled.

"You have nice friends, Landon."

"Sure I do." Notice the careful way I phrased my answer.

After dropping Jamie off—no, I didn't stay for any cider—I started back to my house, grumbling the whole time. By then Jamie's story had left me completely, and I could practically hear my friends laughing about me, all the way from Cecil's Diner.

See what happens when you're a nice guy?

By the next morning everyone at school knew I was walking Jamie home, and this started up a new round of speculation about the two of us. This time it was even worse than before. It was so bad that I had to spend my lunch break in the library just to get away from it all.

That night, the rehearsal was at the Playhouse. It was the last one before the show opened, and we had a lot to do. Right after school, the boys in drama class had to load all the props in the classroom into the rented truck to bring them to the Playhouse. The only problem was that Eddie and I were the only two boys, and he's not exactly the most coordinated individual in history. We'd be walking through a doorway, carrying one of the heavier items, and his Hooville body would work against him. At every critical moment when I really needed his help to balance the load, he'd stumble over some dust or an insect on the floor, and the weight of the prop would come crashing down on my fingers, pinching them against the doorjamb in the most painful way possible.

"S-s-sorry," he'd say. "D-d-did . . . th-th-that hurt?"

I'd stifle the curses rising in my throat and bite out, "Just don't do it again."

But he couldn't stop himself from stumbling around any more than he could stop the rain from falling. By the time we'd finished loading and unloading everything, my fingers looked like Toby's, the roving handyman. And the worst thing was, I didn't even get a chance to eat before rehearsal started. Moving the props had taken three hours, and we didn't finish setting them up until a few minutes before everyone else arrived to begin. With everything else that had happened that day, suffice it to say I was in a pretty bad mood.

I ran through my lines without even thinking about them, and Miss Garber didn't say the word *marvelous* all night long. She had this concerned look in her eyes afterward, but Jamie simply smiled and told her not to worry, that everything was going to be all right. I knew Jamie was just trying to make things better for me, but when she asked me to walk her home, I told her no. The Playhouse was in the middle of town, and to walk her home, I'd have to walk a good distance out of my way. Besides, I didn't want to be seen again doing it. But Miss Garber had overheard Jamie's request and she said, very firmly, that I'd be glad to do it. "You two can talk about the play," she said. "Maybe you can work out the kinks." By kinks, of course, she meant me specifically.

So once more I ended up walking Jamie home, but she could tell I wasn't really in the mood to talk because I walked a little bit in front of her, my hands in my pockets, without even really turning back to see whether she was following. It went this way for the first few minutes, and I hadn't said a word to her.

"You're not in a very good mood, are you?" she finally asked. "You didn't even try tonight."

"You don't miss a thing, do you?" I said sarcastically without looking at her.

"Maybe I can help," she offered. She said it kind of happily, which made me even a little angrier.

"I doubt it," I snapped.

"Maybe if you told me what was wrong—"

I didn't let her finish.

"Look," I said, stopping, turning to face her. "I've just spent all day hauling crap, I haven't eaten since lunch, and now I have to trek a mile out of my way to make sure you get home, when we both know you don't even need me to do it."

It was the first time I'd ever raised my voice to her. To tell you the truth, it felt kind of good. It had been building up for a long time. Jamie was too surprised to respond, and I went on.

"And the only reason I'm doing this is because of your father, who doesn't even like me. This whole thing is dumb, and I wish I had never agreed to do it."

"You're just saying this because you're nervous about the play—"

I cut her off with a shake of my head. Once I got on a roll, it was sometimes hard for me to stop. I could take her optimism and cheerfulness only so long, and today wasn't the day to push me too far.

"Don't you get it?" I said, exasperated. "I'm not nervous about the play, I just don't want to be here. I don't want to walk you home, I don't want my friends to keep talking about me, and I don't want to spend time with you. You keep acting like we're friends, but we're not. We're not anything. I just want the whole thing to be over so I can go back to my normal life."

She looked hurt by my outburst, and to be honest, I couldn't blame her.

"I see," was all she said. I waited for her to raise her voice at me, to defend herself, to make her case again, but she didn't. All she did was look toward the ground. I think part of her wanted to cry, but she didn't, and I finally stalked away, leaving her standing by herself. A moment later, though, I heard her start moving, too. She was about five yards behind me the rest of the way to her house, and she didn't try to talk to me again until she started up the walkway. I was already moving down the sidewalk when I heard her voice.

"Thank you for walking me home, Landon," she called out.

I winced as soon as she said it. Even when I was mean to her face and said the most spiteful things, she could find some reason to thank me. She was just that kind of girl, and I think I actually hated her for it.

Or rather, I think, I hated myself.

Chapter 8

The night of the play was cool and crisp, the sky absolutely clear without a hint of clouds. We had to arrive an hour early, and I'd been feeling pretty bad all day about the way I'd talked to Jamie the night before. She'd never been anything but nice to me, and I knew that I'd been a jerk. I saw her in the hallways between classes, and I wanted to go up to apologize to her for what I'd said, but she'd sort of slip back into the crowd before I got the chance.

She was already at the Playhouse by the time I finally arrived, and I saw her talking to Miss Garber and Hegbert, off to one side, over by the curtains. Everyone was in motion, working off nervous energy, but she seemed strangely lethargic. She hadn't put on her costume yet—she was supposed to wear a white, flowing dress to give that angelic appearance—and she was still wearing the same sweater she'd worn at school. Despite my trepidation at how she might react, I walked up to the three of them.

"Hey, Jamie," I said. "Hello, Reverend . . . Miss Garber."
Jamie turned to me.

"Hello, Landon," she said quietly. I could tell she'd been thinking about the night before, too, because she didn't smile at me like she always did when she saw me. I asked if I could talk to her alone, and the two of us excused ourselves. I could see Hegbert and Miss Garber watching us as we took a few steps off to the side, out of hearing distance.

I glanced around the stage nervously.

"I'm sorry about those things I said last night," I began. "I know they probably hurt your feelings, and I was wrong to have said them."

She looked at me, as if wondering whether to believe me.

"Did you mean those things you said?" she finally asked.

"I was just in a bad mood, that's all. I get sort of wound up sometimes." I knew I hadn't really answered her question.

"I see," she said. She said it as she had the night before, then turned toward the empty seats in the audience. Again she had that sad look in her eyes.

"Look," I said, reaching for her hand, "I promise to make it up to you." Don't ask me why I said it—it just seemed like the right thing to do at that moment.

For the first time that night, she began to smile.

"Thank you," she said, turning to face me.

"Jamie?"

Jamie turned. "Yes, Miss Garber?"

"I think we're about ready for you." Miss Garber was motioning with her hand.

"I've got to go," she said to me.

"I know."

"Break a leg?" I said. Wishing someone luck before a play

is supposed to be bad luck. That's why everyone tells you to "break a leg."

I let go of her hand. "We both will. I promise."

After that, we had to get ready, and we went our separate ways. I headed toward the men's dressing room. The Playhouse was fairly sophisticated, considering that it was located in Beaufort, with separate dressing rooms that made us feel as if we were actual actors, as opposed to students.

My costume, which was kept at the Playhouse, was already in the dressing room. Earlier in the rehearsals we'd had our measurements taken so that they could be altered, and I was getting dressed when Eric walked in the door unannounced. Eddie was still in the dressing room, putting on his mute bum's costume, and when he saw Eric he got a look of terror in his eyes. At least once a week Eric gave him a wedgie, and Eddie kind of hightailed it out of there as fast as he could, pulling one leg up on his costume on the way out the door. Eric ignored him and sat on the dressing table in front of the mirror.

"So," Eric said with a mischievous grin on his face, "what are you going to do?"

I looked at him curiously. "What do you mean?" I asked.

"About the play, stupid. You gonna flub up your lines or something?"

I shook my head. "No."

"You gonna knock the props over?" Everyone knew about the props.

"I hadn't planned on it," I answered stoically.

"You mean you're going to do this thing straight up?"

I nodded. Thinking otherwise hadn't even occurred to me.

He looked at me for a long time, as if he were seeing someone he'd never seen before.

"I guess you're finally growing up, Landon," he said at last. Coming from Eric, I wasn't sure whether it was intended as a compliment.

Either way, though, I knew he was right.

In the play, Tom Thornton is amazed when he first sees the angel, which is why he goes around helping her as she shares Christmas with those less fortunate. The first words out of Tom's mouth are, "You're beautiful," and I was supposed to say them as if I meant them from the bottom of my heart. This was the pivotal moment in the entire play, and it sets the tone for everything else that happens afterward. The problem, however, was that I still hadn't nailed this line yet. Sure, I said the words, but they didn't come off too convincingly, seeing as I probably said the words like anyone would when looking at Jamie, with the exception of Hegbert. It was the only scene where Miss Garber had never said the word *marvelous,* so I was nervous about it. I kept trying to imagine someone else as the angel so that I could get it just right, but with all the other things I was trying to concentrate on, it kept getting lost in the shuffle.

Jamie was still in her dressing room when the curtains finally opened. I didn't see her beforehand, but that was okay. The first few scenes didn't include her anyway—they were mainly about Tom Thornton and his relationship with his daughter.

Now, I didn't think I'd be too nervous when I stepped out on stage, being that I'd rehearsed so much, but it hits you right between the eyes when it actually happens. The Playhouse was absolutely packed, and as Miss Garber had predicted, they'd had to set up two extra rows of seats all the way across the back.

Normally the place sat four hundred, but with those seats there were at least another fifty people sitting down. In addition, people were standing against the walls, packed like sardines.

As soon as I stepped on stage, everyone was absolutely quiet. The crowd, I noticed, was mainly old ladies of the blue-haired type, the kind that play bingo and drink Bloody Marys at Sunday brunch, though I could see Eric sitting with all my friends near the back row. It was downright eerie, if you know what I mean, to be standing in front of them while everyone waited for me to say something.

So I did the best I could to put it out of my mind as I did the first few scenes in the play. Sally, the one-eyed wonder, was playing my daughter, by the way, because she was sort of small, and we went through our scenes just as we'd rehearsed them. Neither of us blew our lines, though we weren't spectacular or anything. When we closed the curtains for act two, we had to quickly reset the props. This time everyone pitched in, and my fingers escaped unscathed because I avoided Eddie at all costs.

I still hadn't seen Jamie—I guess she was exempt from moving props because her costume was made of light material and would rip if she caught it on one of those nails—but I didn't have much time to think about her because of all we had to do. The next thing I knew, the curtain was opening again and I was back in Hegbert Sullivan's world, walking past storefronts and looking in windows for the music box my daughter wants for Christmas. My back was turned from where Jamie entered, but I heard the crowd collectively draw a breath as soon as she appeared on stage. I thought it was silent before, but now it went absolutely hush still. Just then, from the corner of my eye and off to the side of the stage, I saw Hegbert's jaw quivering.

I readied myself to turn around, and when I did, I finally saw what it was all about.

For the first time since I'd known her, her honey-colored hair wasn't pulled into a tight bun. Instead it was hanging loosely, longer than I imagined, reaching below her shoulder blades. There was a trace of glitter in her hair, and it caught the stage lights, sparkling like a crystal halo. Set against her flowing white dress tailored exactly for her, it was absolutely amazing to behold. She didn't look like the girl I'd grown up with or the girl I'd come recently to know. She wore a touch of makeup, too—not a lot, just enough to bring out the softness of her features. She was smiling slightly, as if she were holding a secret close to her heart, just like the part called for her to do.

She looked exactly like an angel.

I know my jaw dropped a little, and I just stood there looking at her for what seemed like a long time, shocked into silence, until I suddenly remembered that I had a line I had to deliver. I took a deep breath, then slowly let it out.

"You're beautiful," I finally said to her, and I think everyone in the whole auditorium, from the blue-haired ladies in front to my friends in the back row, knew that I actually meant it.

I'd nailed that line for the very first time.

Chapter 9

To say that the play was a smashing success was to put it mildly. The audience laughed and the audience cried, which is pretty much what they were supposed to do. But because of Jamie's presence, it really became something special—and I think everyone in the cast was as shocked as I was at how well the whole thing had come off. They all had that same look I did when I first saw her, and it made the play that much more powerful when they were performing their parts. We finished the first performance without a hitch, and the next evening even more people showed up, if you can believe it. Even Eric came up to me afterward and congratulated me, which after what he'd said to me before was somewhat of a surprise.

"The two of you did good," he said simply. "I'm proud of you, buddy."

While he said it, Miss Garber was crying out, "Marvelous!" to anyone who would listen to her or who just happened to be walking past, repeating it over and over so much that I kept on hearing it long after I went to bed that night. I looked for Jamie after we'd pulled the curtains closed for the final time, and spotted her off to the side, with her father. He had tears in his eyes—it was the first time I'd ever seen him cry—and Jamie went into his arms, and they held each other for a long time. He was stroking her hair and whispering, "My angel," to her while her eyes were closed, and even I felt myself choking up.

The "right thing," I realized, wasn't so bad after all.

After they finally let go of each other, Hegbert proudly motioned for her to visit with the rest of the cast, and she got a boatload of congratulations from everyone backstage. She knew she'd done well, though she kept on telling people she didn't know what all the fuss was about. She was her normal cheerful self, but with her looking so pretty, it came across in a totally different way. I stood in the background, letting her have her moment, and I'll admit there was a part of me that felt like old Hegbert. I couldn't help but be happy for her, and a little proud as well. When she finally saw me standing off to one side, she excused herself from the others and walked over, finally stopping when she was close.

Looking up at me, she smiled. "Thank you, Landon, for what you did. You made my father very happy."

"You're welcome," I said, meaning it.

The strange thing was, when she said it, I realized that Hegbert would be driving her home, and for once I wished that I would have had the opportunity to walk her there.

The following Monday was our last week of school before Christmas break, and finals were scheduled in every class. In addition, I had to finish my application for UNC, which I'd sort of been putting off because of all the rehearsals. I planned on hitting the books pretty hard that week, then doing the application at night before I went to bed. Even so, I couldn't help but think about Jamie.

Jamie's transformation during the play had been startling, to say the least, and I assumed it had signaled a change in her. I don't know why I thought that way, but I did, and so I was amazed when she showed up our first morning back dressed like her usual self: brown sweater, hair in a bun, plaid skirt, and all.

One look was all it took, and I couldn't help but feel sorry for her. She'd been regarded as normal—even special—over the weekend, or so it had seemed, but she'd somehow let it slip away. Oh, people were a little nicer to her, and the ones who hadn't talked to her yet told her what a good job she'd done, too, but I could tell right off that it wasn't going to last. Attitudes forged since childhood are hard to break, and part of me wondered if it might even get worse for her after this. Now that people actually knew she could look normal, they might even become more heartless.

I wanted to talk to her about my impressions, I really did, but I was planning to do so after the week was over. Not only did I have a lot to do, but I wanted a little time to think of the best way to tell her. To be honest, I was still feeling a little guilty about the things I'd said to her on our last walk home, and it wasn't just because the play had turned out great. It had more to do with the fact that in all our time together, Jamie had never once been anything but kind, and I knew that I'd been wrong.

I didn't think she wanted to talk to me, either, to tell you the truth. I knew she could see me hanging out with my friends at lunch while she sat off in the corner, reading her Bible, but she never made a move toward us. But as I was leaving school that day, I heard her voice behind me, asking me if I wouldn't mind walking her home. Even though I wasn't ready to tell her yet about my thoughts, I agreed. For old times' sake, you see.

A minute later Jamie got down to business.

"Do you remember those things you said on our last walk home?" she asked.

I nodded, wishing she hadn't brought it up.

"You promised to make it up to me," she said.

For a moment I was confused. I thought I'd done that already with my performance in the play. Jamie went on.

"Well, I've been thinking about what you could do," she continued without letting me get a word in edgewise, "and this is what I've come up with."

She asked if I wouldn't mind gathering the pickle jars and coffee cans she'd set out in businesses all over town early in the year. They sat on the counters, usually near the cash registers, so that people could drop their loose change in. The money was to go to the orphans. Jamie never wanted to ask people straight out for the money, she wanted them to give voluntarily. That, in her mind, was the Christian thing to do.

I remembered seeing the containers in places like Cecil's Diner and the Crown Theater. My friends and I used to toss paper clips and slugs in there when the cashiers weren't looking, since they sounded sort of like a coin being dropped inside, then we'd chuckle to ourselves about how we were putting something over on Jamie. We used to joke about how she'd open one of her cans, expecting something good because of the weight, and she'd dump it out and find nothing but slugs and paper clips. Sometimes, when you remember the things you used to do, it makes you wince, and that's exactly what I did.

Jamie saw the look on my face.

"You don't have to do it," she said, obviously disappointed. "I was just thinking that since Christmas is coming up so quickly and I don't have a car, it'll simply take me too long to collect them all..."

"No," I said cutting her off, "I'll do it. I don't have much to do anyway."

So that's what I did starting Wednesday, even though I had tests to study for, even with that application needing to be finished. Jamie had given me a list of every place she'd placed a can, and I borrowed my mom's car and started at the far end of town the following day. She'd put out about sixty cans in all, and I figured that it would take only a day to collect them all. Compared to putting them out, it would be a piece of cake. It had taken Jamie almost six weeks to do because she'd first had to find sixty empty jars and cans and then she could put out only two or three a day since she didn't have a car and could carry only so many at a time. When I started out, I felt sort of funny about being the one who picked up the cans and jars, being that it was Jamie's project, but I kept telling myself that Jamie had asked me to help.

I went from business to business, collecting the cans and jars, and by the end of the first day I realized it was going to take a little longer than I'd thought. I'd picked up only about twenty containers or so, because I'd forgotten one simple fact of life in Beaufort. In a small town like this, it was impossible to simply run inside and grab the can without chatting with the proprietor or saying hello to someone else you might recognize. It just wasn't done. So I'd sit there while some guy would be talking about the marlin he'd hooked last fall, or they'd ask me how school was going and mention that they needed a hand unloading a few boxes in the back, or maybe they wanted my opinion on whether they should move the magazine rack over to the other side of the store. Jamie, I knew, would have been good at this, and I tried to act like I thought she would want me to. It was her project after all.

To keep things moving, I didn't stop to check the take in between the businesses. I just dumped one jar or can into the next, combining them as I went along. By the end of the first day all the change was packed in two large jars, and I carried them up to my room. I saw a few bills through the glass—not too many—but I wasn't actually nervous until I emptied the contents onto my floor and saw that the change consisted primarily of pennies. Though there weren't nearly as many slugs or paper clips as I'd thought there might be, I was still disheartened when I counted up the money. There was $20.32. Even in 1958 that wasn't a lot of money, especially when divided among thirty kids.

I didn't get discouraged, though. Thinking that it was a mistake, I went out the next day, hauled a few dozen boxes, and chatted with another twenty proprietors while I collected cans and jars. The take: $23.89.

The third day was even worse. After counting up the money, even I couldn't believe it. There was only $11.52. Those were from the businesses down by the waterfront, where the tourists and teenagers like me hung out. We were really something, I couldn't help but think.

Seeing how little had been collected in all—$55.73—made me feel awful, especially considering that the jars had been out for almost a whole year and that I myself had seen them countless times. That night I was supposed to call Jamie to tell her the amount I'd collected, but I just couldn't do it. She'd told me how she'd wanted something extra special this year, and this wasn't going to do it—even I knew that. Instead I lied to her and told her that I wasn't going to count the total until the two of us could do it together, because it was her project, not mine. It was just too depressing. I promised to bring over the money the following afternoon, after school let out. The next day was December 21, the shortest day of the year. Christmas was only four days away.

"Landon," she said to me after counting it up, "this is a miracle!"

"How much is there?" I asked. I knew exactly how much it was.

"There's almost two hundred and forty-seven dollars here!" She was absolutely joyous as she looked up at me. Since Hegbert was home, I was allowed to sit in the living room, and that's where Jamie had counted the money. It was stacked in neat little piles all over the floor, almost all quarters and dimes. Hegbert was in the kitchen at the table, writing his sermon, and even he turned his head when he heard the sound of her voice.

"Do you think that's enough?" I asked innocently.

Little tears were coming down her cheeks as she looked around the room, still not believing what she was seeing right in front of her. Even after the play, she hadn't been nearly this happy. She looked right at me.

"It's...wonderful," she said, smiling. There was more emotion than I'd ever heard in her voice before. "Last year, I only collected seventy dollars."

"I'm glad it worked out better this year," I said through the lump that had formed in my throat. "If you hadn't placed those jars out so early in the year, you might not have collected nearly as much."

I know I was lying, but I didn't care. For once, it was the right thing to do.

I didn't help Jamie pick out the toys—I figured she'd know better what the kids would want anyway—but she'd insisted that I go with her to the orphanage on Christmas Eve so that I could be there when the children opened their gifts. "Please, Landon," she'd said, and with her being so excited and all, I just didn't have the heart to turn her down.

So three days later, while my father and mother were at a party at the mayor's house, I dressed in a houndstooth jacket and my best tie and walked to my mom's car with Jamie's present beneath my arm. I'd spent my last few dollars on a nice sweater because that was all I could think to get her. She wasn't exactly the easiest person to shop for.

I was supposed to be at the orphanage at seven, but the bridge was up near the Morehead City port, and I had to wait until an outbound freighter slowly made its way down the channel. As a result, I arrived a few minutes late. The front door was already locked by that time, and I had to pound on it until Mr. Jenkins finally heard me. He fiddled through his set of keys until he found the right one, and a moment later he opened the door. I stepped inside, patting my arms to ward off the chill.

"Ah . . . you're here," he said happily. "We've been waiting for you. C'mon, I'll take you to where everyone is."

He led me down the hall to the rec room, the same place I'd been before. I paused for just a moment to exhale deeply before finally heading in.

It was even better than I'd imagined.

In the center of the room I saw a giant tree, decorated with tinsel and colored lights and a hundred different handmade ornaments. Beneath the tree, spread in all directions, were wrapped gifts of every size and shape. They were piled high, and the children were on the floor, sitting close together in a large semicircle. They were dressed in their best clothes, I assumed— the boys wore navy blue slacks and white collared shirts, while the girls had on navy skirts and long-sleeved blouses. They all looked as if they'd cleaned up before the big event, and most of the boys had had their hair cut.

On the table beside the door, there was a bowl of punch and platters of cookies, shaped like Christmas trees and sprinkled with green sugar. I could see some adults sitting with the children; a few of the smaller kids were sitting on the adults' laps, their faces rapt with attention as they listened to " 'Twas the Night Before Christmas."

I didn't see Jamie, though, at least not right off the bat. It was her voice that I recognized first. She was the one reading the story, and I finally located her. She was sitting on the floor in front of the tree with her legs bent beneath her.

To my surprise, I saw that tonight her hair hung loosely, just as it had the night of the play. Instead of the old brown cardigan I'd seen so many times, she was wearing a red V-neck sweater that somehow accentuated the color of her light blue eyes. Even without sparkles in her hair or a long white flowing dress, the sight of her was arresting. Without even noticing it, I'd been holding my breath, and I could see Mr. Jenkins smiling at me out of the corner of my eye. I exhaled and smiled, trying to regain control.

Jamie paused only once to look up from the story. She noticed me standing in the doorway, then went back to reading to the children. It took her another minute or so to finish, and when she did, she stood up and smoothed her skirt, then walked around the children to make her way toward me. Not knowing where she wanted me to go, I stayed where I was.

By then Mr. Jenkins had slipped away.

"I'm sorry we started without you," she said when she finally reached me, "but the kids were just so excited."

"It's okay," I said, smiling, thinking how nice she looked.

"I'm so glad you could come."

"So am I."

Jamie smiled and reached for my hand to lead the way. "C'mon with me," she said. "Help me hand out the gifts."

We spent the next hour doing just that, and we watched as the children opened them one by one. Jamie had shopped all over town, picking up a few things for each child in the room, individual gifts that they'd never received before. The gifts that Jamie bought weren't the only ones the children received, however—both the orphanage and the people who worked there had bought some things as well. As paper was tossed around the room in excited frenzy, there were squeals of delight everywhere. To me, at least, it seemed that all of the children had received far more than they'd expected, and they kept thanking Jamie over and over.

By the time the dust had finally settled and all the children's gifts were opened, the atmosphere began to calm down. The room was tidied up by Mr. Jenkins and a woman I'd never met, and some of the smaller children were beginning to fall asleep beneath the tree. Some of the older ones had already gone back to their rooms with their gifts, and they'd dimmed the overhead lights on the way out the door. The tree lights cast an ethereal glow as "Silent Night" played softly on a phonograph that had been set up in the corner. I was still sitting on the floor next to Jamie, who was holding a young girl who'd fallen asleep in her lap. Because of all the commotion, we hadn't really had a chance to talk, not that either of us had minded. We were both gazing up at the lights on the tree, and I wondered what Jamie was thinking. If truth be told, I didn't know, but she had a tender look about her. I thought—no, *I knew*—she was pleased with how the evening had gone, and deep down, so was I. To this point it was the best Christmas Eve I'd ever spent.

I glanced at her. With the lights glowing on her face, she looked as pretty as anyone I'd ever seen.

"I bought you something," I finally said to her. "A gift, I mean." I spoke softly so I wouldn't wake the little girl, and I hoped it would hide the nervousness in my voice.

She turned from the tree to face me, smiling softly. "You didn't have to do that." She kept her voice low, too, and it sounded almost musical.

"I know," I said. "But I wanted to." I'd kept the gift off to one side, and I reached for it, handing the gift-wrapped package to her.

"Could you open it for me? My hands are kind of full right now." She looked down at the little girl, then back to me.

"You don't have to open it now, if you'd rather not," I said, shrugging, "it's really not that big of a deal."

"Don't be silly," she said. "I would only open it in front of you."

To clear my mind, I looked at the gift and started opening it, picking at the tape so that it wouldn't make much noise, then unwrapping the paper until I reached the box. After setting the paper off to the side, I lifted the cover and pulled out the sweater, holding it up to show her. It was brown, like the ones she usually wore. But I figured she could use a new one.

Compared with the joy I'd seen earlier, I didn't expect much of a reaction.

"See, that's all. I told you it wasn't much," I said. I hoped she wasn't disappointed in it.

"It's beautiful, Landon," she said earnestly. "I'll wear it the next time I see you. Thank you."

We sat quietly for a moment, and once again I began to look at the lights.

"I brought you something, too," Jamie finally whispered. She looked toward the tree, and my eyes followed her gaze. Her gift was still beneath the tree, partially hidden by the stand, and I reached for it. It was rectangular, flexible, and a little heavy. I brought it to my lap and held it there without even trying to open it.

"Open it," she said, looking right at me.

"You can't give this to me," I said breathlessly. I already knew what was inside, and I couldn't believe what she had done. My hands began to tremble.

"Please," she said to me with the kindest voice I'd ever heard, "open it. I want you to have it."

Reluctantly I slowly unwrapped the package. When it was finally free of the paper, I held it gently, afraid to damage it. I stared at it, mesmerized, and slowly ran my hand over the top, brushing my fingers over the well-worn leather as tears filled my eyes. Jamie reached out and rested her hand on mine. It was warm and soft.

I glanced at her, not knowing what to say.

Jamie had given me her Bible.

"Thank you for doing what you did," she whispered to me. "It was the best Christmas I've ever had."

I turned away without responding and reached off to the side where I'd set my glass of punch. The chorus of "Silent Night" was still playing, and the music filled the room. I took a sip of the punch, trying to soothe the sudden dryness in my throat. As I drank, all the times I'd spent with Jamie came flooding into my mind. I thought about the homecoming dance and what she'd done for me that night. I thought about the play and how angelic she'd looked. I thought about the times I'd walked her home and how I'd helped collect jars and cans filled with pennies for the orphans.

As these images were going through my head, my breathing suddenly went still. I looked at Jamie, then up to the ceiling and around the room, doing my best to keep my composure, then back to Jamie again. She smiled at me and I smiled at her and all I could do was wonder how I'd ever fallen in love with a girl like Jamie Sullivan.

Questions and Explanations for Chapters 7, 8, and 9

The twenty questions on chapters 7, 8, and 9 focus on grammar and usage, vocabulary, literary terms, characterization, theme, making inferences, using context clues, and the effects of style. Some of the questions combine two or more of these areas, requiring you to synthesize your knowledge, make inferences, and interpret the text. The questions are designed to determine both your current level of understanding of the novel and your ability to answer higher-level questions.

The following sentence tests your ability to recognize grammar and usage errors. The sentence contains either a single error or no error at all. If the sentence contains an error, select the one underlined part that must be changed to make the sentence correct. If there is no error, select answer choice D.

1. Landon <u>decides</u> to lash out at Jamie instead of <u>whom-</u>
   A   B
   <u>ever</u> teases him about his involvement with the <u>Christ-</u>
                                                        C
   <u>mas play</u>. <u>No error</u>
                   D

In order to answer this question, you need to realize what you are being asked to evaluate. For choice A you must determine if the subject/verb agreement between *Landon* and *decides* is correct. Choice B is asking you to differentiate between *whoever* and *whomever*. Remember, *whoever* is used with the subjective case, and *whomever* is used with the objective case. The subjective case is used when the word is the subject of the sentence or clause, the doer of an action. *Whoever* is the subjective form—for example, "Whoever crosses the finish line first wins the race." *Whomever* is the objective form—for example, "He invited *whomever* he felt like to his party." For choice C you need to verify that it's the appropriate usage of a proper adjective. A proper adjective is an adjective form of a proper noun, which is a noun that is capitalized. For example, China is a proper noun, and in the phrase *Chinese food*, the word *Chinese* is the proper adjective. You need to determine if *Christmas* should be capitalized.

Question 2 asks you to analyze the impact onomatopoeia has on a passage.

2. The first time Landon walks Jamie home, she initiates a conversation about the time he spends in the graveyard at night, and asks him, "Do you ever just sit around and listen to the sounds?...Like the crickets chirping, or

the rustling of leaves when the wind blows?" The use of onomatopoeia achieves all of the following EXCEPT:

A. enable readers to get a sense of what it might be like to be in the graveyard at night

B. create a harsh tone that captures the mood of the cemetery at night

C. contrast Jamie's view of spending time at night in the graveyard with Landon's actual experience

D. demonstrate Jamie's appreciation of nature

Onomatopoeia is a sound word that suggests the very sound it describes. The two examples of onomatopoeia in the passage are *chirping* and *rustling*. Ask yourself: What effect do these words have on the scene? Picture the scene in your mind and hear the sounds. Now determine how hearing these sounds affects your appreciation of the scene. The word *except* in the question indicates that three out of the four responses are effects of the onomatopoeia; and you can eliminate those three choices.

If the words *chirping* and *rustling* provide a sense of the sounds that might be heard in the cemetery at night, eliminate choice A. If you think the sounds of chirping and rustling are harsh, eliminate choice B. If you think the sounds indicate the type of experience Jamie imagines in the graveyard as opposed to what Landon actually does while he is there, eliminate choice C; and if the sounds indicate that Jamie has an appreciation for nature, eliminate choice D.

Read the following passage and then answer question 3, which asks you to differentiate among the different types of irony.

You might think I'd be getting excited about [the play], too, but I really wasn't. My friends were still teasing me at school, and I hadn't had an afternoon off in what seemed like forever. The only thing that kept me going was the fact that I was doing the "right thing." I know it's not much, but frankly, it was all I had. Occasionally I even felt sort of good about it, too, though I never admitted it to anyone. I could practically imagine the angels in heaven, standing around and staring wistfully down at me with little tears filling the corners of their eyes, talking about how wonderful I was for all my sacrifices. [Landon]

3. Which type of irony is best illustrated in the preceding paragraph?

    A. dramatic irony

    B. situational irony

    C. verbal irony

    D. cosmic irony

A good definition and understanding of *irony* is "an incongruity between appearance and reality." *Dramatic irony*, choice A, occurs when the words and actions of the characters have a different meaning to the reader than they do to the characters themselves. This is the result of the reader having more background information than the character has. For example, the audience knows that Juliet is not really dead when Romeo discovers her body in the crypt, but he does not, and thus he stabs himself.

Situational irony, choice B, exists when there is a discrepancy between what the reader expects and what actually occurs. In the Shakespeare play, Macbeth's misinterpretation of the witches' prophecies is an example of situational irony, because he expects their words to mean one thing but in reality they mean something else.

Verbal irony, choice C, exists when a character says one thing and means another. Sarcasm is often considered to be a form of verbal irony. When Mark Antony is talking about the conspirators as he stands over the dead body of Caesar, he says, "And Brutus is an honorable man." Clearly, Antony does not think Brutus is really honorable.

Cosmic irony, choice D, also known as irony of fate, is a situation where no matter what a character attempts to do, he cannot escape his fate. The most famous example of this is the Greek myth of Oedipus, who was fated to grow up and kill his father and marry his mother, no matter how he or anyone else tried to prevent it.

Question 4 tests your comprehension of the text as well as your ability to analyze details and examples from the text to draw a conclusion regarding character development.

4. All of the following contribute to Landon's growing resentment and frustration regarding Jamie EXCEPT:

   A. his friends' teasing

   B. his teenage value system

   C. his paradoxical attraction to someone he thought he could never like

   D. his desire to perform for the orphans

Three out of the four choices *do* contribute to Landon's growing resentment and frustration. If you eliminate these incorrect choices, then you will be left with the correct answer. Or, you can determine which choice *does not* add to his growing resentment.

Asking yourself these questions about the choices will help you determine the correct answer: Is Landon getting annoyed because his friends keep teasing him about his involvement with Jamie and the play? If so, eliminate choice A. Does Landon seem to have typical teenage concerns, as contrasted to Jamie's concerns? Is it true that the things she cares about are not what most teenagers think about? If yes, then eliminate choice B. Is Landon finding himself somewhat attracted to Jamie, even though she is not the type of girl he ever imagined himself dating? If this is the case, eliminate choice C. Finally, does his desire to perform well for the orphans conflict with Jamie's desire? If that is the case, eliminate choice D.

Question 5 tests your comprehension as well as your ability to analyze details and examples from the text to draw a conclusion regarding character development.

5. When Landon's frustration and resentment overflow in chapter 7, he is tired of the way his friends continually tease him about his relationship with Jamie, he is caught up participating in the play to please Jamie's father, who "doesn't even like me," and he just wants his life to return to the way it was prior to the drama class and interacting with Jamie, the social outcast. After being told by Miss Garber to walk Jamie home one night, he lashes out at Jamie and unfurls all of his frustrations toward her, badly

hurting her feelings. Yet, even though Jamie is upset by Landon's unkind words, she still thanks him for walking her home. Why does this upset Landon?

A. He wants her to feel as bad as he does.

B. He doesn't want her to think that they are friends.

C. He doesn't want to like Jamie, but fears that he is beginning to.

D. Jamie's thanking him for walking him home makes him feel self-centered and selfish.

All of the choices have some truth in them, but as you take the SAT, ACT, or end-of-year assessments, you are sometimes asked to find the answer choice that BEST answers the question. We know that Jamie causes some discomfort in Landon's life by causing him to think and react differently than he normally does. Because Jamie does not look like or act like or display the values of Landon's teenaged friends, this causes him some distress.

If you think that Landon truly wants to make Jamie feel bad, select choice A. If you think Landon has no desire whatsoever to be friends with Jamie, select choice B. If you think his fear of liking her is causing him to lash out, select choice C. And if you think Jamie's comments cause him to evaluate himself and consider his own words and actions, select choice D.

Question 6 tests your comprehension as well as your ability to analyze the details and examples from the text to draw a conclusion regarding character development.

6. What is the primary reason Landon claims "Or rather, I think, I hated myself" at the end of chapter 7?

    A. He just yelled at Jamie.

    B. He has low self-esteem.

    C. He does not understand what type of girl Jamie is.

    D. He is mad at himself for being more concerned with his own well-being than with Jamie's feelings.

This question is related to the previous one, and it is designed to help you make connections between a character's thoughts, words, and actions and his overall development. This question is also requiring you to ascertain the BEST answer. If Landon says he hates himself mostly because he just yelled at Jamie, select choice A. If you believe Landon has low self-esteem and this is the reason he claims to hate himself, select choice B. If you think that Landon hates himself for not understanding Jamie as a person, select choice C, and if you think Landon is torn up because of concern for his own reputation and the realization that he was inconsiderate of Jamie's feelings, select choice D.

Question 7 asks you to determine the central idea of the text based on an analysis of the author's specific word choice.

7. The night after Landon says all the mean and hurtful things to Jamie, he apologizes and promises to make it up to her. He adds, "Don't ask me why I said it—it just seemed like the right thing to do at that moment." Thematically, what is significant about Landon's comments?

A. These comments illustrate that Landon is becoming a dynamic character.

B. The words are an example of Landon's reverting to his sarcastic tendencies from earlier in the novel.

C. Landon is learning that sometimes it is important to follow your instincts and your feelings, even if it means sometimes feelings will override logic.

D. These words illustrate the classic theme that "actions speak louder than words."

In order to answer a question about theme correctly, you must remember that *theme* refers to a main idea and that a theme is expressed in a complete sentence. A single word like *love, trust,* or *friendship* is not a theme but rather a thematic topic.

Ask yourself: What is the relationship between character development and thematic development? Although the two are interrelated, they are not the same thing. Are Landon's words sarcastic, and are they being used to develop a character or develop a theme? Is Landon learning something that is valuable and is a universal idea that might be essential to our understanding of the novel as a whole? Are the best themes just a trite moral to the story, or do they offer something more than that?

Nicholas Sparks uses multiple clues in his text in order to create varied types of inferences, such as cause-and-effect inferences, literary inferences, occupational inferences, cultural inferences, emotional inferences, and time/era inferences.

The following four questions (8–11) will test your ability to make inferences by connecting the background knowledge you already have about the characters and linking it to textual clues.

Match the lines of dialogue with the correct speaker from the choices listed below:

8. "My angel, I cannot tell you how much this means to me." _____

9. "The two of you did good. I'm really proud of you, buddy." _____

10. "This is the proudest moment I have ever had in all of my years as the drama teacher. You should all be proud of your achievement tonight as well." _____

11. "I feel horrible about putting paper clips in those cans. Sometimes when you look back and think about the things you used to do, they seem so irresponsible. I can't envision doing anything like that now." _____

    A. Landon Carter

    B. Reverend Sullivan

    C. Worth Carter

    D. Miss Garber

    E. Eric Hunter

In question 8, the best context clue is the word *angel*. Which character from the choices listed is most likely to refer to another as angel?

In question 9, focus on the colloquial language "you did *good*" (as opposed to *well*) and the term of endearment *buddy*. Which character is most likely to speak that way?

In question 10, the words "as the drama teacher" clearly indicate that the speaker of these statements is in fact the drama teacher. Who is the drama teacher?

In question 11, the speaker is referring to when he and his friends found it was amusing to fill Jamie's Christmas containers for the orphans with paper clips instead of coins, causing Jamie to temporarily believe that the weight of the can indicated a large quantity of coins. In retrospect, he feels foolish for doing anything that would cause her disappointment. Which character has this change of heart?

The following five sentences (12–16) test your vocabulary and ability to understand words used in context. By studying context clues, you will perceive a clear connection between the underlined word and the words that surround it. Choose the best meaning for the underlined word or phrase in each of the following five sentences. Circle the letter of the meaning you choose.

12. She asked her father to <u>reconsider</u> letting her go to the party.

    A. forget about

    B. not worry about

C. speak again about

D. reevaluate

From the context clues, you know that her father would not permit her to go to the party, and she would like to change his mind; *reconsider* also has the prefix *re-*, which means again. Substitute the words from each choice to determine which one fits the context.

13. Because he was a congressman, he always received <u>preferential</u> treatment at the restaurant.

   A. poor

   B. partisan

   C. standard

   D. superior

The context reveals that the type of treatment he receives is based upon the fact he is a congressman. You need to infer what type of treatment a congressman would receive. In addition, recognize that the root word in *preferential* is *prefer*. How does knowledge of the root word aid you in finding a synonym for *preferential*?

14. His loyal support of his friend was <u>admirable</u>.

   A. commendable

   B. peculiar

   C. foolish

   D. shameful

Ask yourself: Is "loyal support of a friend" a good or bad thing? That alone should reveal the answer. If not, realize that the root word for *admirable* is *admire*. Find the word that means something similar to *admire*.

15. I got <u>the willies</u> at the mention of visiting the graveyard alone.

    A. a vision of a ghost

    B. an uncomfortable feeling

    C. an excited feeling

    D. an irresistible urge

The willies is a colloquialism, so you are not able to use a root of the word to help figure out the meaning. You must rely solely on the context clues. Consider what type of feeling most people would get if it is suggested they visit a graveyard alone.

16. I heard the crowd <u>collectively</u> draw a breath as soon as she appeared on stage.

    A. jointly

    B. scornfully

    C. halfheartedly

    D. individually

If you recognize that *crowd* is a collective noun—a word that appears to be singular but actually denotes a group—you are well on your way to answering this question correctly. Also notice that the root word *collective* means combined, forming a whole. If you are not familiar with either of these words, you can also use the context clues in the sentence. Realize that the crowd is drawing a breath and think about what that means and what that would look like. If you can visualize that scene, you should be able to answer the question.

Question 17 checks your comprehension and asks you to draw an inference from the text.

17. While apologizing to Jamie about his deplorable behavior during their last walk home, Landon tells her that he will make it up to her. At a later date, Jamie asks him to do her a favor and gather the pickle jars and coffee cans she left on store counters around town in an effort to collect donations for the orphans. Why is Landon so surprised that she would ask something more of him?

   A. Landon thinks that he has gone out of his way numerous times walking her home after play practice and that is sufficient.

   B. Landon thinks that by participating in the play, he has already fulfilled his obligation to her.

   C. Landon thinks that Jamie is asking too much.

   D. Landon thinks that Jamie is not letting him get a word in edgewise so he can tell her why he shouldn't have to do anything more.

This question is designed to check your reading comprehension. Although a few of the choices may have been mentioned in the novel, there is only one BEST answer. If you don't remember the reason from your reading, you may either reread the text or use the following questions to jog your memory. First, consider the timing of events in the narrative: that is, when does his promise to make it up to her occur? Does Landon feel that his extraordinary performance in the play was enough? Does Jamie ever ask too much of anyone? And does Landon feel he is unable to speak because Jamie monopolizes the conversation?

Read the following passage and then answer question 18, which tests your application of literary terms, specifically those that relate to discussing characters.

Landon does not tell Jamie that it was he who added money to the collection cans for the orphans. This shows that, inspired by the example of Jamie's selflessness, he wants to emulate her and aspires to be the kind of person she is.

> "I'm glad it worked out better this year," I said through the lump...in my throat. "If you hadn't placed those jars out so early in the year, you might not have collected nearly as much."
> I know I was lying, but I didn't care. For once, it was the right thing to do. [Landon]

18. As exemplified in the dialogue above, Landon's character changes dramatically throughout *A Walk to Remember*, making him what type of character?

    A. static

    B. a foil

    C. dynamic

    D. a stock character

Knowledge of literary terms that are used to discuss characters is necessary in order to answer this question correctly. A *static* character, choice A, represents a character that remains mainly the same throughout the novel. Static characters are often minor characters. Cinderella's stepmother doesn't change at all during the story, so she is a static character.

A *foil*, choice B, is a character that is used to enhance another character through contrast. Gale and Peeta from *The Hunger Games* are foils for each other.

A *dynamic* character, choice C, is one that goes through a change. Most protagonists are dynamic characters, but not all dynamic characters have to be protagonists. Ebenezer Scrooge changes from the beginning of *A Christmas Carol* to the end; thus, he is a dynamic character.

A *stock character*, choice D, is one who is typically the same in all kinds of novels, stories, or movies. He or she is easily recognizable and typically does not develop over time. A wicked stepmother, a dumb jock, and a computer nerd are all stock characters.

Question 19 checks your comprehension and asks you to draw an inference based on the details and examples from the text.

19. In the past, Landon and his friends spent a lot of time mocking Jamie and her Bible, but now he owns it, since she gave it to him as a Christmas gift. Never once does he think about what his friends might say. He has moved well beyond those immature times and now is engulfed in the richness of life as Jamie sees it and understands

what a treasured item of hers this is. Which choice would NOT be a reason why Jamie gave the Bible to Landon?

A. Jamie realizes that Landon put money of his own into the collection cans to help make it a special Christmas for the orphans, and she wants to appropriately thank him.

B. She wants him to become religious like her father.

C. Jamie knows that Landon might need comfort in the future, and having something that represents her love of God would provide comfort to him.

D. Jamie knows more about her future than he does, and her gift will serve as a source of strength for Landon as well as serving as a symbol of her to him.

Three out of the four choices are reasons that Jamie would give her beloved Bible to Landon. She knows he understands the importance the Bible has to her and knows that it will be treasured by him in years to come. She never loses her faith in God, and she wants Landon to see this as well. The choices that illustrate this attitude must be eliminated, and the single choice that does not serve as a reason for Jamie to have given the Bible to Landon is the correct answer. Landon gave almost all the money he had to the collection; does the Bible represent all that Jamie has? If so, eliminate choice A. Do you think Jamie has the desire or expectation that Landon will become like her father? If so, eliminate choice B. Do we have clues that something is going to happen to Jamie? Both choice C and choice D depend on foreshadowing. Don't forget what you read in the prologue and the other bits of foreshadowing sprinkled throughout the novel.

Question 20 asks you to analyze how the choices an author makes contribute to the overall meaning and aesthetic impact of the text.

20. Stylistically, the single-sentence paragraph at the end of chapter 8—"I'd nailed that line for the very first time"—does each of the following EXCEPT:

 A. reveal Landon's true feelings

 B. demonstrate that Landon believes he has fulfilled his promise to Jamie

 C. prove that Landon has developed into a solid actor

 D. indicate Landon's newfound maturity while simultaneously maintaining his narrative voice

You will eliminate three out of the four choices because three of them *are* effects of the single-sentence paragraph. If Landon believes that he really did nail that line, then eliminate choice A. If the fact that he finally said the line correctly is enough for him to think he fulfilled his promise to Jamie, then eliminate choice B. If it does indeed demonstrate that Landon has developed into an excellent actor, eliminate choice C. If Landon really is recognizing Jamie's beauty for the first time and is also expressing himself using conversational language, then eliminate choice D.

Chapter 10

I drove Jamie home from the orphanage later that night. At first I wasn't sure whether I should pull the old yawn move and put my arm around her shoulder, but to be honest, I didn't know exactly how she was feeling about me. Granted, she'd given me the most wonderful gift I'd ever received, and even though I'd probably never open it and read it like she did, I knew it was like giving a piece of herself away. But Jamie was the type of person who would donate a kidney to a stranger she met walking down the street, if he really needed one. So I wasn't exactly sure what to make of it.

Jamie had told me once that she wasn't a dimwit, and I guess I finally came to the conclusion that she wasn't. She may have been . . . well, different . . . but she'd figured out what I'd done for the orphans, and looking back, I think she knew even as we were sitting on the floor of her living room. When she'd called it a miracle, I guess she was talking specifically about me.

Hegbert, I remembered, came into the room as Jamie and I were talking about it, but he really didn't have much to say. Old Hegbert hadn't been himself lately, at least as far as I could tell. Oh, his sermons were still on the money, and he still talked about the fornicators, but lately his sermons were shorter than usual, and occasionally he'd pause right in the middle of one and this strange look would come over him, kind of like he was thinking of something else, something sad.

I didn't know what to make of it, being that I really didn't know him that well. And Jamie, when she talked about him, seemed to describe someone else entirely. I could no more imagine Hegbert with a sense of humor than I could imagine two moons in the sky.

So anyway, he came into the room while we counted the money, and Jamie stood up with those tears in her eyes, and Hegbert didn't even seem to realize I was there. He told her that he was proud of her and that he loved her, but then he shuffled back to the kitchen to continue working on his sermon. He didn't even say hello. Now, I knew I hadn't exactly been the most spiritual kid in the congregation, but I still found his behavior sort of odd.

As I was thinking about Hegbert, I glanced at Jamie sitting beside me. She was looking out the window with a peaceful look on her face, kind of smiling, but far away at the same time. I smiled. Maybe she was thinking about me. My hand started scooting across the seat closer to hers, but before I reached it, Jamie broke the silence.

"Landon," she finally asked as she turned toward me, "do you ever think about God?"

I pulled my hand back.

Now, when I thought about God, I usually pictured him

like those old paintings I'd seen in churches—a giant hovering over the landscape, wearing a white robe, with long flowing hair, pointing his finger or something like that—but I knew she wasn't talking about that. She was talking about the Lord's plan. It took a moment for me to answer.

"Sure," I said. "Sometimes, I reckon."

"Do you ever wonder why things have to turn out the way they do?"

I nodded uncertainly.

"I've been thinking about it a lot lately."

Even more than usual? I wanted to ask, but I didn't. I could tell she had more to say, and I stayed quiet.

"I know the Lord has a plan for us all, but sometimes, I just don't understand what the message can be. Does that ever happen to you?"

She said this as though it were something I thought about all the time.

"Well," I said, trying to bluff, "I don't think that we're meant to understand it all the time. I think that sometimes we just have to have faith."

It was a pretty good answer, I admit. I guess that my feelings for Jamie were making my brain work a little faster than usual. I could tell she was thinking about my answer.

"Yes," she finally said, "you're right."

I smiled to myself and changed the subject, since talking about God wasn't the sort of thing that made a person feel romantic.

"You know," I said casually, "it sure was nice tonight when we were sitting by the tree earlier."

"Yes, it was," she said. Her mind was still elsewhere.

"And you sure looked nice, too."

"Thank you."

This wasn't working too well.

"Can I ask you a question?" I finally said, in the hopes of bringing her back to me.

"Sure," she said.

I took a deep breath.

"After church tomorrow, and, well...after you've spent some time with your father...I mean..." I paused and looked at her. "Would you mind coming over to my house for Christmas dinner?"

Even though her face was still turned toward the window, I could see the faint outlines of a smile as soon as I'd said it.

"Yes, Landon, I would like that very much."

I sighed with relief, not believing I'd actually asked her and still wondering how all this had happened. I drove down streets where windows were decorated with Christmas lights, and through the Beaufort City Square. A couple of minutes later when I reached across the seat, I finally took hold of her hand, and to complete the perfect evening, she didn't pull it away.

When we pulled up in front of her house, the lights in the living room were still on and I could see Hegbert behind the curtains. I supposed he was waiting up because he wanted to hear how the evening went at the orphanage. Either that, or he wanted to make sure I didn't kiss his daughter on the doorstep. I knew he'd frown on that sort of thing.

I was thinking about that—what to do when we finally said good-bye, I mean—when we got out of the car and started toward the door. Jamie was quiet and content at the same time, and I think she was happy that I'd asked her to come over the next day. Since she'd been smart enough to figure out what I'd done for the orphans, I figured that maybe she'd been smart enough to figure out the homecoming situation as well. In her mind, I think even she realized that this was the first time I'd actually asked her to join me of my own volition.

Just as we got to her steps, I saw Hegbert peek out from behind the curtains and pull his face back. With some parents, like Angela's, for instance, that meant they knew you were home and you had about another minute or so before they'd open the door. Usually that gave you both time to sort of bat your eyes at each other while each of you worked up the nerve to actually kiss. It usually took about that long.

Now I didn't know if Jamie would kiss me; in fact, I actually doubted that she would. But with her looking so pretty, with her hair down and all, and everything that had happened tonight, I didn't want to miss the opportunity if it came up. I could feel the little butterflies already starting to form in my stomach when Hegbert opened the door.

"I heard you pull up," he said quietly. His skin was that sallow color, as usual, but he looked tired.

"Hello, Reverend Sullivan," I said dejectedly.

"Hi, Daddy," Jamie said happily a second later. "I wish you could have come tonight. It was wonderful."

"I'm so glad for you." He seemed to gather himself then and cleared his throat. "I'll give you a bit to say good night. I'll leave the door open for you."

He turned around and went back into the living room. From where he sat down, I knew he could still see us. He pretended to be reading, though I couldn't see what was in his hands.

"I had a wonderful time tonight, Landon," Jamie said.

"So did I," I answered, feeling Hegbert's eyes on me. I wondered if he knew I'd been holding her hand during the car ride home.

"What time should I come over tomorrow?" she asked.

Hegbert's eyebrow raised just a little.

"I'll come over to get you. Is five o'clock okay?" She looked over her shoulder. "Daddy, would you mind if I visited with Landon and his parents tomorrow?"

Hegbert brought his hand to his eyes and started rubbing them. He sighed.

"If it's important to you, you can," he said.

Not the most stirring vote of confidence I'd ever heard, but it was good enough for me.

"What should I bring?" she asked. In the South it was tradition to always ask that question.

"You don't need to bring anything," I answered. "I'll pick you up at a quarter to five."

We stood there for a moment without saying anything else, and I could tell Hegbert was growing a little impatient. He hadn't turned a page of the book since we'd been standing there.

"I'll see you tomorrow," she said finally.

"Okay," I said.

She glanced down at her feet for a moment, then back up at me. "Thank you for driving me home," she said.

With that, she turned around and walked inside. I could barely see the slight smile playing gently across her lips as she peeked around the door, just as it was about to close.

The next day I picked her up right on schedule and was pleased to see that her hair was down once more. She was wearing the sweater I'd given her, just like she'd promised.

Both my mom and dad were a little surprised when I'd asked if it would be all right if Jamie came by for dinner. It wasn't a big deal—whenever my dad was around, my mom would have Helen, our cook, make enough food for a small army.

I guess I didn't mention that earlier, about the cook, I mean. In our house we had a maid and a cook, not only because my family could afford them, but also because my mom wasn't the greatest homemaker in the world. She was all right at making sandwiches for my lunch now and then, but there'd been times when the mustard would stain her nails, and it would take her at least three or four days to get over it. Without Helen I would have grown up eating burned mashed potatoes and crunchy steak. My father, luckily, had realized this as soon as they married, and both the cook and the maid had been with us since before I was born.

Though our house was larger than most, it wasn't a palace or anything, and neither the cook nor the maid lived with us because we didn't have separate living quarters or anything like that. My father had bought the home because of its historical value. Though it wasn't the house where Blackbeard had once lived, which would have been more interesting to someone like me, it *had* been owned by Richard Dobbs Spaight, who'd signed the Constitution. Spaight had also owned a farm outside of New Bern, which was about forty miles up the road, and that was where he was buried. Our house might not have been as famous as the one where Dobbs Spaight was buried, but it still afforded my father some bragging rights in the halls of Congress, and whenever he walked around the garden, I could see him dreaming about the legacy he wanted to leave. In a way it made me sad, because no matter what he did, he'd never top old Richard Dobbs Spaight. Historical events like signing the Constitution come along only once every few hundred years, and no matter how you sliced it, debating farm subsidies for tobacco farmers or talking about the "Red influence" was never going to cut it. Even someone like me knew that.

The house was in the *National Historic Register*—still is, I suppose—and though Jamie had been there once before, she was still kind of awed when she walked inside. My mother and father were both dressed very nicely, as was I, and my mother kissed Jamie hello on the cheek. My mother, I couldn't help but think as I watched her do it, had scored before I did.

We had a nice dinner, fairly formal with four courses, though it wasn't stuffy or anything like that. My parents and Jamie carried on the most marvelous conversation—think Miss Garber here—and though I tried to inject my own brand of humor, it didn't really go over too well, at least as far as my parents were concerned. Jamie, however, would laugh, and I took that as a good sign.

After dinner I invited Jamie to walk around the garden, even though it was winter and nothing was in bloom. After putting on our coats, we stepped outside into the chilled winter air. I could see our breaths coming out in little puffs.

"Your parents are wonderful people," she said to me. I guess she hadn't taken Hegbert's sermons to heart.

"They're nice," I responded, "in their own way. My mom's especially sweet." I said this not only because it was true, but also because it was the same thing that kids said about Jamie. I hoped she would get the hint.

She stopped to look at the rosebushes. They looked like gnarled sticks, and I didn't see what her interest was in them.

"Is it true about your grandfather?" she asked me. "The stories that people tell?"

I guess she didn't get my hint.

"Yes," I said, trying not to show my disappointment.

"That's sad," she said simply. "There's more to life than money."

"I know."

She looked at me. "Do you?"

I didn't meet her eyes as I answered. Don't ask me why.

"I know that what my grandfather did was wrong."

"But you don't want to give it back, do you?"

"I've never really thought about it, to tell you the truth."

"Would you, though?"

I didn't answer right away, and Jamie turned from me. She was staring at the rosebushes with their gnarled sticks again, and I suddenly realized that she'd wanted me to say yes. It's what she would have done without thinking twice about it.

"Why do you do things like that?" I blurted out before I could stop myself, blood rushing into my cheeks. "Making me feel guilty, I mean. I wasn't the one who did it. I just happened to be born into this family."

She reached out and touched a branch. "That doesn't mean you can't undo it," she said gently, "when you get the opportunity."

Her point was clear, even to me, and deep down I knew she was right. But that decision, if it ever came, was a long way off. To my way of thinking, I had more important things on my mind. I changed the subject back to something I could relate to better.

"Does your father like me?" I asked. I wanted to know if Hegbert would allow me to see her again.

It took a moment for her to answer.

"My father," she said slowly, "worries about me."

"Don't all parents?" I asked.

She looked at her feet, then off to the side again before turning back to me.

"I think that with him, it's different from most. But my father does like you, and he knows that it makes me happy to see you. That's why he let me come over to your house for dinner tonight."

"I'm glad he did," I said, meaning it.

"So am I."

We looked at each other under the light of a waxing crescent moon, and I almost kissed her right then, but she turned away a moment too soon and said something that sort of threw me.

"My father worries about you, too, Landon."

The way she said it—it was soft and sad at the same time—let me know that it wasn't simply because he thought I was irresponsible, or that I used to hide behind the trees and call him names, or even that I was a member of the Carter family.

"Why?" I asked.

"For the same reason that I do," she said. She didn't elaborate any further, and I knew right then that she was holding something back, something that she couldn't tell me, something that made her sad as well. But it wasn't until later that I learned her secret.

Being in love with a girl like Jamie Sullivan was without a doubt the strangest thing I'd ever been through. Not only was she a girl that I'd never thought about before this year—even though we'd grown up together—but there was something different in the whole way my feelings for her had unfolded. This wasn't like being with Angela, whom I'd kissed the first time I was ever alone with her. I still hadn't kissed Jamie. I hadn't even hugged her or taken her to Cecil's Diner or even to a movie. I hadn't done any of the things that I normally did with girls, yet somehow I'd fallen in love.

The problem was, I still didn't know how she felt about me.

Oh sure, there were some indications, and I hadn't missed them. The Bible was, of course, the biggie, but there was also the way she'd looked at me when she'd closed the door on Christmas Eve, and she'd let me hold her hand on the ride home from the orphanage. To my way of thinking there was definitely something there—I just wasn't exactly sure of how to take the next step.

When I'd finally taken her home after Christmas dinner, I'd asked if it would be okay if I came by from time to time, and she'd said it would be fine. That's exactly how she'd said it, too—"That would be fine." I didn't take the lack of enthusiasm personally—Jamie had a tendency to talk like an adult, and I think that's why she got along with older people so well.

The following day I walked to her house, and the first thing I noticed was that Hegbert's car wasn't in the driveway. When she answered the door, I knew enough not to ask her if I could come in.

"Hello, Landon," she said as she always did, as if it were a surprise to see me. Again her hair was down, and I took this as a positive sign.

"Hey, Jamie," I said casually.

She motioned to the chairs. "My father's not home, but we can sit on the porch if you'd like…"

Don't even ask me how it happened, because I still can't explain it. One second I was standing there in front of her, expecting to walk to the side of the porch, and in the next second I wasn't. Instead of moving toward the chairs, I took a step closer to her and found myself reaching for her hand. I took it in mine and looked right at her, moving just a little closer. She didn't exactly step back, but her eyes widened just a little, and for a tiny, flickering moment I thought I'd done the wrong thing and debated going any further. I paused and smiled, sort of tilting my head to the side, and the next thing I saw was that she'd closed her eyes and was tilting her head, too, and that our faces were moving closer together.

It wasn't that long, and it certainly wasn't the kind of kiss you see in movies these days, but it was wonderful in its own way, and all I can remember about the moment is that when our lips first touched, I knew the memory would last forever.

Chapter 11

Y ou're the first boy I've ever kissed," she said to me.

It was a few days before the new year, and Jamie and I were standing at the Iron Steamer Pier in Pine Knoll Shores. To get there, we'd had to cross the bridge that spans the Intracoastal Waterway and drive a little way down the island. Nowadays the place has some of the most expensive beachfront property in the entire state, but back then it was mainly sand dunes nestled against the Maritime National Forest.

"I figured I might have been," I said.

"Why?" she asked innocently. "Did I do it wrong?" She didn't look like she'd be too upset if I'd said yes, but it wouldn't have been the truth.

"You're a great kisser," I said, giving her hand a squeeze.

She nodded and turned toward the ocean, her eyes getting that far-off look again. She'd been doing that a lot lately. I let it go on for a while before the silence sort of got to me.

"Are you okay, Jamie?" I finally asked.

Instead of answering, she changed the subject.

"Have you ever been in love?" she asked me.

I ran my hand through my hair and gave her one of those looks. "You mean before now?"

I said it like James Dean would have, the way Eric had told me to say it if a girl ever asked me that question. Eric was pretty slick with girls.

"I'm serious, Landon," she said, tossing me a sidelong glance.

I guess Jamie had seen those movies, too. With Jamie, I'd come to realize, I always seemed to be going from high to low and back to high again in less time than it takes to swat a mosquito. I wasn't quite sure if I liked that part of our relationship yet, though to be honest, it kept me on my toes. I was still feeling off balance as I thought about her question.

"Actually, I have," I said finally.

Her eyes were still fixed on the ocean. I think she thought I was talking about Angela, but looking back, I'd realized that what I'd felt for Angela was totally different from what I was feeling right now.

"How did you know it was love?" she asked me.

I watched the breeze gently moving her hair, and I knew that it was no time to pretend I was something that I actually wasn't.

"Well," I said seriously, "you know it's love when all you want to do is spend time with the other person, and you sort of know that the other person feels the same way."

Jamie thought about my answer before smiling faintly.

"I see," she said softly. I waited for her to add something else, but she didn't, and I came to another sudden realization.

Jamie may not have been all that experienced with boys, but to tell you the truth, she was playing me like a harp.

During the next two days, for instance, she wore her hair in a bun again.

On New Year's Eve I took Jamie out to dinner. It was the very first real date she'd ever been on, and we went to a small waterfront restaurant in Morehead City, a place called Flauvin's. Flauvin's was the kind of restaurant with tablecloths and candles and five different pieces of silverware per setting. The waiters wore black and white, like butlers, and when you looked out the giant windows that completely lined the wall, you could watch moonlight reflecting off the slowly moving water.

There was a pianist and a singer, too, not every night or even every weekend, but on holidays when they thought the place would be full. I had to make reservations, and the first time I called they said they were filled, but I had my mom call them, and the next thing you knew, something had opened up. I guess the owner needed a favor from my father or something, or maybe he just didn't want to make him angry, knowing that my grandfather was still alive and all.

It was actually my mom's idea to take Jamie out someplace special. A couple of days before, on one of those days Jamie was wearing her hair in a bun, I talked to my mom about the things I was going through.

"She's all I think about, Mom," I confessed. "I mean, I know she likes me, but I don't know if she feels the same way that I do."

"Does she mean that much to you?" she asked.

"Yes," I said quietly.

"Well, what have you tried so far?"

"What do you mean?"

My mom smiled. "I mean that young girls, even Jamie, like to be made to feel special."

I thought about that for a moment, a little confused. Wasn't that what I was trying to do?

"Well, I've been going to her house every day to visit," I said.

My mom put her hand on my knee. Even though she wasn't a great homemaker and sometimes stuck it to me, like I said earlier, she really was a sweet lady.

"Going to her house is a nice thing to do, but it's not the most romantic thing there is. You should do something that will really let her know how you feel about her."

My mom suggested buying some perfume, and though I knew that Jamie would probably be happy to receive it, it didn't sound right to me. For one thing, since Hegbert didn't allow her to wear makeup—with the single exception being the Christmas play—I was sure she couldn't wear perfume. I told my mom as much, and that was when she'd suggested taking her out to dinner.

"I don't have any money left," I said to her dejectedly. Though my family was wealthy and gave me an allowance, they never gave me more if I ran through it too quickly. "It builds responsibility," my father said, explaining it once.

"What happened to your money in the bank?"

I sighed, and my mom sat in silence while I explained what I had done. When I finished, a look of quiet satisfaction crossed her face, as if she, too, knew I was finally growing up.

"Let me worry about that," she said softly. "You just find out if she'd like to go and if Reverend Sullivan will allow it. If she can, we'll find a way to make it happen. I promise."

The following day I went to the church. I knew that Hegbert would be in his office. I hadn't asked Jamie yet because I figured she would need his permission, and for some reason I wanted to be the one who asked. I guess it had to do with the fact that Hegbert hadn't exactly been welcoming me with open arms when I visited. Whenever he'd see me coming up the walkway—like Jamie, he had a sixth sense about it—he'd peek out the curtains, then quickly pull his head back behind them, thinking that I hadn't seen him. When I knocked, it would take a long time for him to answer the door, as if he had to come from the kitchen. He'd look at me for a long moment, then sigh deeply and shake his head before finally saying hello.

His door was partially open, and I saw him sitting behind his desk, spectacles propped on his nose. He was looking over some papers—they looked almost financial—and I figured he was trying to figure out the church budget for the following year. Even ministers had bills to pay.

I knocked at the door, and he looked up with interest, as if he expected another member of the congregation, then furrowed his brow when he saw that it was me.

"Hello, Reverend Sullivan," I said politely. "Do you have a moment?"

He looked even more tired than usual, and I assumed he wasn't feeling well.

"Hello, Landon," he said wearily.

I'd dressed sharply for the occasion, by the way, with a jacket and tie. "May I come in?"

He nodded slightly, and I entered the office. He motioned for me to sit in the chair across from his desk.

"What can I do for you?" he asked.

I adjusted myself nervously in the chair. "Well, sir, I wanted to ask you something."

He stared at me, studying me before he finally spoke. "Does it have to do with Jamie?" he asked.

I took a deep breath.

"Yes, sir. I wanted to ask if it would be all right with you if I took her to dinner on New Year's Eve."

He sighed. "Is that all?" he said.

"Yes, sir," I said. "I'll bring her home any time you'd need me to."

He took off his spectacles and wiped them with his handkerchief before putting them back on. I could tell he was taking a moment to think about it.

"Will your parents be joining you?" he asked.

"No, sir."

"Then I don't think that will be possible. But thank you for asking my permission first." He looked down at the papers, making it clear it was time for me to leave. I stood from my chair and started toward the door. As I was about to go, I faced him again.

"Reverend Sullivan?"

He looked up, surprised I was still there.

"I'm sorry for those things I used to do when I was younger, and I'm sorry that I didn't always treat Jamie the way she should have been treated. But from now on, things will change. I promise you that."

He seemed to look right through me. It wasn't enough.

"I love her," I said finally, and when I said it, his attention focused on me again.

"I know you do," he answered sadly, "but I don't want to see her hurt." Even though I must have been imagining it, I thought I saw his eyes begin to water.

"I wouldn't do that to her," I said.

He turned from me and looked out the window, watching as the winter sun tried to force its way through the clouds. It was a gray day, cold and bitter.

"Have her home by ten," he finally said, as though he knew he'd made the wrong decision.

I smiled and wanted to thank him, though I didn't. I could tell that he wanted to be alone. When I glanced over my shoulder on my way out the door, I was puzzled to see his face in his hands.

I asked Jamie an hour later. The first thing she said was that she didn't think she could go, but I told her that I'd already spoken to her father. She seemed surprised, and I think it had an effect on how she viewed me after that. The one thing I didn't tell her was that it looked almost as though Hegbert had been crying as I'd made my way out the door. Not only didn't I understand it completely, I didn't want her to worry. That night, though, after talking to my mom again, she provided me with a possible explanation, and to be honest, it made perfect sense to me. Hegbert must have come to the realization that his daughter was growing up and that he was slowly losing her to me. In a way, I hoped that was true.

I picked her up right on schedule. Though I hadn't asked her to wear her hair down, she'd done it for me. Silently we drove over the bridge, down the waterfront to the restaurant. When we got to the hostess stand, the owner himself appeared and walked us to our table. It was one of the better ones in the place.

It was crowded by the time we arrived, and all around us people were enjoying themselves. On New Year's people dressed fashionably, and we were the only two teenagers in the place. I didn't think we looked too out of place, though.

Jamie had never been to Flauvin's before, and it took her just a few minutes to take it all in. She seemed nervously happy, and I knew right away that my mom had made the right suggestion.

"This is wonderful," she said to me. "Thank you for asking me."

"My pleasure," I said sincerely.

"Have you been here before?"

"A few times. My mother and father like to come here sometimes when my father comes home from Washington."

She looked out the window and stared at a boat that was passing by the restaurant, its lights blazing. For a moment she seemed lost in wonder. "It's beautiful here," she said.

"So are you," I answered.

Jamie blushed. "You don't mean that."

"Yes," I said quietly, "I do."

We held hands while we waited for dinner, and Jamie and I talked about some of the things that had happened in the past few months. She laughed when we talked about the homecoming dance, and I finally admitted the reason I'd asked her in the first place. She was a good sport about it—she sort of laughed it off cheerfully—and I knew that she'd already figured it out on her own.

"Would you want to take me again?" she teased.

"Absolutely."

Dinner was delicious—we both ordered the sea bass and salads, and when the waiter finally removed our plates, the music started up. We had an hour left before I had to bring her home, and I offered her my hand.

At first we were the only ones on the floor, everyone watching us as we glided around the floor. I think they all knew how we were feeling about each other, and it reminded them of when they were young, too. I could see them smiling wistfully at us. The lights were dim, and when the singer began a slow melody, I held her close to me with my eyes closed, wondering if anything in my life had ever been this perfect and knowing at the same time that it hadn't.

I was in love, and the feeling was even more wonderful than I ever imagined it could be.

After New Year's we spent the next week and a half together, doing the things that young couples did back then, though from time to time she seemed tired and listless. We spent time down by the Neuse River, tossing stones in the water, watching the ripples while we talked, or we went to the beach near Fort Macon. Even though it was winter, the ocean the color of iron, it was something that both of us enjoyed doing. After an hour or so Jamie would ask me to take her home, and we'd hold hands in the car. Sometimes, it seemed, she would almost nod off before we even got home, while other times she would keep up a stream of chatter all the way back so that I could barely get a word in edgewise.

Of course, spending time with Jamie also meant doing the things she enjoyed as well. Though I wouldn't go to her Bible study class—I didn't want to look like an idiot in front of her— we did visit the orphanage twice more, and each time we went there, I felt more at home. Once, though, we'd had to leave early, because she was running a slight fever. Even to my untrained eyes, it was clear that her face was flushed.

We kissed again, too, though not every time we were together, and I didn't even think of trying to make it to second base. There wasn't any need to. There was something nice when I kissed her, something gentle and right, and that was enough for me. The more I did it, the more I realized that Jamie had been misunderstood her entire life, not only by me, but by everyone.

Jamie wasn't simply the minister's daughter, someone who

read the Bible and did her best to help others. Jamie was also a seventeen-year-old girl with the same hopes and doubts that I had. At least, that's what I assumed, until she finally told me.

I'll never forget that day because of how quiet she had been, and I had the funny feeling all day long that something important was on her mind.

I was walking her home from Cecil's Diner on the Saturday before school started up again, a day blustery with a fierce, biting wind. A nor'easter had been blowing in since the previous morning, and while we walked, we'd had to stand close to each other to stay warm. Jamie had her arm looped through mine, and we were walking slowly, even more slowly than usual, and I could tell she wasn't feeling well again. She hadn't really wanted to go with me because of the weather, but I'd asked her because of my friends. It was time, I remember thinking, that they finally knew about us. The only problem, as fate would have it, was that no one else was at Cecil's Diner. As with many coastal communities, things were quiet on the waterfront in the middle of winter.

She was quiet as we walked, and I knew that she was thinking of a way to tell me something. I didn't expect her to start the conversation as she did.

"People think I'm strange, don't they?" she finally said, breaking the silence.

"Who do you mean?" I asked, even though I knew the answer.

"People at school."

"No, they don't," I lied.

I kissed her cheek as I squeezed her arm a little tighter to me. She winced, and I could tell that I'd hurt her somehow.

"Are you okay?" I asked, concerned.

"I'm fine," she said, regaining her composure and keeping the subject on track. "Will you do me a favor, though?"

"Anything," I said.

"Will you promise to tell me the truth from now on? I mean always?"

"Sure," I said.

She stopped me suddenly and looked right at me. "Are you lying to me right now?"

"No," I said defensively, wondering where this was going. "I promise that from now on, I'll always tell you the truth."

Somehow, when I said it, I knew that I'd come to regret it.

We started walking again. As we moved down the street, I glanced at her hand, which was looped through mine, and I saw a large bruise just below her ring finger. I had no idea where it had come from, since it hadn't been there the day before. For a second I thought it might have been caused by me, but then I realized that I hadn't even touched her there.

"People think I'm strange, don't they?" she asked again.

My breath was coming out in little puffs.

"Yes," I finally answered. It hurt me to say it.

"Why?" She looked almost despondent.

I thought about it. "People have different reasons," I said vaguely, doing my best not to go any further.

"But why, exactly? Is it because of my father? Or is it because I try to be nice to people?"

I didn't want anything to do with this.

"I suppose," was all I could say. I felt a little queasy.

Jamie seemed disheartened, and we walked a little farther in silence.

"Do you think I'm strange, too?" she asked me.

The way she said it made me ache more than I thought it would. We were almost at her house before I stopped her and held her close to me. I kissed her, and when we pulled apart, she looked down at the ground.

I put my finger beneath her chin, lifting her head up and making her look at me again. "You're a wonderful person, Jamie. You're beautiful, you're kind, you're gentle...you're everything that I'd like to be. If people don't like you, or they think you're strange, then that's their problem."

In the grayish glow of a cold winter day, I could see her lower lip begin to tremble. Mine was doing the same thing, and I suddenly realized that my heart was speeding up as well. I looked in her eyes, smiling with all the feeling I could muster, knowing that I couldn't keep the words inside any longer.

"I love you, Jamie," I said to her. "You're the best thing that ever happened to me."

It was the first time I'd ever said the words to another person besides a member of my immediate family. When I'd imagined saying it to someone else, I'd somehow thought it would be hard, but it wasn't. I'd never been more sure of anything.

As soon as I said the words, though, Jamie bowed her head and started to cry, leaning her body into mine. I wrapped my arms around her, wondering what was wrong. She was thin, and I realized for the first time that my arms went all the way around her. She'd lost weight, even in the last week and a half, and I remembered that she'd barely touched her food earlier. She kept crying into my chest for what seemed like a long time. I wasn't sure what to think, or even if she felt the same way I did. Even so, I didn't regret the words. The truth is always the truth, and I'd just promised her that I would never lie again.

"Please don't say that," she said to me. "Please..."

"But I do," I said, thinking she didn't believe me.

She began to cry even harder. "I'm sorry," she whispered to me through her ragged sobs. "I'm so, so sorry..."

My throat suddenly went dry.

"Why're you sorry?" I asked, suddenly desperate to understand what was bothering her. "Is it because of my friends and what they'll say? I don't care anymore—I really don't." I was reaching for anything, confused and, yes—scared.

It took another long moment for her to stop crying, and in time she looked up at me. She kissed me gently, almost like the breath of a passerby on a city street, then ran her finger over my cheek.

"You can't be in love with me, Landon," she said through red and swollen eyes. "We can be friends, we can see each other... but you *can't* love me."

"Why not?" I shouted hoarsely, not understanding any of this.

"Because," she finally said softly, "I'm very sick, Landon."

The concept was so absolutely foreign that I couldn't comprehend what she was trying to say.

"So what? You'll take a few days..."

A sad smile crossed her face, and I knew right then what she was trying to tell me. Her eyes never left mine as she finally said the words that numbed my soul.

"I'm dying, Landon."

Questions and Explanations for
Chapters 10 and 11

T he ten questions from chapters 10 and 11 focus on grammar and usage, literary terms, characterization, making inferences, thematic development, and stylistic choices. Some of the questions combine two or more of these areas, requiring you to synthesize your knowledge, make inferences, and interpret the text. The questions are designed to determine both your current level of understanding of the novel and your ability to answer higher-level questions.

The following sentences (1–3) test your ability to recognize grammar and usage errors. Each sentence contains either a single error or no error at all. If the sentence contains an error, select the one underlined part that must be changed to make the sentence correct. If there is no error, select answer choice D.

1. <u>Who</u> <u>did</u> Reverend Sullivan confide in regarding his
     A   B
   <u>daughter's</u> medical condition? <u>No error</u>
     C   D

To answer this question, you need to know what to evaluate. Choice A requires you to differentiate between *who* and *whom*. Remember that *who* is used subjectively—the doer of an action; an example would be, "Who is the best singer?" And *whom* is used objectively—the receiver of the action; an example would be, "Whom did Sally call?" Some people find it easier to rearrange a question in order to determine the subject and any objects. Instead of "Whom did Sally call?" change it to "Sally called whom?" Others find it easier to rearrange the question into a statement and substitute *he* or *him* for *who* or *whom* to determine subject (he or who) or object (him or whom). For example, "[Who or Whom] left his cell phone here?" is similar to the statement "He left his cell phone here," thus *who* is the correct choice.

Choice B calls attention to the subject and verb agreement between *Reverend Sullivan* and *did confide*. Choice C is assessing the use of the apostrophe to show possession.

2. Everyone in the orphanage <u>loved</u> it when <u>they</u> <u>received</u>
                              A   B   C
   a visit from Jamie. <u>No error</u>
                       D

While reading this sentence think about the difference between conversational English and formal written English. Conversational English is the way we talk in everyday life. Choice A is questioning whether the subject and verb, *everyone* and *loved,* agree. Technically, *everyone* is singular. It's correct to say, "Everyone is going to the party," and not correct to say, "Everyone are going to the party." For choice B, you need to determine if the pronoun *they* has agreement with its antecedent. The antecedent of a pronoun is the word that the pronoun takes the place of. In the sentence "Frodo gave him the ring," the word *him* is the singular pronoun, taking place of the word *Sam*. So *Sam* is the antecedent for *him*. Choice C is pointing out the tense of the verb *received*.

3. Daily, Jamie usually <u>likes</u> to pray, help others, and <u>reading</u>
        A   B

   the <u>Bible</u>. <u>No error</u>
        C   D

Choice A is questioning the subject and verb agreement between *Jamie* and *likes*. For choice B you need to make sure that the item in a series, *reading*, is in parallel form. Parallel form means the words have the same structure. In the example "I like running, swimming, and playing tennis," everything I like ends in *-ing*; that is parallel form. Choice C is questioning whether the word *Bible* needs to be capitalized.

Question 4 tests your comprehension as well as your ability to analyze the impact an author's word choice has on character development.

4. Landon claims Jamie was "playing me like a harp." Which details from chapter 11 help demonstrate this simile?

   A. Jamie wears her hair in a bun for the next two days.

   B. Jamie asks Landon if he has ever been in love before.

C. Jamie comments that Landon is the first boy she ever kissed.

D. Jamie agrees to go to the restaurant Flauvin's on New Year's Eve.

This question asks you to find more than one correct answer. In order to be able to answer this question, you need to understand two things: the colloquialism, which is conversational language, and the simile. "Playing you" is a colloquialism for claiming someone is toying with you, flirting with you, or having fun with you, usually at your expense. The simile is "playing me like a harp." The best way to understand the simile is to envision someone playing a harp, a notoriously difficult instrument to master, and to realize that one who plays the harp well makes it appear effortless. Thus, someone "playing me like a harp" may be having fun at my expense, though it is hardly noticeable. The *s* at the end of the word *details* indicates that more than one answer will be correct.

If you think Jamie is purposely wearing her hair up because she knows Landon likes it down, select choice A. If her questions about being in love enable her to steer the conversation in a direction that Landon didn't envision it going, thus illustrating that Jamie is in control, select choice B. If Jamie controls the conversation about first kisses and coyly turns it into a means to get a compliment out of Landon, select choice C. If Jamie has some ulterior motive for going out to dinner on New Year's Eve and is involved in controlling some aspect of the date, select choice D.

Read the following passage and then answer question 5, which asks you to draw an inference based on details and examples from the text.

Landon has a conversation with his mother where he relates his feelings for Jamie and his concern about not knowing if she feels the same way about him. His mother suggests taking Jamie out for dinner.

"I don't have any money left," I said to her dejectedly. Though my family was wealthy and gave me an allowance, they never gave me more if I ran through it too quickly. "It builds responsibility," my father said, explaining it once.

"What happened to your money in the bank?"

I sighed, and my mother sat in silence while I explained what I had done. When I finished, a look of quiet satisfaction crossed her face, as if she, too, knew I was finally growing up.

5. It can be inferred from reading the selection that:

A. Landon's mother will not give him any extra money because in the past she has always gone along with her husband's wishes, and his father's word is the law in the Carter household

B. she is proud that Landon has thought of others before himself and given his money to a worthy cause

C. she feels that once again, Landon is not responsible with handling money

D. Landon is playing his mother in a manner similar to the way he realizes Jamie is playing him

Landon's mother is seldom mentioned in the story other than to express that she was kind and gentle. However, it is a certainty that all mothers want their children to develop to be thoughtful, insightful, responsible adults. This passage is the first time that Mrs. Carter can see Landon has matured from the self-centered teen that he was at the beginning of the story to the mature person that he is today.

You need to determine the BEST answer. That means that not only must every aspect of the answer be correct, but the answer taken as a whole must be superior to all the other choices. The most important part of the passage is the final line, when his mother has a "look of quiet satisfaction," realizing that her son is "finally growing up." This is clearly a compliment to Landon. Which response best demonstrates this newfound admiration?

Question 6 checks your comprehension and asks you to use textual evidence to draw an inference from the text.

6. What do you think is the reason that Landon doesn't take notice of the changes that Jamie is going through, such as losing weight, having a bruise below her ring finger, listlessness, lack of eating, and on occasion falling asleep on the way home from an afternoon out together?

   A. He doesn't want his friends to know they've been spending time with each other, so he is more concerned with who might see them together.

   B. He is so in love with her that he is oblivious to anything else.

   C. He doesn't want to acknowledge that anything is wrong with her.

D. He is so self-centered that he is more focused on advancing their physical relationship.

In order to determine the BEST answer, first analyze the accuracy of each choice. Does Landon want his friends to see them together? If so, you can eliminate choice A. Does the characterization of Landon in choice B seem accurate and is that effect of his love plausible? If so, consider choice B as a possible answer. Choice C is similar to choice B, but at this time in the story, does Landon realize that anything is wrong with Jamie? When Jamie tells him that she is very sick, the idea of her being near death is so incomprehensible to him that his first reaction is to tell her to "take a few days." Although Landon has talked about wanting to get romantic and was talking about kissing, is he still as self-centered as he was at the beginning of the novel?

Question 7 checks your comprehension.

7. The first time Jamie asks Landon about people thinking she is strange, he answers, "No, they don't." Why does Landon respond the way he does?

   A. because he thinks he is protecting Jamie's feelings

   B. because people do not think she is strange

   C. because he promised Eric he would never tell Jamie the truth

   D. because Jamie couldn't handle hearing the truth

This question is designed to check your comprehension. Although all of these reasons are plausible, the one correct answer is clearly stated in the text. If you don't know the answer, reread the chapter.

Question 8 asks you to analyze the development of a theme throughout a text.

8. What is the most important thematic significance developed through Jamie's asking Landon if people think she is strange?

   A. Landon's character has the opportunity to demonstrate his newfound maturity.

   B. Jamie is forcing Landon to be honest, and honesty is the best policy.

   C. The conversation emphasizes the idea that doing good is more important than being popular.

   D. The repeated questioning emphasizes the need for honesty in a committed relationship.

Remember that theme refers to a main idea. If you have multiple ideas to choose from, determine which one is most encompassing and may include the others; that is how you determine the BEST answer.

Is characterization the same thing as theme? If not, eliminate choice A. In order to distinguish between the three thematic ideas presented in choices B, C, and D, think about both Jamie's question and Landon's response. Reread the reasons people cite for having this opinion and Landon's response when Jamie asks Landon if he also thinks she is strange. What do Landon's words in response to Jamie's question mean?

Question 9 does a number of things: It checks your comprehension, asks you to use textual evidence to draw an inference about character development, and asks you to analyze the impact of the author's choices on various elements of the novel.

9. Which choices below indicate why the conversation Jamie and Landon have regarding how people view her is important?

   A. Jamie is seen in a new light.

   B. Landon has the opportunity to be entirely honest with Jamie.

   C. The conversation provides a natural progression for the news at the end of the chapter.

   D. It advances the plot toward its tragic conclusion.

This question indicates that there are multiple correct answers. Has Jamie ever given any indication that she is concerned about how others view her? If the answer is no, select choice A. Does the repeated questioning provide Landon the chance to keep his promise about always telling Jamie the truth? If yes, select choice B. Does the conversation turn from how others view Jamie to Landon's view and his profession of love? And does that profession of love lead to Jamie's sobbing, fearful confession of her secret? If yes, select choice C. And if Landon's confession of love mixed with Jamie's revelation point toward the ending of the story, then select choice D.

Question 10 asks you to analyze how the author's choices concerning structure contribute to the overall meaning of the text.

10. Which of the following choices are important stylistic effects of the single-sentence last paragraph of chapter 11, "I'm dying, Landon"?

   A. It is the culmination of all the foreshadowing throughout the novel.

   B. It helps mirror for readers Landon's reaction to the news, because both are almost simultaneously figuring out the truth as Jamie shares her horrible news.

   C. It continues the motifs of rebirth and second chances.

   D. It builds suspense.

This question indicates that there are multiple correct answers. Chapter, scene, or story endings are usually points of emphasis, and a single-sentence paragraph definitely has multiple effects. Recalling your own initial reading of the novel may assist you in analyzing the four choices. Some of the effects may not have been obvious during your initial reading, but as you read the choices, consider the novel as a whole to determine some of the authorial intentions with this stylistic choice. Also, realize that the question indicates *at least two* of the choices are going to be correct.

If there have been many instances and examples of foreshadowing that were hinting at some potentially shocking news, select choice A. Although some insightful readers may have guessed at Jamie's news, the information wasn't confirmed until they actually read it. Does the pacing and timing of

Jamie's news permit readers to learn the truth at the same time Landon does? If so, select choice B. Choice C requires two different things to be occurring in order to be true. First, are motifs of *rebirth* and *second chances* important in the novel? If not, eliminate choice C. If they are important to the novel, are they addressed in the words "I'm dying, Landon"? If they are, select choice C; if not, eliminate it. Finally, does the news that Jamie is dying prompt the reader to want to continue reading (thus building suspense)? If yes, select choice D.

Chapter 12

She had leukemia; she'd known it since last summer.

The moment she told me, the blood drained from my face and a sheaf of dizzying images fluttered through my mind. It was as though in that brief moment, time had suddenly stopped and I understood everything that had happened between us. I understood why she'd wanted me to do the play: I understood why, after we'd performed that first night, Hegbert had whispered to her with tears in his eyes, calling her his angel; I understood why he looked so tired all the time and why he fretted that I kept coming by the house. Everything became absolutely clear.

Why she wanted Christmas at the orphanage to be so special...

Why she didn't think she'd go to college...

Why she'd given me her Bible...

It all made perfect sense, and at the same time, nothing seemed to make any sense at all.

Jamie Sullivan had leukemia...

Jamie, sweet Jamie, was dying...

My Jamie...

"No, no," I whispered to her, "there has to be some mistake..."

But there wasn't, and when she told me again, my world went blank. My head started to spin, and I clung to her tightly to keep from losing my balance. On the street I saw a man and a woman, walking toward us, heads bent and their hands on their hats to keep them from blowing away. A dog trotted across the road and stopped to smell some bushes. A neighbor across the way was standing on a stepladder, taking down his Christmas lights. Normal scenes from everyday life, things I would never have noticed before, suddenly making me feel angry. I closed my eyes, wanting the whole thing to go away.

"I'm so sorry, Landon," she kept saying over and over. It was I who should have been saying it, however. I know that now, but my confusion kept me from saying anything.

Deep down, I knew it wouldn't go away. I held her again, not knowing what else to do, tears filling my eyes, trying and failing to be the rock I think she needed.

We cried together on the street for a long time, just a little way down the road from her house. We cried some more when Hegbert opened the door and saw our faces, knowing immediately that their secret was out. We cried when we told my mother later that afternoon, and my mother held us both to her bosom and sobbed so loudly that both the maid and the cook wanted to call the doctor because they thought something had happened to my father. On Sunday Hegbert made the announcement to his congregation, his face a mask of anguish and fear, and he had to be helped back to his seat before he'd even finished.

Everyone in the congregation stared in silent disbelief at the words they'd just heard, as if they were waiting for a punch line to some horrible joke that none of them could believe had been told. Then all at once, the wailing began.

We sat with Hegbert the day she told me, and Jamie patiently answered my questions. She didn't know how long she had left, she told me. No, there wasn't anything the doctors could do. It was a rare form of the disease, they'd said, one that didn't respond to available treatment. Yes, when the school year had started, she'd felt fine. It wasn't until the last few weeks that she'd started to feel its effects.

"That's how it progresses," she said. "You feel fine, and then, when your body can't keep fighting, you don't."

Stifling my tears, I couldn't help but think about the play.

"But all those rehearsals...those long days...maybe you shouldn't have—"

"Maybe," she said, reaching for my hand and cutting me off, "doing the play was the thing that kept me healthy for so long."

Later, she told me that seven months had passed since she'd been diagnosed. The doctors had given her a year, maybe less.

These days it might have been different. These days they could have treated her. These days Jamie would probably live. But this was happening forty years ago, and I knew what that meant.

Only a miracle could save her.

"Why didn't you tell me?"

This was the one question I hadn't asked her, the one that I'd been thinking about. I hadn't slept that night, and my eyes were still swollen. I'd gone from shock to denial to sadness to anger and back again, all night long, wishing it weren't so and praying that the whole thing had been some terrible nightmare.

We were in her living room the following day, the day that Hegbert had made the announcement to the congregation. It was January 10, 1959.

Jamie didn't look as depressed as I thought she would. But then again, she'd been living with this for seven months already. She and Hegbert had been the only ones to know, and neither of them had trusted even me. I was hurt by that and frightened at the same time.

"I'd made a decision," she explained to me, "that it would be better if I told no one, and I asked my father to do the same. You saw how people were after the services today. No one would even look me in the eye. If you had only a few months left to live, is that what you would want?"

I knew she was right, but it didn't make it any easier. I was, for the first time in my life, completely and utterly at a loss.

I'd never had anyone close to me die before, at least not anyone that I could remember. My grandmother had died when I was three, and I don't remember a single thing about her or the services that had followed or even the next few years after her passing. I'd heard stories, of course, from both my father and my grandfather, but to me that's exactly what they were. It was the same as hearing stories I might otherwise read in a newspaper about some woman I never really knew. Though my father would bring me with him when he put flowers on her grave, I never had any feelings associated with her. I felt only for the people she'd left behind.

No one in my family or my circle of friends had ever had to

confront something like this. Jamie was seventeen, a child on the verge of womanhood, dying and still very much alive at the same time. I was afraid, more afraid than I'd ever been, not only for her, but for me as well. I lived in fear of doing something wrong, of doing something that would offend her. Was it okay to ever get angry in her presence? Was it okay to talk about the future anymore? My fear made talking to her difficult, though she was patient with me.

My fear, however, made me realize something else, something that made it all worse. I realized I'd never even known her when she'd been healthy. I had started to spend time with her only a few months earlier, and I'd been in love with her for only eighteen days. Those eighteen days seemed like my entire life, but now, when I looked at her, all I could do was wonder how many more days there would be.

On Monday she didn't show up for school, and I somehow knew that she'd never walk the hallways again. I'd never see her reading the Bible off by herself at lunch, I'd never see her brown cardigan moving through the crowd as she made her way to her next class. She was finished with school forever; she would never receive her diploma.

I couldn't concentrate on anything while I sat in class that first day back, listening as teacher after teacher told us what most of us had already heard. The responses were similar to those in church on Sunday. Girls cried, boys hung their heads, people told stories about her as if she were already gone. What can we do? they wondered aloud, and people looked to me for answers.

"I don't know," was all I could say.

I left school early and went to Jamie's, blowing off my classes after lunch. When I knocked at the door, Jamie answered it the way she always did, cheerfully and without, it seemed, a care in the world.

"Hello, Landon," she said, "this is a surprise." When she leaned in to kiss me, I kissed her back, though the whole thing made me want to cry.

"My father isn't home right now, but if you'd like to sit on the porch, we can."

"How can you do this?" I asked suddenly. "How can you pretend that nothing is wrong?"

"I'm not pretending that nothing is wrong, Landon. Let me get my coat and we'll sit outside and talk, okay?"

She smiled at me, waiting for an answer, and I finally nodded, my lips pressed together. She reached out and patted my arm.

"I'll be right back," she said.

I walked to the chair and sat down, Jamie emerging a moment later. She wore a heavy coat, gloves, and a hat to keep her warm. The nor'easter had passed, and the day wasn't nearly as cold as it had been over the weekend. Still, though, it was too much for her.

"You weren't in school today," I said.

She looked down and nodded. "I know."

"Are you ever going to come back?" Even though I already knew the answer, I needed to hear it from her.

"No," she said softly, "I'm not."

"Why? Are you that sick already?" I started to tear up, and she reached out and took my hand.

"No. Today I feel pretty good, actually. It's just that I want to be home in the mornings, before my father has to go to the office. I want to spend as much time with him as I can."

Before I die, she meant to say but didn't. I felt nauseated and couldn't respond.

"When the doctors first told us," she went on, "they said that I should try to lead as normal a life as possible for as long as I could. They said it would help me keep my strength up."

"There's nothing normal about this," I said bitterly.

"I know."

"Aren't you frightened?"

Somehow I expected her to say *no*, to say something wise like a grown-up would, or to explain to me that we can't presume to understand the Lord's plan.

She looked away. "Yes," she finally said, "I'm frightened all the time."

"Then why don't you act like it?"

"I do. I just do it in private."

"Because you don't trust me?"

"No," she said, "because I know you're frightened, too."

I began to pray for a miracle.

They supposedly happen all the time, and I'd read about them in newspapers. People regaining use of their limbs after being told they'd never walk again, or somehow surviving a terrible accident when all hope was lost. Every now and then a traveling preacher's tent would be set up outside of Beaufort, and people would go there to watch as people were healed. I'd been to a couple, and though I assumed that most of the healing was no more than a slick magic show, since I never recognized the people who were healed, there were occasionally things that even I couldn't explain. Old man Sweeney, the baker here in town, had been in the Great War fighting with an artillery unit behind the trenches, and months of shelling the enemy had left him deaf in one ear. It wasn't an act—he really couldn't hear a single thing, and there'd been times when we were kids that we'd been able to sneak off with a cinnamon roll because of it. But the preacher started praying feverishly and finally laid his hand upon the side of Sweeney's head. Sweeney screamed out loud, making people practically jump out of their seats. He had a terrified look on his face, as if the guy had touched him with a white-hot poker, but then he shook his head and looked around, uttering the words "I can hear again." Even he couldn't believe it. "The Lord," the preacher had said as Sweeney made his way back to his seat, "can do anything. The Lord listens to our prayers."

So that night I opened the Bible that Jamie had given me for Christmas and began to read. Now, I'd heard all about the Bible in Sunday school or at church, but to be frank, I just remembered the highlights—the Lord sending the seven plagues so the Israelites could leave Egypt, Jonah being swallowed by a whale, Jesus walking across the water or raising Lazarus from the dead. There were other biggies, too. I knew that practically every chapter of the Bible has the Lord doing something spectacular, but I hadn't learned them all. As Christians we leaned heavily on teachings of the New Testament, and I didn't know the first things about books like Joshua or Ruth or Joel. The first night I read through Genesis, the second night I read through Exodus. Leviticus was next, followed by Numbers and then Deuteronomy. The going got a little slow during certain parts, especially as all the laws were being explained, yet I couldn't put it down. It was a compulsion that I didn't fully understand.

It was late one night, and I was tired by the time I eventually reached Psalms, but somehow I knew this was what I was looking for. Everyone has heard the Twenty-third Psalm, which starts, "The Lord is my Shepherd, I shall not want," but I wanted to read the others, since none of them were supposed to be more important than the others. After an hour I came across an underlined section that I assumed Jamie had noted because it meant something to her. This is what it said:

I cry to you, my Lord, my rock!
    Do not be deaf to me, for if you are silent, I shall go down to the pit like the rest. Hear my voice raised in petition as I cry to you for help, as I raise my hands, my Lord, toward your holy of holies.

I closed the Bible with tears in my eyes, unable to finish the psalm.

Somehow I knew she'd underlined it for me.

"I don't know what to do," I said numbly, staring into the dim light of my bedroom lamp. My mom and I were sitting on my bed. It was coming up on the end of January, the most difficult month of my life, and I knew that in February things would only get worse.

"I know this is hard for you," she murmured, "but there's nothing you can do."

"I don't mean about Jamie being sick—I know there's nothing I can do about that. I mean about Jamie and me."

My mother looked at me sympathetically. She was worried about Jamie, but she was also worried about me. I went on.

"It's hard for me to talk to her. All I can do when I look at her is think about the day when I won't be able to. So I spend all my time at school thinking about her, wishing I could see her right then, but when I get to her house, I don't know what to say."

"I don't know if there's anything you can say to make her feel better."

"Then what should I do?"

She looked at me sadly and put her arm around my shoulder. "You really love her, don't you?" she said.

"With all my heart."

She looked as sad as I'd ever seen her. "What's your heart telling you to do?"

"I don't know."

"Maybe," she said gently, "you're trying too hard to hear it."

The next day I was better with Jamie, though not much. Before I'd arrived, I'd told myself that I wouldn't say anything that might get her down—that I'd try to talk to her like I had before—and that's exactly how it went. I sat myself on her couch and told her about some of my friends and what they were doing; I caught her up on the success of the basketball team. I told her that I still hadn't heard from UNC, but that I was hopeful I'd know within the next few weeks. I told her I was looking forward to graduation. I spoke as though she'd be back to school the following week, and I knew I sounded nervous the entire time. Jamie smiled and nodded at the appropriate times, asking questions every now and then. But I think we both knew by the time I finished talking that it was the last time I would do it. It didn't feel right to either of us.

My heart was telling me exactly the same thing.

I turned to the Bible again, in the hope that it would guide me.

"How are you feeling?" I asked a couple of days later.

By now Jamie had lost more weight. Her skin was beginning to take on a slightly grayish tint, and the bones in her hands were starting to show through her skin. Again I saw bruises. We were inside her house in the living room; the cold was too much for her to bear.

Despite all this, she still looked beautiful.

"I'm doing okay," she said, smiling valiantly. "The doctors have given me some medicine for the pain, and it seems to help a little."

I'd been coming by every day. Time seemed to be slowing down and speeding up at exactly the same time.

"Can I get anything for you?"

"No, thank you, I'm doing fine."

I looked around the room, then back at her. "I've been reading the Bible," I finally said.

"You have?" Her face lit up, reminding me of the angel I'd seen in the play. I couldn't believe that only six weeks had gone by.

"I wanted you to know."

"I'm glad you told me."

"I read the book of Job last night," I said, "where God stuck it to Job to test his faith."

She smiled and reached out to pat my arm, her hand soft on my skin. It felt nice. "You should read something else. That's not about God in one of his better moments."

"Why would he have done that to him?"

"I don't know," she said.

"Do you ever feel like Job?"

She smiled, a little twinkle in her eyes. "Sometimes."

"But you haven't lost your faith?"

"No." I knew she hadn't, but I think I was losing mine.

"Is it because you think you might get better?"

"No," she said, "it's because it's the only thing I have left."

After that, we started reading the Bible together. It somehow seemed like the right thing to do, but my heart was nonetheless telling me that there still might be something more.

At night I lay awake, wondering about it.

Reading the Bible gave us something to focus on, and all of a sudden everything started to get better between us, maybe because I wasn't as worried about doing something to offend her. What could be more right than reading the Bible? Though I didn't know nearly as much as she did about it, I think she appreciated the gesture, and occasionally when we read, she'd put her hand on my knee and simply listen as my voice filled the room.

Other times I'd be sitting beside her on the couch, looking at the Bible and watching Jamie out of the corner of my eye at the same time, and we'd come across a passage or a psalm, maybe even a proverb, and I'd ask her what she thought about it. She always had an answer, and I'd nod, thinking about it. Sometimes she asked me what I thought, and I did my best, too, though there were moments when I was bluffing and I was sure that she could tell. "Is that what it really means to you?" she'd ask, and I'd rub my chin and think about it before trying again. Sometimes, though, it was her fault when I couldn't concentrate, what with that hand on my knee and all.

One Friday night I brought her over for dinner at my house. My mom joined us for the main course, then left the table and sat in the den so that we could be alone.

It was nice there, sitting with Jamie, and I knew she felt the same way. She hadn't been leaving her house much, and this was a good change for her.

Since she'd told me about her illness, Jamie had stopped wearing her hair in a bun, and it was still as stunning as it had been the first time I'd seen her wear it down. She was looking at the china cabinet—my mom had one of those cabinets with the lights inside—when I reached across the table and took her hand.

"Thank you for coming over tonight," I said.

She turned her attention back to me. "Thanks for inviting me."

I paused. "How's your father holding up?"

Jamie sighed. "Not too well. I worry about him a lot."

"He loves you dearly, you know."

"I know."

"So do I," I said, and when I did, she looked away. Hearing me say this seemed to frighten her again.

"Will you keep coming over to my house?" she asked. "Even later, you know, when . . . ?"

I squeezed her hand, not hard, but enough to let her know that I meant what I said.

"As long as you want me to come, I'll be there."

"We don't have to read the Bible anymore, if you don't want to."

"Yes," I said softly, "I think we do."

She smiled. "You're a good friend, Landon. I don't know what I'd do without you."

She squeezed my hand, returning the favor. Sitting across from me, she looked radiant.

"I love you, Jamie," I said again, but this time she wasn't frightened. Instead our eyes met across the table, and I watched as hers began to shine. She sighed and looked away, running her hand through her hair, then turned to me again. I kissed her hand, smiling in return.

"I love you, too," she finally whispered.

They were the words I'd been praying to hear.

I don't know if Jamie told Hegbert about her feelings for me, but I somehow doubted it because his routine hadn't changed at all. It was his habit to leave the house whenever I came over after school, and this continued. I would knock at the door and listen as Hegbert explained to Jamie that he would be leaving and would be back in a couple of hours. "Okay, Daddy," I always heard her say, then I would wait for Hegbert to open the door. Once he let me in, he would open the hallway closet and silently pull out his coat and hat, buttoning the coat up all the way before he left the house. His coat was old-fashioned, black and long, like a trench coat without zippers, the kind that was fashionable earlier this century. He seldom spoke directly to me, even after he learned that Jamie and I'd begun to read the Bible together.

Though he still didn't like me in the house if he wasn't there, he nonetheless allowed me to come in. I knew that part of the reason had to do with the fact that he didn't want Jamie to get chilled by sitting on the porch, and the only other alternative was to wait at the house while I was there. But I think Hegbert needed some time alone, too, and that was the real reason for the change. He didn't talk to me about the rules of the house—I could see them in his eyes the first time he'd said I could stay. I was allowed to stay in the living room, that was all.

Jamie was still moving around fairly well, though the winter was miserable. A cold streak blew in during the last part of January that lasted nine days, followed by three straight days of drenching rain. Jamie had no interest in leaving the house in such weather, though after Hegbert had gone she and I might stand on the porch for just a couple of minutes to breathe the fresh sea air. Whenever we did this, I found myself worrying about her.

While we read the Bible, people would knock at the door at least three times every day. People were always dropping by, some with food, others just to say hello. Even Eric and Margaret came over, and though Jamie wasn't allowed to let them in, she did so anyway, and we sat in the living room and talked a little, both of them unable to meet her gaze.

They were both nervous, and it took them a couple of minutes to finally get to the point. Eric had come to apologize, he said, and he said that he couldn't imagine why all this had happened to her of all people. He also had something for her, and he set an envelope on the table, his hand shaking. His voice was choked up as he spoke, the words ringing with the most heartfelt emotion I'd ever heard him express.

"You've got the biggest heart of anyone I've ever met," he said to Jamie, his voice cracking, "and even though I took it for granted and wasn't always nice to you, I wanted to let you know how I feel. I've never been more sorry about anything in my life." He paused and swiped at the corner of his eye. "You're the best person I'll probably ever know."

As he was fighting back his tears and sniffling, Margaret had already given in to hers and sat weeping on the couch, unable to speak. When Eric had finished, Jamie wiped tears from her cheeks, stood slowly, and smiled, opening her arms in what could only be called a gesture of forgiveness. Eric went to her willingly, finally beginning to cry openly as she gently caressed his hair, murmuring to him. The two of them held each other for a long time as Eric sobbed until he was too exhausted to cry anymore.

Then it was Margaret's turn, and she and Jamie did exactly the same thing.

When Eric and Margaret were ready to leave, they pulled on their jackets and looked at Jamie one more time, as if to remember her forever. I had no doubt that they wanted to think of her as she looked right then. In my mind she was beautiful, and I know they felt the same way.

"Hang in there," Eric said on his way out the door. "I'll be praying for you, and so will everybody else." Then he looked toward me, reached out, and patted me on the shoulder. "You too," he said, his eyes red. As I watched them leave, I knew I'd never been prouder of either of them.

Later, when we opened the envelope, we learned what Eric had done. Without telling us, he'd collected over $400 for the orphanage.

I waited for the miracle.

It hadn't come.

In early February the pills Jamie was taking were increased to help offset the heightened pain she was feeling. The higher dosages made her dizzy, and twice she fell when walking to the bathroom, one time hitting her head against the washbasin. Afterward she insisted that the doctors cut back her medicine, and with reluctance they did. Though she was able to walk normally, the pain she was feeling intensified, and sometimes even raising her arm made her grimace. Leukemia is a disease of the blood, one that runs its course throughout a person's body. There was literally no escape from it as long as her heart kept beating.

But the disease weakened the rest of her body as well, preying on her muscles, making even simple things more difficult. In the first week of February she lost six pounds, and soon walking became difficult for her, unless it was only for a short distance. That was, of course, if she could put up with the pain, which in time she couldn't. She went back to the pills again, accepting the dizziness in place of pain.

Still we read the Bible.

Whenever I visited Jamie, I would find her on the couch with the Bible already opened, and I knew that eventually her father would have to carry her there if we wanted to continue. Though she never said anything to me about it, we both knew exactly what it meant.

I was running out of time, and my heart was still telling me that there was something more I could do.

On February 14, Valentine's Day, Jamie picked out a passage from Corinthians that meant a lot to her. She told me that if she'd ever had the chance, it was the passage she'd wanted read at her wedding. This is what it said:

Love is always patient and kind. It is never jealous. Love is never boastful or conceited. It is never rude or selfish. It does not take offense and is not resentful. Love takes no pleasure in other people's sins, but delights in the truth. It is always ready to excuse, to trust, to hope, and to endure whatever comes.

Jamie was the truest essence of that very description.

Three days later, when the temperature slightly warmed, I showed her something wonderful, something I doubted she'd ever seen before, something I knew she would want to see.

Eastern North Carolina is a beautiful and special part of the country, blessed with temperate weather and, for the most part, wonderful geography. Nowhere is this more evident than Bogue Banks, an island right off the coast, near the place we grew up. Twenty-four miles long and nearly a mile wide, this island is a fluke of nature, running from east to west, hugging the coastline a half mile offshore. Those who live there can witness spectacular sunrises and sunsets every day of the year, both taking place over the expanse of the mighty Atlantic Ocean.

Jamie was bundled up heavily, standing beside me on the edge of the Iron Steamer Pier as this perfect southern evening descended. I pointed off into the distance and told her to wait. I could see our breaths, two of hers to every one of mine. I had to support Jamie as we stood there—she seemed lighter than the leaves of a tree that had fallen in autumn—but I knew that it would be worth it.

In time the glowing, cratered moon began its seeming rise from the sea, casting a prism of light across the slowly darkening water, splitting itself into a thousand different parts, each more beautiful than the last. At exactly the same moment, the sun was meeting the horizon in the opposite direction, turning the sky red and orange and yellow, as if heaven above had suddenly opened its gates and let all its beauty escape its holy confines. The ocean turned golden silver as the shifting colors reflected off it, waters rippling and sparkling with the changing light, the vision glorious, almost like the beginning of time. The sun continued to lower itself, casting its glow as far as the eye could see, before finally, slowly, vanishing beneath the waves. The moon continued its slow drift upward, shimmering as it turned a thousand different shades of yellow, each paler than the last, before finally becoming the color of the stars.

Jamie watched all this in silence, my arm tight around her,

her breathing shallow and weak. As the sky was finally turning to black and the first twinkling lights began to appear in the distant southern sky, I took her in my arms. I gently kissed both her cheeks and then, finally, her lips.

"That," I said, "is exactly how I feel about you."

A week later Jamie's trips to the hospital became more regular, although she insisted that she didn't want to stay there overnight. "I want to die at home," was all she said. Since the doctors couldn't do anything for her, they had no choice but to accept her wishes.

At least for the time being.

"I've been thinking about the past few months," I said to her.

We were sitting in the living room, holding hands as we read the Bible. Her face was growing thinner, her hair beginning to lose its luster. Yet her eyes, those soft blue eyes, were as lovely as ever.

I don't think I'd ever seen someone as beautiful.

"I've been thinking about them, too," she said.

"You knew, from the first day in Miss Garber's class that I was going to do the play, didn't you? When you looked at me and smiled?"

She nodded. "Yes."

"And when I asked you to the homecoming dance, you made me promise that I wouldn't fall in love, but you knew that I was going to, didn't you?"

She had a mischievous gleam in her eye. "Yes."

"How did you know?"

She shrugged without answering, and we sat together for a few moments, watching the rain as it blew against the windows.

"When I told you that I prayed for you," she finally said to me, "what did you think I was talking about?"

*   *   *

The progression of her disease continued, speeding up as March approached. She was taking more medicine for pain, and she felt too sick to her stomach to keep down much food. She was growing weak, and it looked like she'd have to go to the hospital to stay, despite her wishes.

It was my mother and father who changed all that.

My father had driven home from Washington, hurriedly leaving although Congress was still in session. Apparently my mother had called him and told him that if he didn't come home immediately, he might as well stay in Washington forever.

When my mother told him what was happening, my father said that Hegbert would never accept his help, that the wounds were too deep, that it was too late to do anything.

"This isn't about your family, or even about Reverend Sullivan, or anything that happened in the past," she said to him, refusing to accept his answer. "This is about our son, who happens to be in love with a little girl who needs our help. And you're going to find a way to help her."

I don't know what my father said to Hegbert or what promises he had to make or how much the whole thing eventually cost. All I know is that Jamie was soon surrounded by expensive equipment, was supplied with all the medicine she needed, and was watched by two full-time nurses while a doctor peeked in on her several times a day.

Jamie would be able to stay at home.

That night I cried on my father's shoulder for the first time in my life.

"Do you have any regrets?" I asked her. She was in her bed under the covers, a tube in her arm feeding her the medication she needed. Her face was pale, her body feather light. She could barely walk, and when she did, she now had to be supported by someone else.

"We all have regrets, Landon," she said, "but I've led a wonderful life."

"How can you say that?" I cried out, unable to hide my anguish. "With all that's happening to you?"

She squeezed my hand, her grip weak, smiling tenderly at me.

"This," she admitted as she looked around her room, "could be better."

Despite my tears I laughed, then immediately felt guilty for doing so. I was supposed to be supporting her, not the other way around. Jamie went on.

"But other than that, I've been happy, Landon. I really have. I've had a special father who taught me about God. I can look back and know that I couldn't have tried to help other people any more than I did." She paused and met my eyes. "I've even fallen in love and had someone love me back."

I kissed her hand when she said it, then held it against my cheek.

"It's not fair," I said.

She didn't answer.

"Are you still afraid?" I asked.

"Yes."

"I'm afraid, too," I said.

"I know. And I'm sorry."

"What can I do?" I asked desperately. "I don't know what I'm supposed to do anymore."

"Will you read to me?"

I nodded, though I didn't know whether I'd be able to make it through the next page without breaking down.

Please, Lord, tell me what to do!

*　　*　　*

"Mom?" I said later that night.

"Yes?"

We were sitting on the sofa in the den, the fire blazing before us. Earlier in the day Jamie had fallen asleep while I read to her, and knowing she needed her rest, I slipped out of her room. But before I did, I kissed her gently on the cheek. It was harmless, but Hegbert had walked in as I'd done so, and I had seen the conflicting emotions in his eyes. He looked at me, knowing that I loved his daughter but also knowing that I'd broken one of the rules of his house, even an unspoken one. Had she been well, I know he would never have allowed me back inside. As it was, I showed myself to the door.

I couldn't blame him, not really. I found that spending time with Jamie sapped me of the energy to feel hurt by his demeanor. If Jamie had taught me anything over these last few months, she'd shown me that actions—not thoughts or intentions—were the way to judge others, and I knew that Hegbert would allow me in the following day. I was thinking about all this as I sat next to my mother on the sofa.

"Do you think we have a purpose in life?" I asked.

It was the first time I'd asked her such a question, but these were unusual times.

"I'm not sure I understand what you're asking," she said, frowning.

"I mean—how do you know what you're supposed to do?"

"Are you asking me about spending time with Jamie?"

I nodded, though I was still confused. "Sort of. I know I'm doing the right thing, but...something's missing. I spend time with her and we talk and read the Bible, but..."

I paused, and my mother finished my thought for me.

"You think you should be doing more?"

I nodded.

"I don't know that there's anything more you *can* do, sweetheart," she said gently.

"Then why do I feel the way I do?"

She moved a little closer on the sofa, and we watched the flames together.

"I think it's because you're frightened and you feel helpless, and even though you're trying, things continue to get harder and harder—for the both of you. And the more you try, the more hopeless things seem."

"Is there any way to stop feeling this way?"

She put her arm around me and pulled me closer. "No," she said softly, "there isn't."

The next day Jamie couldn't get out of bed. Because she was too weak now to walk even with support, we read the Bible in her room.

She fell asleep within minutes.

Another week went by and Jamie grew steadily worse, her body weakening. Bedridden, she looked smaller, almost like a little girl again.

"Jamie," I pleaded, "what can I do for you?"

Jamie, my sweet Jamie, was sleeping for hours at a time now, even as I talked to her. She didn't move at the sound of my voice; her breaths were rapid and weak.

I sat beside the bed and watched her for a long time, thinking how much I loved her. I held her hand close to my heart, feeling the boniness of her fingers. Part of me wanted to cry right then, but instead I laid her hand back down and turned to face the window.

Why, I wondered, had my world suddenly unraveled as it had? Why had all this happened to someone like her? I wondered if there was a greater lesson in what was happening. Was it all, as Jamie would say, simply part of the Lord's plan? Did the Lord want me to fall in love with her? Or was that something of my own volition? The longer Jamie slept, the more I felt her presence beside me, yet the answers to these questions were no clearer than they had been before.

Outside, the last of the morning rain had passed. It had been a gloomy day, but now the late afternoon sunlight was breaking through the clouds. In the cool spring air I saw the first signs of nature coming back to life. The trees outside were budding, the leaves waiting for just the right moment to uncoil and open themselves to yet another summer season.

On the nightstand by her bed I saw the collection of items that Jamie held close to her heart. There were photographs of her father, holding Jamie as a young child and standing outside of school on her first day of kindergarten; there was a collection of cards that children of the orphanage had sent. Sighing, I reached for them and opened the card on top of the stack.

Written in crayon, it said simply:

Please get better soon. I miss you.

It was signed by Lydia, the girl who'd fallen asleep in Jamie's lap on Christmas Eve. The second card expressed the same sentiments, but what really caught my eye was the picture that the child, Roger, had drawn. He'd drawn a bird, soaring above a rainbow.

Choking up, I closed the card. I couldn't bear to look any further, and as I put the stack back where it had been before, I noticed a newspaper clipping, next to her water glass. I reached for the article and saw that it was about the play, published in the Sunday paper the day after we'd finished. In the photograph above the text, I saw the only picture that had ever been taken of the two of us.

It seemed so long ago. I brought the article nearer to my face. As I stared, I remembered the way I felt when I had seen her that night. Peering closely at her image, I searched for any sign that she suspected what would come to pass. I knew she did, but her expression that night betrayed none of it. Instead, I saw only a radiant happiness. In time I sighed and set aside the clipping.

The Bible still lay open where I'd left off, and although Jamie was sleeping, I felt the need to read some more. Eventually I came across another passage. This is what it said:

> *I am not commanding you, but I want to test the sincerity of your love by comparing it to the earnestness of others.*

The words made me choke up again, and just as I was about to cry, the meaning of it suddenly became clear.

God had finally answered me, and I suddenly knew what I had to do.

I couldn't have made it to the church any faster, even if I'd had a car. I took every shortcut I could, racing through people's backyards, jumping fences, and in one case cutting through someone's garage and out the side door. Everything I'd learned about the town growing up came into play, and although I was never a particularly good athlete, on this day I was unstoppable, propelled by what I had to do.

I didn't care how I looked when I arrived because I suspected Hegbert wouldn't care, either. When I finally entered the church, I slowed to a walk, trying to catch my breath as I made my way to the back, toward his office.

Hegbert looked up when he saw me, and I knew why he was here. He didn't invite me in, he simply looked away, back toward the window again. At home he'd been dealing with her illness by cleaning the house almost obsessively. Here, though, papers were scattered across the desk, and books were strewn about the room as if no one had straightened up for weeks. I knew that this was the place he thought about Jamie; this was the place where Hegbert came to cry.

"Reverend?" I said softly.

He didn't answer, but I went in anyway.

"I'd like to be alone," he croaked.

He looked old and beaten, as weary as the Israelites described in David's Psalms. His face was drawn, and his hair had grown thinner since December. Even more than I, perhaps, he had to keep up his spirits around Jamie, and the stress of doing so was wearing him down.

I marched right up to his desk, and he glanced at me before turning back to the window.

"Please," he said to me. His tone was defeated, as though he didn't have the strength to confront even me.

"I'd like to talk to you," I said firmly. "I wouldn't ask unless it was very important."

Hegbert sighed, and I sat in the chair I had sat in before, when I'd asked him if he would let me take Jamie out for New Year's Eve.

He listened as I told him what was on my mind.

When I was finished, Hegbert turned to me. I don't know

what he was thinking, but thankfully, he didn't say no. Instead he wiped his eyes with his fingers and turned toward the window.

Even he, I think, was too shocked to speak.

Again I ran, again I didn't tire, my purpose giving me the strength I needed to go on. When I reached Jamie's house, I rushed in the door without knocking, and the nurse who'd been in her bedroom came out to see what had caused the racket. Before she could speak, I did.

"Is she awake?" I asked, euphoric and terrified at the same time.

"Yes," the nurse said cautiously. "When she woke up, she wondered where you were."

I apologized for my disheveled appearance and thanked her, then asked if she wouldn't mind leaving us alone. I walked into Jamie's room, partially closing the door behind me. She was pale, so very pale, but her smile let me know she was still fighting.

"Hello, Landon," she said, her voice faint, "thank you for coming back."

I pulled up a chair and sat next to her, taking her hand in mine. Seeing her lying there made something tighten deep in my stomach, making me almost want to cry.

"I was here earlier, but you were asleep," I said.

"I know...I'm sorry. I just can't seem to help it anymore."

"It's okay, really."

She lifted her hand slightly off the bed, and I kissed it, then leaned forward and kissed her cheek as well.

"Do you love me?" I asked her.

She smiled. "Yes."

"Do you want me to be happy?" As I asked her this, I felt my heart beginning to race.

"Of course I do."

"Will you do something for me, then?"

She looked away, sadness crossing her features. "I don't know if I can anymore," she said.

"But if you could, would you?"

I cannot adequately describe the intensity of what I was feeling at that moment. Love, anger, sadness, hope, and fear, whirling together, sharpened by the nervousness I was feeling. Jamie looked at me curiously, and my breaths became shallower. Suddenly I knew that I'd never felt as strongly for another person as I did at that moment. As I returned her gaze, this simple realization made me wish for the millionth time that I could make all this go away. Had it been possible, I would have traded my life for hers. I wanted to tell her my thoughts, but the sound of her voice suddenly silenced the emotions inside me.

"Yes," she finally said, her voice weak yet somehow still full of promise. "I would."

Finally getting control of myself, I kissed her again, then brought my hand to her face, gently running my fingers over her cheek. I marveled at the softness of her skin, the gentleness I saw in her eyes. Even now she was perfect.

My throat began to tighten again, but as I said, I knew what I had to do. Since I had to accept that it was not within my power to cure her, what I wanted to do was give her something that she'd always wanted.

It was what my heart had been telling me to do all along.

Jamie, I understood then, had already given me the answer I'd been searching for, the one my heart had needed to find.

She'd told me the answer as we'd sat outside Mr. Jenkins's office, the night we'd asked him about doing the play.

I smiled softly, and she returned my affection with a slight squeeze of my hand, as if trusting me in what I was about to do. Encouraged, I leaned closer and took a deep breath. When I exhaled, these were the words that flowed with my breath.

"Will you marry me?"

Chapter 13

When I was seventeen, my life changed forever.

As I walk the streets of Beaufort forty years later, thinking back on that year of my life, I remember everything as clearly as if it were all still unfolding before my very eyes.

I remember Jamie saying yes to my breathless question and how we both began to cry together. I remember talking to both Hegbert and my parents, explaining to them what I needed to do. They thought I was doing it only for Jamie, and all three of them tried to talk me out of it, especially when they realized that Jamie had said yes. What they didn't understand, and I had to make clear to them, was that I needed to do it for me.

I was in love with her, so deeply in love that I didn't care if she was sick. I didn't care that we wouldn't have long together. None of those things mattered to me. All I cared about was doing something that my heart had told me was the right thing to do. In my mind it was the first time God had ever spoken directly to me, and I knew with certainty that I wasn't going to disobey.

I know that some of you may wonder if I was doing it out of pity. Some of the more cynical may even wonder if I did it because she'd be gone soon anyway and I wasn't committing much. The answer to both questions is no. I would have married Jamie Sullivan no matter what happened in the future. I would have married Jamie Sullivan if the miracle I was praying for had suddenly come true. I knew it at the moment I asked her, and I still know it today.

Jamie was more than just the woman I loved. In that year Jamie helped me become the man I am today. With her steady hand she showed me how important it was to help others; with her patience and kindness she showed me what life is really all about. Her cheerfulness and optimism, even in times of sickness, were the most amazing things I have ever witnessed.

We were married by Hegbert in the Baptist church, my father standing beside me as the best man. That was another thing she did. In the South it's a tradition to have your father beside you, but for me it's a tradition that wouldn't have had much meaning before Jamie came into my life. Jamie had brought my father and me together again; somehow she'd also managed to heal some of the wounds between our two families. After what he'd done for me and for Jamie, I knew in the end that my father was someone I could always count on, and as the years passed our relationship grew steadily stronger until his death.

Jamie also taught me the value of forgiveness and the transforming power that it offers. I realized this the day that Eric and Margaret had come to her house. Jamie held no grudges. Jamie led her life the way the Bible taught.

Jamie was not only the angel who saved Tom Thornton, she was the angel who saved us all.

Just as she'd wanted, the church was bursting with people. Over two hundred guests were inside, and more than that waited outside the doors as we were married on March 12, 1959. Because we were married on such short notice, there wasn't time to make many arrangements, and people came out of the woodwork to make the day as special as they could, simply by showing up to support us. I saw everyone I knew—Miss Garber, Eric, Margaret, Eddie, Sally, Carey, Angela, and even Lew and his grandmother—and there wasn't a dry eye in the house when the entrance music began. Although Jamie was weak and hadn't moved from her bed in two weeks, she insisted on walking down the aisle so that her father could give her away. "It's very important to me, Landon," she'd said. "It's part of my dream, remember?" Though I assumed it would be impossible, I simply nodded. I couldn't help but wonder at her faith.

I knew she planned on wearing the dress she'd worn in the Playhouse the night of the play. It was the only white dress that was available on such short notice, though I knew it would hang more loosely than it had before. While I was wondering how Jamie would look in the dress, my father laid his hand on my shoulder as we stood before the congregation.

"I'm proud of you, son."

I nodded. "I'm proud of you, too, Dad."

It was the first time I'd ever said those words to him.

My mom was in the front row, dabbing her eyes with her handkerchief when the "Wedding March" began. The doors opened and I saw Jamie, seated in her wheelchair, a nurse by her side. With all the strength she had left, Jamie stood shakily as her father supported her. Then Jamie and Hegbert slowly made their way down the aisle, while everyone in the church sat silently in wonder. Halfway down the aisle, Jamie suddenly seemed to tire, and they stopped while she caught her breath. Her eyes closed, and for a moment I didn't think she could go on. I know that no more than ten or twelve seconds elapsed, but it seemed much longer, and finally she nodded slightly. With that, Jamie and Hegbert started moving again, and I felt my heart surge with pride.

It was, I remembered thinking, the most difficult walk any-one ever had to make.

In every way, a walk to remember.

The nurse had rolled the wheelchair up front as Jamie and her father made their way toward me. When she finally reached my side, there were gasps of joy and everyone spontaneously began to clap. The nurse rolled the wheelchair into position, and Jamie sat down again, spent. With a smile I lowered myself to my knees so that I would be level with her. My father then did the same.

Hegbert, after kissing Jamie on the cheek, retrieved his Bible in order to begin the ceremony. All business now, he seemed to have abandoned his role as Jamie's father to some-thing more distant, where he could keep his emotions in check. Yet I could see him struggling as he stood before us. He perched his glasses on his nose and opened the Bible, then looked at Jamie and me. Hegbert towered over us, and I could tell that he hadn't anticipated our being so much lower. For a moment he stood before us, almost confused, then surprisingly decided to kneel as well. Jamie smiled and reached for his free hand, then reached for mine, linking us together.

Hegbert began the ceremony in the traditional way, then

read the passage in the Bible that Jamie had once pointed out to me. Knowing how weak she was, I thought he would have us recite the vows right away, but once more Hegbert surprised me. He looked at Jamie and me, then out to the congregation, then back to us again, as if searching for the right words.

He cleared his throat, and his voice rose so that everyone could hear it. This is what he said:

"As a father, I'm supposed to give away my daughter, but I'm not sure that I'm able to do this."

The congregation went silent, and Hegbert nodded at me, willing me to be patient. Jamie squeezed my hand in support.

"I can no more give Jamie away than I can give away my heart. But what I can do is to let another share in the joy that she has always given me. May God's blessings be with you both."

It was then that he set aside the Bible. He reached out, offering his hand to mine, and I took it, completing the circle.

With that he led us through our vows. My father handed me the ring my mother had helped me pick out, and Jamie gave me one as well. We slipped them on our fingers. Hegbert watched us as we did so, and when we were finally ready, he pronounced us husband and wife. I kissed Jamie softly as my mother began to cry, then held Jamie's hand in mine. In front of God and everyone else, I'd promised my love and devotion, in sickness and in health, and I'd never felt so good about anything.

It was, I remember, the most wonderful moment of my life.

It is now forty years later, and I can still remember everything from that day. I may be older and wiser, I may have lived another life since then, but I know that when my time eventually comes, the memories of that day will be the final images that float through my mind. I still love her, you see, and I've never removed my ring. In all these years I've never felt the desire to do so.

I breathe deeply, taking in the fresh spring air. Though Beaufort has changed and I have changed, the air itself has not. It's still the air of my childhood, the air of my seventeenth year, and when I finally exhale, I'm fifty-seven once more. But this is okay. I smile slightly, looking toward the sky, knowing there's one thing I still haven't told you: I now believe, by the way, that miracles can happen.

Questions and Explanations for Chapters 12 and 13

The ten questions from chapters 12 and 13 focus on grammar and usage, literary terms, characterization, making inferences, analyzing themes, and understanding the author's stylistic choices. Some of the questions combine two or more of these areas, requiring you to synthesize your knowledge, make inferences, and interpret the text. The questions are designed to determine both your current level of understanding of the novel and your ability to answer higher-level questions.

The following sentences (1 and 2) test your ability to recognize grammar and usage errors. Each sentence contains either a single error or no error at all. If the sentence contains an error, select the one underlined part that must be changed to make the sentence correct. If there is no error, select answer choice D.

1. Many of the people in Reverend <u>Sullivan's</u> congregation
      A
   <u>thought</u> he <u>should of</u> told them sooner about Jamie's ill-
      B   C
   ness. <u>No error</u>
      D

Understanding what is being evaluated will assist you in making your determination of whether or not there is an error in this sentence. Choice A is questioning the use of the apostrophe to show possession. Single nouns are made possessive by adding an *'s* to the word. Choice B is questioning the verb tense of *thought.* Is the past tense correct for the sentence? Choice C is asking about the accuracy of the phrase *should of.* Sometimes when a word or phrase is spoken, it sounds like there are two or more different spellings for it. For example, the phrase "could have" is the same as the contraction "could've." This word might sound like "could of" or "coulda" when spoken out loud.

2. <u>Landon's</u> knowledge of <u>Jamie's</u> illness clearly <u>effected</u>
      A   B   C
   his narrative voice. <u>No error</u>
      D

In this sentence, both choices A and B are questioning whether you understand the correct use of the apostrophe. Singular nouns show possession with the addition of an *'s*—for example, *Paul's, Barbara's, Sean's.* Choice C is questioning the use of *effected* versus its homophone *affected.* Remember that *affect* is typically used as a verb, meaning to act on. *Effect* is typically a noun, meaning something that is produced. If someone or something is doing something, usually the correct word choice is *affect,* as in this example: "Research has shown that rereading a passage will affect a student's level of comprehension."

Question 3 checks your understanding of literary terms.

3. When mentally processing Jamie's news about her illness, Landon says, "It all made perfect sense, and at the same time, nothing seemed to make any sense at all." This statement is an example of what?

   A. rhetorical analysis

   B. paradox

   C. oxymoron

   D. hyperbole

Knowledge of literary terms will enable you to apply your understanding to the sentence and determine what the direct quotation is an example of.

Rhetorical analysis is the understanding of a passage based on the devices the author uses. Rhetorical analysis is not concerned with *what* a passage is saying; it is concerned with *how* the writer is saying it. Rhetorical analysis is concerned with sentence structure, point of view, diction, genre, punctuation, rhetorical figures (such as alliteration, allusions, anaphora, or hyperbole), tone, and figures of speech (such as simile, metaphor, and personification).

A *paradox* is an apparent contradiction that upon further analysis seemingly makes sense. Thus, the famous first line of *A Tale of Two Cities*, "It was the best of times; it was the worst of times," initially doesn't make sense. But when you think about how both situations can exist simultaneously, you understand the paradox.

An *oxymoron* is a joining of two contradictory terms—for example, *jumbo shrimp, icy hot,* and *larger half.* Although an oxymoron is a paradoxical expression, the difference between an oxymoron and a paradox is that an oxymoron has just two contradictory terms, whereas a paradox is a complete sentence.

A *hyperbole* is an overexaggeration meant to make a point—for example, "Everyone who has paid attention to this learning guide should know this by now because hyperbole has been explained a bazillion times."

Read the following passage and then answer question 4, which asks you to use details and examples from the text in order to draw inferences.

Landon takes to reading the Bible that Jamie had given to him as a gift. He comes across an underlined section and thinks that it must have meant something special to her.

> *I cry to you, my Lord, my rock!*
> *Do not be deaf to me, for if you are silent, I shall go down to the pit like the rest. Hear my voice raised in petition as I cry to you for help, as I raise my hands, my Lord, toward your holy of holies.*

Landon realizes that the underlining of the psalm was meant for him.

4. We can infer a number of things about Jamie, Landon, and their relationship from the passage above. Which of the following choices are appropriate inferences to make?

    A. If Landon does not obtain help from God, he would despair all of his life.

    B. Jamie wanted to leave this gift, the gift of God's presence, to Landon.

    C. Jamie was destined to show him the depths of the human heart—and the joy and pain of living.

    D. Landon will never be able to read the Bible again because it hurts too much.

This question indicates that there will be more than one correct answer. In order to answer this question correctly, you need to be able to understand it (reread it now if necessary), and you need to be able to relate it to the novel as a whole.

Does the passage suggest that Landon needs to turn to God for help? If so, select choice A. Is there any indication that Jamie meant for Landon to come across this passage in the Bible? If yes, then select choice B. Is determining one's purpose in life an important thematic topic in the novel? Can this passage be interpreted as a sign of Jamie's purpose? If so, select choice C. Is there any indication that Landon will never read the Bible again? If there is support for this interpretation, select choice D.

Question 5 asks you to use strong and thorough textual evidence—details from the book—to support your analysis of the author's choices and how these choices contribute to the aesthetic or stylistic impact of the writing style.

5. What is the most striking change in the narrative that readers should recognize in chapter 12?

    A. Landon continues to use foreshadowing to reveal how he lives his life after his wedding.

    B. The narrative voice shifts entirely to the more mature Landon.

    C. The pacing is extremely slow, to match Landon's desire to keep Jamie alive.

    D. Jamie's debilitating illness is described in painstaking detail.

Something dramatically different is taking place in chapter 12. Choice A indicates a continuation of the use of foreshadowing, but a continuation is not a change, so this choice must be eliminated. Is Landon using the same voice to tell the story that he has been using throughout most of the novel, or has he eliminated the sarcasm and colloquialism that marked the earlier chapters? If he is using the same voice, eliminate choice B; if he is not, select that option. Choice C claims that the rate of the story has slowed down. Did you find the story dragging? If so, select this choice; otherwise eliminate it. If you think that the biggest difference is a focus on the specific details regarding Jamie's disease, then select choice D.

Question 6 asks you to determine a central idea in the text and analyze its development.

6. Thematically speaking, what significance does the wedding have?

    A. The wedding signifies the importance of achieving lifelong desires.

    B. The wedding provides the families a chance to solidify their newfound friendship.

C. The wedding illustrates that a person's actions and not his or her thoughts or intentions are the most important measure of his or her worth.

D. The wedding symbolizes the importance of overcoming your fears.

All four choices may have some element of truth in them. Your job is to determine which is the BEST answer. The best answer may encompass some of the other choices and will also be a complete sentence about an idea. Because a wedding is the joining of two individuals, the best answer will pertain to both Jamie and Landon.

Did both Jamie and Landon have a stated desire to get married? If not, eliminate choice A. Does the wedding focus on both families? And do they have a newfound friendship? If the answer is yes to both of these questions, consider choice B; otherwise, eliminate it. Do the actions of both Jamie and Landon illustrate the sentiment in choice C? Is the wedding an opportunity for the couple to act upon their thoughts and intentions? If yes, select choice C. Does fear play a role in the wedding? If not, eliminate choice D.

Question 7 checks your comprehension as well as your ability to connect details and examples from the text to a developing motif.

7. Which details, from the choices listed below, develop the motif of "coming together," which is instrumental throughout the entire novel?

A. Landon's parents arrange for the medical equipment and personnel at Jamie's house.

B. Landon and his father grow closer together.

C. Jamie and Landon's wedding takes place.

D. Reverend Sullivan both marries and buries his daughter.

This question indicates that there will be more than one correct answer. A *motif* is a recurring object, idea, symbol, image, etc., in a literary work. For example, throughout the Twilight series, there are a number of recurring elements, such as choices, love, good versus evil, and fear. Images of light and darkness permeate the Twilight saga; these are also motifs. Motifs serve as unifying components of a text. They may be actions, details, ideas, images, settings, situations, symbols, themes, types of characters, or words.

The question indicates that "coming together" is indeed a motif in the novel, so you need to apply your understanding of the word and the novel as a whole to determine which of these choices represents a type of reconciliation.

If the arrangements made by Landon's father for Jamie to receive at-home medical care can be considered a type of coming together between the two families, select choice A. If an improving relationship between father and son can be considered a type of coming together, select choice B. If Jamie and Landon's wedding is a type of coming together, select choice C. And if Reverend Sullivan does indeed both marry and bury his daughter and both of these can be considered a coming together, select choice D.

Question 8 asks you to analyze how an author's choices concerning the structure of a specific part of the text contribute to the overall structure and meaning of the work as a whole.

8. Which of the following choices accurately reflects the effect of Sparks's stylistic decisions regarding the first line of chapter 13?

   A. It is the exact sentence that opens the prologue, bringing the narrative full circle.

   B. It emphasizes the importance and impact the events had on Landon's life.

   C. It alludes to Landon's maturity and growth.

   D. It provides a logical springboard for discussion regarding character and thematic development.

This question indicates that there will be more than one correct answer. In order to answer this question, reread the first line of chapter 13. If it is the same sentence that opens the prologue of the novel, select choice A. If the statement indicates that the events had a significant impact on Landon's life, select choice B. If you realize now, having read the novel, that Landon has changed and matured because of these events, select choice C. And if the statement is provocative and can be used to discuss the important characters and thematic topics of the novel, select choice D.

Question 9 asks you to draw an inference based on details and examples from the text.

9. What is the primary purpose of chapter 13?

   A. to bring definitive closure to the narrative

   B. to illustrate Landon's newfound relationship with God

C. to provide opportunities for reconciliation

D. to raise more questions than it answers

Stylistically, chapter 13, in some way, serves as an epilogue, which balances the prologue. The information that Sparks chooses to include (and exclude) is a conscious, artistic choice. Some aspects of each of the choices may be evident in chapter 13; but your job is to select the BEST answer. The best answer is supported by details and examples that exist throughout the entire chapter and thus is a representation of the cumulative weight of the evidence.

If you believe that the chapter provides a complete ending, with no loose ends whatsoever, select choice A. If you think the chapter mainly focuses on Landon's newfound spirituality and his connection with the Almighty, select choice B. If the various acts of reconciliation are the main emphasis of the chapter, select choice C. If you think that the ending, though satisfying, ultimately leaves the reader with more questions than answers, select choice D.

Question 10 asks you to consider multiple interpretations of the text and to draw inferences based on strong and thorough textual evidence.

10. Which of the following statements illustrates Sparks's stylistic choice to have a purposely ambiguous ending regarding miracles in *A Walk to Remember*?

A. Readers are not certain if Jamie lives much past her wedding day.

B. Landon might or might not have become a minister, as Jamie had suggested.

C. Landon might have followed Jamie's idea and used his grandfather's money to attempt to atone for his questionable legacy.

D. Landon's miracle may be a reference to his rapid maturity, which changed the direction of his life.

This question indicates that there will be more than one correct answer. In order to answer this question, you need to do two things: First, you must realize that the two important words in the question are *ambiguous* and *miracles*. A novel with an ambiguous ending is open to multiple interpretations, and the word *miracle* has two important definitions: an extraordinary event that is considered a work of God, and anything considered a wonder or a marvel. The connotation of *miracle* involves some sort of drastic change. After understanding the important terms, you must consider them in relation to the novel as a whole, thinking about the changes characters have gone through and the thematic topics that were addressed throughout the text.

If it is possible that Jamie survives longer than her diagnosis, select choice A. If it is possible that the onetime self-centered and directionless Landon became a minister, select choice B. If Landon might have attempted to "undo" the damage created by his grandfather, then select choice C. And if you believe that Landon is being truthful in his opening line, then select choice D.

Post-Reading Questions and Writing Assignments

Critical Reading Questions

Answer the questions below based on the information in the accompanying passage.

The next night, as I was walking her home, she asked me about my father.

"He's all right, I reckon," I said. "But he's not around much."

"Do you miss that? Not growing up with him around?"

"Sometimes."

"I miss my mom, too," she said, "even though I never even knew her."

It was the first time I'd ever considered that Jamie and I might have something in common. I let that sink in for a while.

"It must be hard for you," I said sincerely. "Even though my father's a stranger to me, at least he's still around."

She looked up at me as we walked, then faced forward again. She tugged gently at her hair again. I was beginning to notice that she did this whenever she was nervous or wasn't sure what to say.

"It is, sometimes. Don't get me wrong—I love my father with all my heart—but there are times when I wonder what it would have been like to have a mother around. I think she and I would have been able to talk about things in a way that my father and I can't."

I assumed she was talking about boys. It wasn't until later that I learned how wrong I was.

"What's it like, living with your father? Is he like how he is in church?"

"No. He's actually got a pretty good sense of humor."

"Hegbert?" I blurted out. I couldn't even imagine it.

I think she was shocked to hear me call him by his first name, but she let me off the hook and didn't respond to my comment. Instead she said, "Don't look so surprised. You'll like him, once you get to know him."

"I doubt if I'll ever get to know him."

"You never know, Landon," she said, smiling, "what the Lord's plan is."

261

1. Which of the following statements best expresses Jamie's attitude toward the narrator?

   A. She is in awe of him and is too embarrassed to confront him about his rudeness.

   B. She sees him as a lost soul whom she needs to lead to God.

   C. She is giddy in his presence, only cautiously asking him personal questions.

   D. She is patronizing toward him because she has an air of superiority.

   E. She is curious about his upbringing, respectful of their differences, and concerned about his future.

2. The passage is primarily concerned with:

   A. developing a biblical allusion

   B. advancing the plot

   C. comparing and contrasting two characters

   D. describing a tone

   E. establishing a mood

3. The narrator would most likely describe himself as:

   A. arrogant

   B. attentive

   C. confident

   D. idealistic

   E. worried

4. The sentence "It was the first time I'd ever considered that Jamie and I might have something in common" conveys:

   A. a developing maturity

   B. an epiphany

   C. foreshadowing

   D. a central conflict

   E. a selfish persona

5. In context, the clause "she tugged gently" (line 17) suggests that Jamie:

   A. is embarrassed by the question that she asked

   B. is responding to the narrator's comments about his own father

   C. is reluctant to agree that sometimes things are difficult for her

   D. is uncomfortable speaking with the narrator

   E. is unwilling to disclose personal details

6. The use of the words "It wasn't until later" in lines 25–26 is an example of:

   A. metaphor

   B. hyperbole

   C. digression

   D. foreshadowing

   E. alliteration

Answer the questions below based on the information in the accompanying passage.

I know that some of you may wonder if I was doing it out of pity. Some of the more cynical may even wonder if I did it because she'd be gone soon anyway and I wasn't committing much. The answer to both questions is no. I would have married Jamie Sullivan no matter what happened in the future. I would have married Jamie Sullivan if the miracle I was praying for had suddenly come true. I knew it at the moment I asked her, and I still know it today.

Jamie was more than just the woman I loved. In that year Jamie helped me become the man I am today. With her steady hand she showed me how important it was to help others; with her patience and kindness she showed me what life is really all about. Her cheerfulness and optimism, even in times of sickness, was the most amazing thing I have ever witnessed.

We were married by Hegbert in the Baptist church, my father standing beside me as the best man. That was another thing she did. In the South it's a tradition to have your father beside you, but for me it's a tradition that wouldn't have had much meaning before Jamie came into my life. Jamie had brought my father and me together again; somehow she'd also managed to heal some of the wounds between our two families. After what he'd done for me and for Jamie, I knew in the end that my father was someone I could always count on, and as the years passed our relationship grew steadily stronger until his death.

Jamie also taught me the value of forgiveness and the transforming power that it offers. I realized this the day that Eric and Margaret had come to her house. Jamie held no grudges. Jamie led her life the way the Bible taught.

Jamie was not only the angel who saved Tom Thornton, she was the angel who saved us all.

1. The passage can best be described as:

    A. narration

    B. analysis

    C. exposition

    D. persuasion

    E. entertainment

2. According to the passage, Jamie is primarily characterized by her:

    A. words

    B. thoughts

    C. feelings

    D. actions

    E. reputation

3. The word "cynical" in line 2 refers to:

    A. the people who believe the narrator acted out of pity

    B. the narrator's own attitude

    C. anyone who can't understand the narrator's intentions

D. Jamie's father

E. those who believe the narrator wasn't risking much

4. To the narrator, Jamie seems to be all of the following EXCEPT:

    A. courageous

    B. giving

    C. inconsiderate

    D. tolerant

    E. wise

5. To demonstrate his growth and maturation, the narrator uses all of the following devices EXCEPT:

    A. a closing metaphor that sums up his view of Jamie

    B. repetition of key ideas

    C. self-reflection on the significance of Jamie's actions

    D. details and analysis regarding Jamie's attitude

    E. comments about his relationship with his own father

6. One can infer from the passage that:

    A. the narrator sometimes has had second thoughts about his marriage

    B. Jamie played a small but significant part in the narrator's life

    C. the narrator and his father always had a strong relationship

D. faith no longer plays an essential part in the narrator's life

E. the narrator believes that he is a better person for having known his wife

Short Answer Questions (paragraph response)

1. Oftentimes, a writer has a seemingly throwaway line or reference that gains significance only after the reader has completed the entire novel. One such example of this in *A Walk to Remember* is the information about Landon and his friends hanging out in the graveyard and Jamie's questions about it. Now that you have read the entire novel, what significance does the graveyard have? Be sure to consider the perspectives of both Landon and Jamie.

2. Symbolism is the sustained use of objects to stand for something else. Thus, a symbol is any object that not only has meaning in and of itself but also is representative of something else. Make a list of anything that may serve as a symbol in *A Walk to Remember*. Then select one of your items and explain its function in the novel as a whole. Be sure to consider character and thematic development.

3. In the final line of the novel, Landon states, "There's one thing I still haven't told you: I now believe, by the way, that miracles can happen." What miracle took place? How do we as readers judge what a miracle is?

4. Jamie and Landon's first date, on New Year's Eve, is a key scene in the development of their relationship.

Reread the passage (in chapter 11) that describes that evening and analyze how that scene is depicted. Be sure to include details that are emphasized in the novel, as well as those that are left out, and discuss how the date impacts Landon's character.

5. What is the significance of the title *A Walk to Remember*? In addition to the obvious plot point, be sure to address both character and thematic development.

Writing Assignments (essay response)

1. One important thematic topic in *A Walk to Remember* is the conflict between the head and the heart. Consider the numerous choices facing Jamie and Landon and determine whether they favor using logic or emotion for making key decisions. Then, using specific details and examples from the text, write an essay in which you analyze what the novel seems to support regarding this conflict.

2. The traditional role of women in the 1950s was as second-class citizens to their husbands. However, Mrs. Carter rises up against her husband and tells him that if he doesn't come home immediately, he may as well stay in Washington forever. It is she who urges Worth Carter to talk to Reverend Sullivan and arrange for home health care and expensive equipment for Jamie. Use Mrs. Carter and the other female characters in the novel as a springboard to discuss what *A Walk to Remember* says regarding the role of women. Research life in the

South, exploring traditional jobs, family life, and roles and responsibilities for women. Then, use this information and the details and examples from the novel to provide an interpretation of the novel that focuses on the role of the female characters in the text.

3. Although Jamie appears to be a social outcast, she seems to be connected to the people in her life. In contrast, Landon seems to be popular, yet he has only superficial connections with others for the most part. Compare and contrast these two main characters, using details and examples from the novel to illustrate the significance of these similarities and differences. Cite strong and thorough textual evidence to support your analysis of the two. Then relate your analysis to important themes addressed in *A Walk to Remember*.

4. Stylistically, Nicholas Sparks made an interesting choice in the structure of *A Walk to Remember*. Although the narrative is told from Landon's adult point of view, he actually relates the story in his seventeen-year-old voice. His narrative voice matures and develops as the story unfolds. Using details and examples from the text, trace the development of Landon's character. Then articulate the effect this change has on the novel as a whole.

5. Select a moment or scene from *A Walk to Remember* that you find especially memorable. Write an essay in which you identify the passage, explain its relationship to the work as a whole, and analyze the reasons for its effectiveness.

Rubric for Essays

CATEGORY	OUTSTANDING	STRONG	MEETS EXPECTATIONS	EMERGING	UNACCEPTABLE
Thesis	A clearly stated, focused, and persuasive opinion	A clearly stated and focused claim	Although the opinion may be legitimate, it is too broad for the scope of the assignment	More of a topic than thesis OR thesis does not address assignment	No thesis evident OR thesis is a retelling of plot
Organization	Introduction grabs attention; variety of transitions used within and between paragraphs; topic sentences have ample support; meaningful conclusion ties together essay well	Introduction sparks some interest; some variety of transitions used within and between paragraphs; topic sentences have support; satisfying conclusion completes the argument	Evidence of an introduction, body paragraphs, and a conclusion; transitions used within and between paragraphs	Introduction and/or conclusion does not flow with rest of argument; body paragraphs lack topic sentences or support; few transitions used	Introduction and/or conclusion missing; topic sentences not evident OR topic sentences are summaries; transitions not used

Support from the Text	Every body paragraph has multiple supports from text; evidence from text persuasively supports your argument; all citations are incorporated smoothly	Every body paragraph has some support from text; evidence supports your argument; most citations are incorporated smoothly	Every body paragraph has support from text, though the evidence may be superficial; some citations stand alone	Evidence does not support topic sentences; most citations stand alone and are not incorporated smoothly into argument	Little or no textual support
Analysis	All support material is introduced and commented upon; cumulative weight of the evidence is convincing	Most support material is introduced and commented upon; analysis is clearly connected to thesis	Ideas support thesis but are obvious and basic	Analysis misrepresents evidence OR is an illogical argument OR ideas are not fully developed	Analysis not attempted OR restates evidence OR does not address the assignment
MUGS (Mechanics, Usage, Grammar, Spelling)	Varied sentences; sophisticated vocabulary; no editing errors	Some variety in sentence structure; advanced vocabulary; few eciting errors	Little sentence variety; adequate vocabulary; some editing errors	Lack of sentence variety and clarity; limited vocabulary; many editing errors	Fragments and/or run-ons; errors with word choice; editing errors handicap readers

Understanding the Rubric

It is important to understand the various sections of the rubric and to use it while you are drafting your essay. The following sections are designed to help you understand the rubric for your literary essay.

Thesis

A strong essay relies on the quality of its thesis. Thus a strong thesis—a precise opinion about a limited topic, a debatable claim, a main idea, a central idea—is essential for a strong, interpretative, analytical essay.

A strong thesis has the following characteristics:

- a clearly defined opinion
- one idea
- something worth saying
- specific terms

A thesis may be weak if it is a retelling of the plot. An example of a weak thesis is: "*A Walk to Remember* is a novel of Landon's maturation as he grows to love and marry Jamie." It is also weak if it merely mentions a topic. An example of this type of weak thesis is: "*A Walk to Remember* is a novel about kindness and understanding."

Your thesis must not be too broad: "In *A Walk to Remember*, Sparks shows in many ways how to encourage religious commitment." Instead, focus your topic: "*A Walk to Remember* demonstrates that kindness and understanding are the best means to encourage religious commitment."

A strong thesis is clearly stated and focused: "In the novel *A Walk to Remember*, teenagers are the main characters in order to illustrate the idea that in life, suffering is unavoidable for all ages, young and old alike."

An outstanding thesis is not only clearly stated and focused but also persuasive: "*A Walk to Remember* demonstrates that decisions are best made by listening to your heart."

Organization

An essay has three distinct sections: the introduction, the body, and the conclusion. The introduction should be about 15 percent of your paper; the body should be about 75 percent; and the conclusion should comprise about 10 percent of the entire essay.

INTRODUCTION

The introduction should contain the following elements:

- motivator
- title and author
- basic plot summary/overview
- thesis

The *motivator* is the first part of your introduction. It is something that captures your reader's attention and entices him to keep on reading. A good introduction announces the topic and sets the tone. For example, an amusing anecdote is not appropriate for a paper about political torture. You want to entice your reader (motivate him) to keep reading. And you want to state—either explicitly or implicitly—your opinion. Here are some suggestions for possible motivators:

- general background
- history
- definitions
- quotation
- anecdote
- personal experience
- arresting statement
- interesting details (facts, figures, statistics)
- directly stated thesis
- a question

Here are some examples of poor beginnings:

- In this paper I intend to . . .
- Wars have always affected mankind.
- As you may know, having too little time is a problem for many of us.
- In the modern world today, . . .

Here are some examples of stronger beginnings:

- Although Jamie is an important character in *A Walk to Remember*, readers are seldom privy to her interior world; rather, we are dependent on her words and actions in order to get to know her.
- Nicholas Sparks's control over point of view in *A Walk to Remember* is essential to his success in showing the maturation process of a typical high school senior.

- Landon creates suspense from the onset of Nicholas Sparks's *A Walk to Remember* by claiming, "When I was seventeen, my life changed forever."
- Do miracles exist? For Landon Carter they do.

BODY

Each body paragraph should have a topic sentence, that is, a sentence that states the main idea of the paragraph. All of the topic sentences in your essay should develop and illustrate your thesis. If they do, your essay will have unity. Within the paragraph, all of your details and examples should develop and illustrate your topic sentence. If they do, then your paragraph will have unity.

In order to allow your reader to follow your train of thought, you need to use transitions—standard devices and hooks to connect ideas—that give your essay coherence. Use transitions within and between paragraphs.

CONCLUSION

Your conclusion is your last chance to make your case. Compare it to an attorney's closing argument in a trial. Rather than restating your thesis and main support for it, you should demonstrate how the cumulative weight of the evidence in your essay works together to prove your point.

Support from the Text

Support from the text can come in one of three forms: summaries, paraphrases, or direct quotations. The most effective support is a direct quotation because you are using the exact words of the original text in support of your assertions.

None of your citations should be used as a stand-alone sentence in your essay; rather, you should incorporate citations into your own sentences. Also, when writing about literature, it is important to differentiate between the author and his characters. Thus, instead of referring to Nicholas Sparks, you should refer to the character saying the lines.

EXAMPLES

Incorrect: One of the most important concepts Sparks writes about is how people understand others. "Actions—not thoughts or intentions—were the way to judge others" (235).

Correct: Through the time he spends with Jamie, Landon learns that actions are "the way to judge others" (235).

Analysis

Although having citations in your essay is important, citations alone are not enough. You must be certain that you are using the citations to develop your ideas.

You do this by following a four-part process:

1. Introduce
2. Use
3. Cite
4. Comment upon

When you make the cited material a part of your own sentence, you integrate it smoothly into your essay by introducing the quoted material before you use it. This prepares the reader of your essay for the information that is going to follow.

After introducing the source material, you use it. Make sure you use quotation marks for all passages that you cite verbatim—that is, exactly—from the novel.

Follow the documentation style required by your teacher, which is typically MLA (Modern Language Association). Sometimes you may be asked to use the *Chicago Manual of Style* or APA (American Psychological Association) documentation guidelines, including footnotes or endnotes. Although the specific formats vary, all documentation styles exist to indicate the location of the cited material in the original text and to credit the original text properly. If in doubt, ask your teacher for documentation guidelines.

The most important aspect of using citations is your explanation of the significance of the text evidence you are citing. When you discuss the passage, quoting lines from the novel helps develop your interpretation. Providing individual instances of textual support is a good thing, and when all of the quotations in your essay work together, they create a cohesive whole.

Another part of your analysis is addressing details and examples that may initially indicate a counterinterpretation. The best interpretations are those that address and incorporate the significant words and actions on both sides of the argument.

MUGS

MUGS refers to the editing portion of your essay. MUGS stands for "mechanics, usage, grammar, and spelling." This is the last step of the writing process, when you clean up any surface-level errors.

Mechanics are the rules regarding how you put a sentence together—using capital letters and punctuation marks. In addition, it requires you to use a variety of sentence types. Sometimes a simple sentence is effective, such as "Landon loves Jamie." Other times, a complex sentence is more effective, such as "Although Landon is falling for Jamie, he is still concerned about his reputation and is worried about what his friends might think."

Usage refers to various forms of agreement—subject and verb agreement (*he is*; *they are*) and pronoun and antecedent agreement (*not* "Landon and me are going to the store," or "Everybody has their equipment")—as well as dangling and misplaced modifiers. A dangling modifier is using a word or group of words to modify something that isn't in the sentence—for example, "Walking along the beach, a ship came into view." In this sentence, the ship wasn't walking along the beach, so the phrase "walking along the beach" is considered dangling. To correct the error, rewrite the sentence: "While I was walking along the beach, a ship came into view." A vague pronoun reference, when a pronoun could possibly refer to more than one word, can create confusion—for example, "Miss Garber threw the chalk at the window and broke it." Did she break the window or the chalk?

Grammar is the overarching term that covers all the rules of language and composition. And spelling is self-evident.

Three Sample Essays and Application of the Rubric

Below is a copy of essay question 4 and three sample essays, each written at different and improving levels, based on the rubric. Sample Essay 1 is an example of a below-level essay. Sample Essay 2 takes some of the shortcomings (as identified on the rubric) from Sample Essay 1, makes some revisions based on the rubric, and thus improves the essay. Sample Essay 3 is an outstanding essay fully utilizing the essential elements of the rubric and thus improving Sample Essay 2.

Essay Question 4. Stylistically, Nicholas Sparks made an interesting choice in the structure of *A Walk to Remember*. Although the narrative is told from Landon's adult point of view, he actually relates the story in his seventeen-year-old voice. His narrative voice matures and develops as the story unfolds. Using details and examples from the text, trace the development of Landon's character. Then articulate the effect this change has on the novel as a whole.

Sample Essay 1 (example of a poor essay)

A Walk to Remember by Nicholas Sparks has an interesting choice in narrative structure. Landon's voice (he is the narrator) matures and develops as the story unfolds. His voice changes from the beginning to the end. He starts off old in the prologue, then is young, and finally ends old again at the end. These changes have an affect on the novel as a whole.

In the prologue Landon is an older man looking back on his life. "When I was seventeen, my life changed forever" (3). By the end of the prologue Landon has become a teenager again. "I'm seventeen years old" (5). Here he changes from old to young.

After the prologue, readers get to experience Landon's senior year of high school with him. He talks like a typical teenage boy, saying things like "you get the picture" (18) and "that's for sure" (19). He goes to homecoming and ends up being in the Christmas play.

As Landon begins to spend more time with Jamie while working on the play, he begins to see things in a different light, like when in chapter 9 he says, "The 'right thing,' I realized, wasn't so bad after all" (148). This is an example of his voice maturing and developing. Landon is learning to do the right thing.

At the end of the novel, Landon is ready to marry Jamie. He really loves her because he says, "You know it's love when all you want to do is spend time with the other person, and you sort of know that the other person feels the same way" (191). And marrying Jamie is the adult, responsible thing to do. This is the change that Landon has in *A Walk to Remember—* growing up.

- thesis is a retelling of plot
- evidence of introduction, body paragraphs, and a conclusion; transitions used between paragraphs
- most citations stand alone and are not incorporated smoothly into argument
- analysis restates evidence and does not address the assignment
- little sentence variety
- some editing errors

Sample Essay 2 (example of a competent essay)

"When I was seventeen, my life changed forever" (Sparks 3). With these words, Landon, the narrator of Nicholas Sparks's *A Walk to Remember* begins to tell his story, the story of his growing up and falling in love—but not necessarily in that order. Landon's narrative voice changes from the beginning to the end of the novel because during his senior year of high school, he not only gets another year older, Landon becomes many years wiser. This change is reflected in his choice of diction throughout the novel. The change in Landon's narrative voice reflects the maturity he as a character gains during his senior year of high school.

In the beginning of the novel in the prologue, Landon is an older man looking back on his life, but by the end of the prologue Landon has become a teenager again, as he says, "I'm seventeen years old" (5). With this sentence, he takes the reader back in time. The younger Landon shares his senior year with readers, who get to experience his senior year of high school with him. During the early chapters of the novel, Landon talks like a typical teenage boy, saying things like "you get the picture" (18) and "that's for sure" (19). This represents typical teenager vocabulary and shows that Landon is a normal kid. He goes to homecoming and ends up being in the Christmas play.

As Landon begins to spend more time with Jamie while working on the play, he begins to see things in a different light. He visits the orphans and after some rough starts and stops, ends up performing the play without any funny stuff. Even Landon's friend Eric says, "I guess you're finally growing up,

Landon" (144). A part of growing up is doing the right thing for the right reason. When Landon doesn't mess up the play for Jamie, he says that "the 'right thing,' I realized, wasn't so bad after all" (148). This is an example of his voice maturing and developing. Landon is learning to do the right thing.

At the end of the novel, Landon marries Jamie. He does this for her but not out of pity. He does it because it is the right thing to do. The final chapter begins with the same sentence as the prologue, "When I was seventeen, my life changed forever" (243). Even though these are the same words, the readers now have a better understanding of what they mean because Landon has grown up and learned that "miracles can happen" (248). Although readers need to interpret what those words mean—what the exact miracle is—Landon in *A Walk to Remember* has learned to love and be loved and develops his faith. These are the important effects of Landon's growing up.

- a clearly stated and focused claim
- introduction sparks some interest
- some variety of transitions used within and between paragraphs
- topic sentences have support
- a conclusion exists
- most support material is introduced and commented upon
- analysis is clearly connected to thesis
- some variety in sentence structure
- few editing errors

Sample Essay 3 (example of an outstanding essay)

<u>"When I was seventeen, my life changed forever"</u> { Uses direct quotation as a strong motivator
<u>(Sparks 3).</u> With these words, Landon, the narrator
of <u>Nicholas Sparks's *A Walk to Remember,*</u> begins to { Mentions the title and author
tell his story, the story of his growing up and fall-
ing in love—but not necessarily in that order. Landon
begins his story as a fifty-seven-year-old man, but in
the course of three pages, he takes readers back in
time to his senior year of high school, with the older
Landon using the voice of his younger self to tell his
tale. <u>Stylistically, the morphing of an adult perspective
with a teenage narrative voice enables the form of the</u> { Demonstrates an attentiveness to the assignment
<u>novel to reinforce the development of its protagonist.</u>
During Landon's senior year of high school, he not
only gets another year older but becomes many years
wiser. <u>And the subtle changes in diction throughout</u> { Strong thesis
<u>the novel mirror this newfound maturity.</u>

In the beginning of the Prologue, Landon is an { Transitional phrase
older man looking back on his life. He admits that
he often says "my life changed forever" (3) yet "seldom bother[s] to explain" (3) his comment, but an
explanation is exactly what *A Walk to Remember* is.
Some readers might claim the novel is Landon's story.
Others might say it is Jamie's story. But actually, it is
their story, for they are each two parts of one whole.
Those who knew Jamie know the external events, the
facts and the major details from forty years ago, but
Landon, "who was closest to it" (3), was the one who
lived the story, experienced it, and was truly changed by
it. After four decades, Landon is finally ready to share

the emotions and feelings of that year. He promises "to leave nothing out" (5) and also forewarns readers that "you will smile, and then you will cry" (5). By the end of the Prologue, Landon has become a teenager again, as he says, <u>"I'm seventeen years old" (5)</u>. With this sentence, <u>he takes readers back in time, so they can get to know, understand, and appreciate Jamie much the same way as he did all those years ago.</u>

Use of direct quotations supports claims

Explanation of support makes this an analysis, not just a retelling

Landon begins by sharing his senior year with readers. During the early chapters of the novel, <u>he talks like a typical teenage boy,</u> saying things like <u>"you get the picture" (18)</u> and <u>"that's for sure" (19)</u>. This <u>represents typical teenager vocabulary and shows that Landon is a normal kid</u> who struggles to find a date for homecoming and ends up being in the Christmas play. Mixed in with this teenage voice, though, is Landon's adult perspective. He foreshadows future events when he inserts comments like "It was a lesson that I would eventually learn in time, though it wasn't Hegbert who taught me" (22). Not only does this line help build suspense, but it draws attention to an important thematic statement of the novel, the idea that "if you put your trust in God, you'll be all right in the end" (22). Thus, from early on, Landon emphasizes the importance of trust, love, and faith. Landon readily admits that his seventeen-year-old self didn't understand this and that he didn't learn this from his preacher. Astute readers will connect this lesson to Landon's relationship with Jamie.

Claim is stated

Claim is supported with textual evidence

Explanation of support

The early chapters of *A Walk to Remember* are interspersed with typical teenage words and phrases such as "a blow-off class" (28) and "He was a real winner, if you know what I mean" (39). These chapters also describe Landon's typical teenage concerns, such as his insecurity regarding his reputation, as he mentions that "being seen with her once was bad enough...but being seen with her every day? What would my friends say?" (81). He doesn't even want to consider being in the play with Jamie because of what other people might think of him—concerned with both being in a play and spending time with Jamie, two very uncool things. Even though Jamie helped Landon out during homecoming, he still has no desire to be involved in any activity that would require him to spend additional time with her and thus be judged negatively by his peers. After his list of suggested male actors results in nothing and Jamie begins to cry, Landon acquiesces and agrees to be in the show. But he ends the chapter with the line "I really didn't have a choice, did I?" (83). By claiming he didn't have a choice, Landon is abdicating responsibility and thus attempting to convince readers and himself that his participation in the play was foisted upon him by forces outside his control. He wants to make it perfectly clear that his involvement is in no way voluntary.

Analysis is an explanation of support for thesis

As Landon begins to spend more time with Jamie while working on the play, he begins to see things in a different light, but his change isn't instantaneous. For example, he not only dismisses Jamie's suggestion that he consider becoming a minister, rejecting the notion as being "absolutely ridiculous" (110), but he also isn't very supportive or even interested in her goal for the future, which is to get married. His first thoughts after hearing this are "it seemed kind of silly to hope for that as your life's goal" (110). Immediately after dismissing her ideas as silly, Landon acts as if he is so understanding of her discomfort that he switches the topic of conversation. Then he claims Jamie makes him "feel guilty" (111), which is "one of the reasons it was so hard to put up with her" (111). Throughout the entire course of this conversation, Landon is oblivious to Jamie's pain. Yet, immediately after this, when her plan to perform the play for the orphans is rejected, Landon does notice her pain, suggests that she visit the orphans, and agrees to visit them with her—even though it is the last thing that Landon personally wants to do. This action is one of the first times that Landon does something for someone else, a sign of his maturation.

Paragraph has a nice balance of textual support and explanation of support

This maturation is not a complete role reversal for Landon, though. When everyone finds out that he has been walking Jamie home from school, Landon retreats to his self-centered, immature self, getting irritated and annoyed, worried more about what others think of him than what he thinks of himself. And then he lashes out at Jamie, telling her, "You keep acting like we're friends, but we're not. We're not anything. I just want the whole thing to be over so I can go back to my normal life" (139). Yet, after his outburst when Jamie still thanks Landon for walking her home, he redirects his anger and negative energy toward himself. The next night Landon is sincere in his apology to Jamie and knows that he will do his best without even contemplating purposely messing up the performance. When he admits this to Eric, his friend tells him, "I guess you're finally growing up, Landon" (144). Eric's line is directed toward readers as well as Landon, in order to ensure that they also notice Landon's growth. A part of growing up is doing the right thing for the right reason. When Landon doesn't mess up the play for Jamie, he says that "the 'right thing,' I realized, wasn't so bad after all" (148). This is an example not only of Landon's character development but of the development and maturation of his narrative voice as well. Landon is learning to do the right thing.

Learning to do the right thing is a part of Landon's maturation process. He initially thinks that performing the play was his way of making up for all his mean words to Jamie, but she has other ideas. Landon reluctantly agrees to collect money from the jars that Jamie left around town. This experience leads to Landon's selfless action of adding some of his own money to the collection totals. This experience also lends itself to Landon's falling in love with Jamie. Although he initially tries to act all suave and debonair regarding the topic, he eventually provides Jamie a working definition of love, telling her that "you know it's love when all you want to do is spend time with the other person, and you sort of know that the other person feels the same way" (191). Landon's attitude toward spending time with Jamie clearly has moved one hundred and eighty degrees from where it once was. And soon after, Landon says that Jamie is the first person he loves who isn't a family member, and he had "never been more sure of anything" (201). Landon's words and actions

Use of a hook as a transitional device

287

are now those of a mature young adult—a young man who learns the importance of "doing something that my heart had told me was the right thing to do" (243). And that thing was, of course, marrying Jamie.

At the end of the novel, when Landon marries Jamie, he does this for her but not out of pity. He does it because it is the right thing to do. The final chapter begins with the same sentence as the prologue, "When I was seventeen, my life changed forever" (243). Even though these are the same words, the readers now have a better understanding of what they mean because Landon has grown up and learned that "miracles can happen" (248). Although readers need to interpret what these words mean—what the exact miracle is—Landon has learned to love and be loved while simultaneously developing his faith. All three of these things are essential to Landon's growing up. And they are essential to our appreciation of *A Walk to Remember*.

Stylistically, a return to the motivator; essay mirrors the device used in the novel

Ending has a sense of closure and finality

About the Author

With over 77 million copies of his books sold, Nicholas Sparks is one of the world's most beloved storytellers. His novels include ten #1 *New York Times* bestsellers, and all his books, including *Three Weeks with My Brother*, the memoir he wrote with his brother, Micah, have been *New York Times* and international bestsellers, and were translated into more than forty languages. Seven of Nicholas Sparks's novels—*The Lucky One, The Last Song, Dear John, Nights in Rodanthe, Message in a Bottle, A Walk to Remember*, and *The Notebook*—were also adapted into major motion pictures. The author lives in North Carolina with his wife and family. You can visit him at www.nicholassparks.com.

Available Books in the Novel Learning Series™

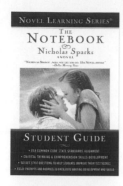

Novel Learning Series:
The Notebook by Nicholas
Sparks
ISBN: 978-1-4555-1559-2

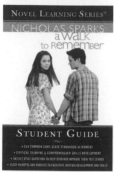

Novel Learning Series:
A Walk to Remember by
Nicholas Sparks
ISBN: 978-1-4555-0856-3

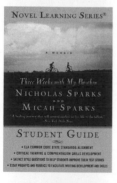

Novel Learning Series:
Three Weeks with My Brother:
A Memoir by Nicholas and Micah
Sparks
ISBN: 978-1-4555-1561-5

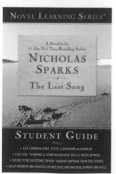

Novel Learning Series:
The Last Song by Nicholas
Sparks
ISBN: 978-1-4555-1560-8

For more information
www.novellearningseries.com